"You just won't get the message about me, will you?"

"Joe, I..." Her throat closed up and her mouth went dry as she watched him step around the coffee table and close the distance between them.

"How many years," he was asking too softly as he came toward her, "have I protected you... from me?"

She stared into those eyes that burned her through the darkness, and she had to swallow before managing on a husky sigh, "About twenty."

He stopped coming toward her only when he stood so close she could feel his breath on her upturned face. She looked into those strange wolfish eyes and saw pure emptiness, flat deadness. At first. But then she looked harder, and beneath the emptiness, she saw despair.

"You're so innocent," he muttered, and his amber eyes seemed to devour her. "So damned naive, even after all these years."

Dear Reader,

Last year, I requested that you send me your opinions on the books that we publish—and on romances in general. Thank you so much for the many thoughtful comments. For the next couple of months, I'd like to share with you quotes from those letters. This seems very appropriate now, while we are in the midst of the THAT SPECIAL WOMAN! promotion. Each one of our readers is a special woman, as heroic as the heroines in our books.

This August has some wonderful books coming your way. *More Than He Bargained For* by Carole Halston, a warm, poignant story, is the THAT SPECIAL WOMAN! selection. Debbie Macomber also brings us the first book in her FROM THIS DAY FORWARD series—*Groom Wanted*. MORGAN'S MERCENARIES, Lindsay McKenna's action-packed trio concludes this month with *Commando*. And don't miss books from other favorite authors: Marie Ferrarella, Susan Mallery and Christine Rimmer.

I hope you enjoy this book, and all of the stories to come! Have a wonderful August!

Sincerely,

Tara Gavin
Senior Editor
Silhouette Books

Quote of the Month: ''Romance books provide the escape that is needed from the sometimes crazy and hard-to-live-in world. It takes me away for that three or four hours a day to a place no one else can come into. That is why I read romances. Because sometimes there is not a happy ending, and going to a place where there is can uplift the spirit that really needs it.''

—J. Majeski
New Jersey

CHRISTINE RIMMER

BORN INNOCENT

Silhouette®

SPECIAL EDITION®

Published by Silhouette Books New York

America's Publisher of Contemporary Romance

For my aunts, Katherine Clunie, Anna Marie Folsom,
Emma Schofield and Janice Trotter, because their doors
have always been open to me.

Also, thanks to Lou Foxworthy, Deputy of the Sierra
County Sheriff's Office, and to Marianne Ruhling LVN, for
answering so graciously every question I put to them. Any
police procedural or medical errors are strictly my own.

SILHOUETTE BOOKS
300 East 42nd St., New York, N.Y. 10017

BORN INNOCENT

Copyright © 1993 by Christine Rimmer

All rights reserved. Except for use in any review, the reproduction
or utilization of this work in whole or in part in any form by any
electronic, mechanical or other means, now known or hereafter
invented, including xerography, photocopying and recording, or in
any information storage or retrieval system, is forbidden without
the permission of the publisher, Silhouette Books, 300 E. 42nd St.,
New York, N.Y. 10017

ISBN: 0-373-09833-2

First Silhouette Books printing August 1993

Printed in the U.S.A.

Books by Christine Rimmer

CHRISTINE RIMMER,

a third-generation Californian, came to her profession the long way around. Before settling down to write about the magic of romance, she'd been an actress, a salesclerk, a janitor, a model, a phone sales representative, a teacher, a waitress, a playwright and an office manager. Now that she's finally found work that suits her perfectly, she insists she never had a problem keeping a job—she was merely gaining "life experience" for her future as a novelist. Those who know her best withhold comment when she makes such claims; they are grateful that she's at last found steady work. Christine is grateful, too—not only for the joy she finds in writing, but for what awaits her when the day's work is through: a man she loves, who loves her right back, and the privilege of watching their children grow and change day to day.

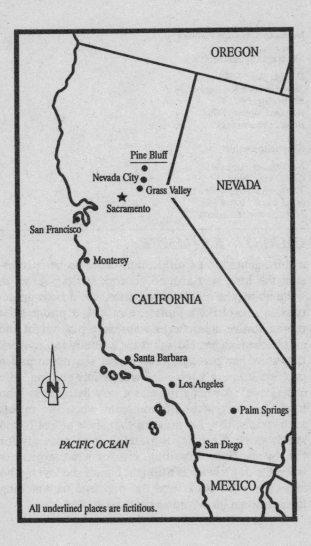

OREGON

Pine Bluff
●
Nevada City ●
● Grass Valley

NEVADA

★
Sacramento

San Francisco ●

● Monterey

CALIFORNIA

● Santa Barbara

● Los Angeles

● Palm Springs

● San Diego

PACIFIC OCEAN

N

MEXICO

All underlined places are fictitious.

Chapter One

Claire recognized the battered pickup just as she was pulling into her own parking slot two spaces away.

She stopped her van. After that, she sat there for a moment, hands clutching the steering wheel, wishing she could see through the walls of the trim, wood-sided cottage in front of her, to know for sure if Joe Tally was actually there, waiting for her.

But then she closed her eyes and discovered she didn't really need to see him. She could *feel* him. He was there.

And though she'd loved him with every fiber of her being for most of her life, right then she hated him.

They'd made an agreement, which they'd both stood by for well over a month. Why in heaven's name did he have to choose today of all days to break it? Did he *know*, somehow? Did he sense . . . ?

Claire cut off the thought before it was even complete. Joe knew nothing. There was no way he *could* know. She herself didn't even know for sure yet.

With a soft sigh, Claire rested her cheek on the steering wheel and stared at the sign hung from a wrought-iron frame on the grass by the front walk.

SNOW'S INN
Your Sierra Retreat
in Friendly Pine Bluff
Reasonable Rates
NO Vacancy

It was a sign she herself had painted not long ago, and she was proud of it. She had a firm, bold hand. The letters were straight and clear. The little border of pine boughs could have been drawn by a professional.

The motel, which consisted of a rather motley collection of small cottages and one large L-shaped building, had been somewhat run down when she'd bought it five years ago. But with time and care, she'd made it special. Now, during the summer months, she was always booked up solid for weeks in advance.

She'd done well for herself, made herself a good life. Even if Joe Tally wouldn't have her, she was doing just fine.

Claire tipped her head so she could see a patch of the powder blue sky. From the pool area about fifty feet away, she could hear splashing and laughter. Her customers were enjoying themselves on this gorgeous summer day. Everything was just as it should be. Nothing had changed. The world kept turning and life went on—just as she would keep on, no matter what happened when she went through the door to the lobby and confronted the man who waited for her there.

She breathed deep, feeling better . . . and then she jumped in her seat and cried "Oh!" as behind her in the street there was a chain of sharp explosions. For a frightened, suspended moment, she thought someone was shooting at her. Then she remembered; tomorrow was July 4th, Independence Day.

She turned her head just in time to see a local boy speed off down the street as fast as his skinny legs would take him.

Claire smiled then, and dashed away the one tear that had escaped her lids. She would not hope, nor would she dread. She would simply put one foot in front of the other and do what must be done.

Beside her on the passenger seat was a big stack of mail, which Claire had just picked up from the post office. It was her personal mail, along with all the correspondence belonging to the guests of her motel. Next to the mail sat a bag from a Grass Valley drugstore. The bag contained a bottle of sunblock, a lipstick Claire had thought pretty, a few bars of the glycerine soap she liked—and the real reason Claire had taken three hours off to drive to Grass Valley and back: a pregnancy test kit.

Claire hooked her purse over her shoulder, scooped the mail into her arms and then hesitated. Should she leave the bag in the van for now? She could just as easily come out and get it later, after Joe was gone.

But no. Joe Tally seemed to have eyes in the back of his head sometimes, it was true. But she was reasonably sure he did not possess X-ray vision. If she just kept her face composed, then her secret—and she didn't know for certain yet if there really *was* a secret, now did she?—would be safe, brown bag or not.

Claire snatched up the bag and got out of the van. Shoulders back and eyes dry, she strode up the steps to the porch of the cottage. She opened the glass-topped front door and entered the air-conditioned comfort of the front room that served as the lobby of her motel.

From behind the check-in desk, Claire's head housekeeper, Verna Higgins, glanced up. "You got a visitor, Claire." Verna tipped her head toward the man in faded jeans who waited near a lace-curtained window.

Claire turned and forced herself to meet those tawny eyes of his. He didn't move, but his long body seemed to gather a little, to ready itself.

"Hello, Claire."

She granted the briefest of nods. "Joe."

"I need to talk to you. Alone." He flicked a quick glance at Verna.

Claire smiled at the woman who relieved her at the desk and also cleaned the rooms. "Thanks, Verna. I'll take over now. Go ahead and finish up the rooms."

"Okay." Verna came around from behind the desk and went out the way Claire had come in.

When Verna was gone, neither Claire nor Joe spoke for a moment. Claire found the silence dangerous. Just standing there staring at him was a mistake. He looked much better than he had on that forbidden night almost six weeks ago, yet the lines of time and care were there. Life had not been kind to Joe Tally; it had hardened and tempered him—and left a haunted look in his strange amber eyes.

Claire felt the old, pointless urge take hold of her. She yearned to rush to him, to hold out her arms, to offer her whole self as a comfort to him, as a salve to his lonely, troubled soul.

She cut her eyes away from him and set the mail behind the counter. Then she carefully positioned the service bell in the center of the check-in desk, where anyone who came in would be sure to see it.

"Come on in back," she said, and went through the door behind the desk into the tiny foyer that led to her own living quarters. Beyond the foyer was her dining and living room, and beyond that was a kitchen, her bedroom and bath.

"Have a seat," she offered over her shoulder once she'd reached her living room. "I'll only be a moment."

Not pausing to see if he took her suggestion, she went through the short hall to her bedroom and set the bag and her purse on the little table by the bed. She closed the door behind her on her way back out to him, though she knew the precaution accomplished nothing. Joe was not the type to wander into rooms just because the door happened to be ajar. Joe went where he went on purpose, or not at all.

He was still standing when she returned to the living room. He'd gone over to one of the long double-hung windows on the west wall. The afternoon sun had begun to slant that way. It cut a sharp brightness across one side of his face. Once more, from outside, she was aware of the splashing and laughter at the pool.

"Okay, Joe. What is it?" She barely moved into the room, choosing instead to hover near the entrance to the hall.

A tightness pinched his mouth, as if he didn't know how to begin. But then he did begin, his low voice even and matter-of-fact. "Look, I haven't forgotten the agreement."

A sharp pain pierced her, and it took every ounce of will she possessed to keep her brow smooth, her expression serene. She had told herself she wouldn't hope. But hope was a weed of an emotion—it sprung up again no matter what you did to kill it. She lifted her chin. "Then why are you here?"

He turned away from the window to face her more directly. Now the light was behind him, creating a faint nimbus around his dark brown hair. "It's about Alan Henson."

Claire almost murmured "Who?," but somehow she held the word back. She felt her cheeks warm slightly at how close she'd come to embarrassing herself, when all she had left now was her pride. Of course she knew who Alan was. But with Joe near, she had trouble remembering anyone else existed.

"What about Alan?" She was proud of her voice. It was cool and steady, the exact opposite of how she felt inside.

"I hear you've been seeing him."

"So? What if I have?"

Joe's response was flat and final. "I don't like it, that's what. I want it to stop."

Something sharp and fiery arrowed through her veins then. Anger. What was his problem? *He* didn't want her, but he didn't want anyone else to have her, either?

The anger made her reckless. She spoke with flagrant challenge. "Excuse me, but who exactly do you think you are?"

He took one step toward her, and no more. Then, very deliberately, he looked her up and down. Her skin burned in the wake of his glance.

"I'm your *friend*. I only want to help," he said with quiet emphasis.

Claire couldn't suppress her slight gasp. They were her own words of that night nearly six weeks ago, her own exact words, given back.

Joe went on, with some irony, "And part of what I do for a living is knowing a suspicious character when I see one."

Staring at him, grimly doing her best to push back images of that unforgettable night, Claire tried to absorb what he was saying about Alan. But it just didn't make sense. Alan Henson, with his soft brown eyes and quiet ways, was just about the most harmless individual Claire had ever met. She shook her head. "Come on, Joe. There is nothing suspicious about Alan Henson."

"There isn't?"

"No."

"Then why the hell is he hanging around this town all alone, doing nothing week after week?"

She remembered what Alan had explained to her that first morning she'd run into him over at Mandy's Café. "He's...getting away from it all."

"That's what he's told you?"

"Yes."

"What else has he said—about himself, about his life?"

"What do you mean?"

He gave her a look so patient it was condescending. "I mean, who is this guy? What do you know about him? Where does he come from? Who are his people? And what the hell is he 'getting away from'?"

Claire sank to the straight chair by the hall entrance. Now that she really thought about it, Alan actually hadn't told her much about himself. She recalled, a little defensively, "He's a businessman. From San Francisco."

"What business?" Joe demanded. "And how do you know he's really from San Francisco?"

Claire held back a moan of frustration. *Who cares about Alan Henson?* she thought. He was a guest. He'd been renting the back bungalow for the past four weeks. She'd shared a few "dutch" lunches with him at Mandy's Café, and once he'd bought her a drink over at O'Donovan's Tavern. To Claire, he seemed a nice enough man, and that was about all.

Alan Henson was no problem for her. She had *real* problems to worry over, problems that she was trying her best not to let Joe suspect.

"Claire, look at me. This is important. You're too damn trusting, and you know it."

She forced herself once again to meet Joe's eyes. "You're making a big issue out of nothing. Just let it go."

"No, Claire. I won't let it go. I don't like what I've heard about this guy. He shows up in town out of nowhere and spreads the word around that he's looking for vacation property—and then he's vague and unenthusiastic when Bob Buntley calls him.'' Bob was the local real estate agent. ''He also spends a hell of a lot of time in his room, with the blinds drawn. Or down at the river sitting on a rock, staring into the current.

''When he thinks no one's paying attention, he acts like a man with something serious on his mind. But then the minute anyone actually talks to him, he pastes on a big smile and suddenly he hasn't got a care in the world.'' Joe paused, looked away, then snared her glance again. ''Damn it, Claire. There's something . . . not right about the guy.'' His frustration was evident in the tightness of his voice. ''I just...I don't like to see you mixed up with him.'' He turned his back on her and went to stare out the window again.

Claire began to feel ashamed. Even if Joe would never give her his love, he'd meant what he said a few moments ago. He *was* her friend. Her welfare mattered to him. He must have gone to some trouble to discover whatever there was to learn about Henson. And from the points he'd just made, his suspicions had some merit. She saw now just how petty and mean she'd been to mislead him about herself and a man in whom she had no interest at all.

She rose, and carefully approached him. ''Look, Joe.'' She spoke with gentle firmness. ''You know how people are in this town. A woman goes to lunch with a man, and they have her married to him by dinnertime. But whatever people are saying, I'm not dating Alan Henson. He's just a casual acquaintance, and that's all he'll ever be. If he's got problems I don't know about, well, they don't concern me because there's nothing at all between Alan and me.''

Joe turned from the window. ''You're sure?''

''Yes. Honestly. There's nothing between Alan Henson and me. And there never will be.'' How could there be, a desolate inner voice added, when Alan Henson isn't you?

Joe looked down at her. She found herself doing what she'd always done when close to him: memorizing him, from the high, fine forehead to the bladelike nose, the thin slash of mouth. His skin was toughened, freckled, from long hours in the sun. His straight black brows had the slightest arch at the outer edges.

The longing grew, like something warm expanding from the core of her. Just one touch, her heart cried. Only one. Just to reach up and lay her hand softly along the line of that rough cheek—

Clenching her fists, Claire cut off the treacherous thought. She made herself step back. Joe blinked when she moved. He glanced away, and then back at her.

She forced herself to say the words, "If that's all, then I think you'd better go."

Joe didn't reply. He was looking steadily at her once more. For one forbidden moment she allowed herself to again imagine the impossible—that he would reach for her, take her in his arms, and swear he couldn't live another millisecond without her at his side.

But then bitter reality returned. "Yeah," he muttered gruffly. "I'd better go."

As always, except for that one taboo night, he was stronger than she was. He turned on his heel and stalked out the way he'd come.

Chapter Two

For Claire, there was one overwhelming desire right then: to chase after him and beg him to give what they might share a chance, to plead with him to let himself love her. But begging for his love had never worked before. She'd done it twice. Once at eighteen, and then again six years ago, when she was twenty-four. Both times he'd turned her down flat. So she knew by hard experience that chasing after Joe Tally would get her nowhere at all.

Claire sighed and rubbed her eyes. Then, though she despised herself for doing it, she wandered forlornly out to the lobby and peeked through the curtain as Joe started up his truck and drove away. Only the sound of more firecrackers going off—this time a string of loud ones tossed right onto the porch of the cottage—snapped her out of her self-pitying reverie.

Claire almost flung open the door to chase the errant neighbor boy down the street and yell at him to cut it out.

But she controlled herself, and finally smiled. It was only a prank, after all. And it was high time she stopped mooning over a man who would never allow himself to return her love.

Right now, she'd do better to cheer up and get on with her day. She forced a smile, but it wavered when she recalled the pregnancy test that was waiting on her bedside table in its plain brown bag.

She knew she probably ought to take it and be done with it. Within three minutes, she'd have the results. But there were hours of dealing with the public still ahead of her—not to mention the barbecue tonight at her mother's house, which she'd promised to attend.

No, if the result was positive, she'd rather find out at the end of the day, when she would be guaranteed a block of time alone, time to absorb the fact that she was carrying Joe's baby.

She would wait a little longer. Until tonight. And then, no matter what, she'd get it over with.

Over at the desk, the outside line rang.

Life goes on, Claire thought, as she marched across the room to answer the call.

After turning the desk over to Verna again at five-thirty, Claire walked to her mother's house. It was a pleasant half-mile stroll. She crossed the bridge that spanned the Yuba River, which flowed through the center of town. Then she walked through the commercial area of town and on up the street to where Main became North Main and the stores gave way to houses.

Ella Snow no longer lived in the big house on Serpentine Street where Claire had grown up. Instead, when Claire's father had died ten years ago, Ella sold the big house and bought a smaller place on North Main, a place with only two bedrooms and no yard to worry about.

The white-trimmed blue house perched on the river side of the street, right below where Cemetery Road branched off. The entry porch could be reached by ascending a flight of stairs. In back, the house was supported on stilts to keep it dry during high water. Claire went through the front screen door to the kitchen, which faced the street.

At the squeak of the door, her mother turned from the sink where she was busily slicing summer squash. "There you are. About time." Ella held out her cheek to be kissed. "Where's the German potato salad?"

Claire extended the casserole dish she'd carried with her from the motel. "Right here."

"Good. Just set it down. No, not there." Ella pointed farther down the counter. "Over there."

From the other side of the kitchen peninsula, at the big, round oak table, Ella's other guests, two couples she played Bingo with on Thursday nights and her best friend, Dinah Richter, called greetings. Claire smiled at them and gave a wave. "Hi, everybody." She turned back to her mother. "What can I do?"

Ella shot her a swift, sneaky glance. Claire should probably have known instantly that her mother was up to something. "Why don't you go out on the deck and see if you can be of some help with the barbecue?"

Claire frowned. Ella had said she was inviting her Bingo friends and Dinah, so everyone was inside. "Help who?"

Her mother's fatuous smile told it all. "Why, Alan Henson, of course. Didn't I mention I'd asked him to join us?"

Twenty minutes later, Claire slid around the door of her mother's bedroom and closed it softly behind her.

Ella, who'd excused herself "to freshen up," was standing in front of her dresser mirror and carefully blotting her lipstick with a folded tissue.

"Mother, you have got to stop interfering in my life."

Ella gave a little gasp of surprise as she realized she'd been trapped in her own bedroom. "What is the matter with you, Claire? We have guests." Ella grimaced at herself in the mirror; the lipstick had smeared. "Now is hardly the time to—"

"*You* have guests, Mother," Claire pointed out. "This isn't my house. As a matter of fact, I'm a guest, too."

"Oh, stop pouting." Ella scrubbed at her lips with a fresh tissue and prepared to begin again. "You know what I mean. You're my daughter, the substitute hostess in my absence. We shouldn't both be back here at once."

Claire decided to drop the relatively unimportant question of her responsibility toward her mother's guests. She went straight to the real issue. "Why did you invite Alan Henson tonight?"

Ella reapplied the lipstick and blotted it with great care. "I thought you liked Alan. After all, you *are* dating the man."

"I am not dating him." Claire watched her mother as she smoothed the gray wings of her hair. "He's a casual acquaintance, that's all."

"So *you* say. But everyone in town says..."

Claire gritted her teeth. She'd had about enough of people jumping to conclusions about herself and a man she hardly knew. "Who cares what everyone in town says, Mother? If you want to know who I'm dating, the best person to ask is me."

"Well." In the mirror, Ella's reflection wore a wounded look. "I certainly didn't think you'd *mind* if I invited him. He's such a nice man, after all."

"You were matchmaking, Mother. Just admit it."

Ella turned then and faced her daughter. "And what if I was? I can't see how my creating a pleasant opportunity for you to enjoy the company of a decent man is going to hurt you."

"I'm not interested in him, Mother. Get that through your head."

"Oh, no? And why not?"

"I'm just not."

"That's no answer."

"It's answer enough."

"Oh, stop this. Let's be honest, at least, just between you and me. Let's have it out in the open. You're not interested in a nice, respectable man because—"

"Mother, don't start," Claire warned.

But it had no effect. Her mother finished triumphantly, "You're too busy waiting around for a single glance from that no-good bounty hunter, Joe Tally!"

Claire said nothing for a moment. She was trying to keep from defending Joe, because defending Joe would only play into her mother's hands. But, in the end, she couldn't stand the unfairness. Joe was a good man who'd never had a single break in his whole life. And Claire wouldn't stand by and let people run him down. She softly advised, "Don't call Joe names, Mother."

"Names? What names? I suppose you're going to try to tell me he isn't a bounty hunter?"

"You know what I mean. You said he was no good."

"It's only the truth."

"It is not. Joe is . . ." Claire contained herself, reminding herself of the true issue here. "Joe's got nothing to do with this discussion."

With a snort of pure disdain, Ella waved her hand in front of her face. "Good heavens, how you do delude yourself. But you can't delude me. Joe Tally has *everything* to do with why you won't give a decent man a chance. I've watched you since you were little more than a baby, chasing after him, following him around like a lovesick calf. And even though you tell me there's nothing between you, I know what's before my eyes."

"It's none of your business, Mother." Claire tried to sound strong and purposeful, but her mother became nothing short of an emotional battering ram once she got going. Claire found herself wishing she'd kept her mouth shut about Alan Henson. She should have just left well enough alone and ignored her mother's embarrassing attempts at matchmaking.

But it was too late. Ella, who was a tall woman, anyway, drew herself up even taller. "None of my business? How can you say that? My only daughter is ruining her life and she tries to tell me it's none of my affair?"

"I'm not—"

"Don't tell me what you're *not* doing. I can see. And don't fool yourself. I know what's best for my own child. And what's more, I will never stop providing opportunities for you to get to know nice men—*any* men—as long as they're not that trouble-making loser, Joe Tally!"

Claire was reaching the end of her rope on the subject of Joe. She spoke very precisely. "Joe is not a troublemaker, Mother. Nor is he a loser."

But Ella would not be silenced. "He is and always has been *nothing* but bad news. And if you weren't so blinded by your sick infatuation with him, you'd realize the truth. It is purely a miracle that he's managed to end up on the right-hand side of the law. Why, when he was a boy—"

"Stop it, Mother. I'm not telling you again. Just leave Joe out of this."

"Well, that would be just fine with me. There is nothing I'd like better than to leave that—"

"Stop. Stop right there. I mean it. No more about Joe, or I will leave this house now."

Ella must have decided Claire was serious, because for several seconds she said nothing, only glared and fumed. Claire took those precious seconds to make her other point. "And be warned. The next time you provide one of these *opportunities* for me, you'd better anticipate that I'll be tossing the German potato salad on the counter, and walking right out the door."

Ella continued to glare at her daughter. She said tightly, "Unfortunately, you are too old to spank. I imagine you'll do what you want to do, whether it mortifies your mother or not."

"At last you understand," Claire said quietly.

Ella made a small, tight sound of exasperation, then turned to the mirror once more and gave her hair a final pat. When she faced Claire again, she wore a determined smile. "Well," she said carefully, "since that's settled, let's return to our guests."

"Fine," Claire agreed, admiring her mother in spite of her frustration with her. Ella Whitney Snow's father had been a minister, and her grandfather a judge. She had married Pine Bluff's one doctor and devoted her life to her family and a number of worthy causes, for which she worked unstintingly and without pay. A true pillar of her community, she knew how to put a proper face on things when there was nothing more to say.

Somehow, Claire got through the evening. But it was grueling. Her mother listened, enthralled, every time Alan Henson opened his mouth. And her mother's friends kept tittering and whispering to each other whenever they thought Claire wouldn't notice.

By eight-forty-five Claire had had enough. The dishes were done and put away, and everyone sat in the living area explaining to Alan all about the Independence Day parade and the annual races, both of which would be held on Main Street tomorrow.

Claire waited awhile for an appropriate opening, but everyone kept filling each smidgen of silence with another tale of how Gerry Hines won the potato sack race last year, and why little Pookie Evans cried every time the starting gun went off. Claire's mind began to wander—to the test from the drugstore, which she intended to finally put behind her as soon as she'd achieved the privacy of her own cottage.

She stood, aware that the move was abrupt, but past caring if anyone noticed her eagerness to be gone. "Well, I should get back to relieve Verna. Dinner was great, Mother. Good to see you all."

Alan shot out of his seat as if Ella had pinched him—which Claire would not have put past her for a minute. "I should get back, too. I'll walk you."

Claire restrained a sigh and realized this was probably as good a time as any to explain to Alan that she would never be getting any more involved with him than she was right now.

She smiled. "Sure. Why not?"

Ella, Dinah and the others made approving little clucking sounds. Ella rose to see her guests out.

"Ella, it was wonderful," Alan enthused when the three of them had formed an awkward knot by the kitchen door. "I honestly can't say when I've had a more satisfying evening." Claire shot him a glance, thinking he was laying it on a little thick. He went on, "And from now on, I'm adding that dash of fresh chopped jalapeño to my own barbecue sauce."

"Oh, well, now..." Ella was actually blushing. Claire glanced from Alan to her mother and wondered if she'd read this whole situation wrong. Was it possible her mother might be after Alan Henson herself? Ella simpered, "All cooks have their little secrets."

"Thank you for sharing yours," Alan said with a perfectly straight face. Her mother gave a gracious nod. Claire tried to keep from rolling her eyes, deciding with some irony that she *must* be pregnant—because listening to this exchange, she felt like throwing up.

Alan added, as if it were an afterthought, "And I *will* drop by, if you'd like. Tomorrow or the next day. We'll go over those figures, and I'll show you just what I mean."

"That would be so helpful." Ella serenely smiled.

Claire looked at Alan. "What figures?"

Her mother waved a dismissing hand. "Oh, nothing, Claire. Before you arrived, Alan and I were talking. He mentioned that he can show me a few ways to increase the income from what your father left me." Ella handed Claire her clean casserole dish. "But enough about money. You youngsters be on your way now. Thanks so much for coming, Alan. You two have a lovely walk home."

"We will," Alan promised, and led the way out the door.

As Claire and Alan set off down the street, Claire was careful not to sway too close to him. She didn't want to give him any encouragement—and she was thinking that she didn't like the idea of Alan advising her mother on her finances. Joe's cautionary remarks about the man had stuck with her.

When they'd reached the main part of town and were strolling the sidewalk toward the turn to the bridge, Claire observed lightly, "You know, Alan, you've never told me exactly what it is you do for a living."

Alan turned to smile at her, his even teeth flashing white through the gathering darkness. "You're kidding. I haven't?"

"No." She waited for him to volunteer something—anything. When he didn't, she asked more directly, "What is your work, really?"

A quick glance told her that his pleasant face had grown thoughtful. "Well, to anyone who isn't in finance, it's a little hard to explain."

"Try me. I took a few business classes in college. I might be able to understand."

"Well, I'm a financial planner. I advise people. On how to use their money to make more money. They come to me and I show them sound investments."

"What kind of investments?"

"Well, now. That's a little complicated. I'd have to really sit down with you, to go into all that."

They had reached Sierra Street and the turn to the bridge. Claire stopped and faced Alan. She said as gently as she could manage, "Alan, I'd prefer if you didn't give my mother any financial advice. Fair enough?"

He blinked, and then pasted on a smile. "Well. Ahem. Certainly. If that's how you feel."

"Yes, that's how I feel."

"Well." Even through the shadows of coming night, she could see that his soft brown eyes looked wounded. "All right, then."

Feeling like a first-class jerk, she muttered a thank-you and turned toward the bridge. Alan strolled along beside her, saying nothing for a few moments. As they reached the center of the old bridge, someone set off a rocket that rose screaming into the sky and exploded over the river like a bursting star.

Alan chuckled. "I thought those were illegal around here."

Claire was relieved. The tension had been broken. "They are, unless you're talking about a professional fireworks display. But that doesn't stop some people."

"Will the sheriff be after them?"

"If they keep it up. *And* if he can find them."

Alan chuckled again, and the rest of the walk passed in amicable silence.

When they reached the motel, Alan put his hand on her arm just before Claire mounted the steps to her cottage. As far as she could recall, it was the first time he'd touched her, except in passing, since she'd met him.

His hand felt soft and cool. It was a light, gentle touch. There was nothing pushy or offensive about it, yet Claire recoiled from it. Deep in her heart, she cursed Joe Tally, not only for refusing to love her, but also for making any other man's touch seem all wrong.

Alan offered, "Come to my bungalow for a drink."

She hesitated, not wanting to go, but remembering her resolve to get things clear between them.

He urged, "Come on, Claire. Just one."

"All right. One." She set the empty casserole dish on the edge of the porch to pick up when she returned.

"Great." He turned and led the way along the strip of grass beside her cottage and the middle bungalow, to his bungalow in the southeast corner of the motel lot. He opened the door and gestured her inside. "Welcome to my castle."

Smiling weakly, she went in and sat on the beige couch in the small sitting room. Over against one wall there was a pine credenza on which sat a tray with a collection of liquor bottles and a few of the motel's plain water glasses.

"Scotch? Vodka?"

"Just a club soda will be fine."

He grinned. "Sit tight." He held up the room ice bucket. "Be right back."

"It's okay. I don't need ice."

"Ah, but I do." And he was gone.

He was back quickly, as he'd promised, sliding in the door to the accompaniment of a volley of exploding firecrackers from somewhere out on the street.

Efficiently, he dropped the ice into the glasses and poured himself two fingers of Scotch, then emptied a bottle of club soda for her. He handed Claire her drink. "To...fireworks."

Feeling awkward, she clicked her glass with his and took a tiny sip. She set the glass down. "Alan, I..."

He dropped down next to her and slithered an arm along the back of the couch behind her. "What? Go ahead. I'm here to listen."

She slid away a little. "Look. I came here to explain something to you."

"Oh, really?" He looked nervous, and she felt a little sorry for him. He drank again, draining the glass. Then he got up, refilled the glass, and returned, plunking down beside her again, closer than before. "Fire away."

She slid back, this time to the far arm of the couch. "Listen. I just want you to understand. As far as I'm concerned, you and I are just . . . friendly acquaintances. And that's all we'll ever be."

He knocked back another swallow, and then set his drink on the low table in front of the couch. He looked at her, frowning. "Excuse me?"

She dragged in a breath. "I said, I hope you haven't gotten the wrong idea about how I feel about you. Because there can never be anything...romantic between us. I'm not looking for anything like that."

He craned closer to her and peered at her, a measuring kind of look that she didn't like at all. "Do you really expect me to believe that?"

She wondered what in the world could be going on behind those soft brown eyes. "Yes," she said quietly. "I do."

He chuckled. "Oh, come on. You're here, aren't you?"

She felt totally at a loss. He was behaving so strangely, nervous one minute, then looking her over with insolent appraisal the next.

Joe had been right. She really knew nothing at all about this man. She'd thought him a pleasant lunch companion, and not much else. But tonight, after Joe's warning, she'd been paying a little more attention—and she didn't like what she was seeing. It was time to go.

"Listen. I only came here to tell you that I'm not interested in you." She winced a little at her own bluntness. But trying to be tactful had achieved nothing. She understood now she must be perfectly clear with this man. She started to rise. "Good night."

He grabbed her arm and yanked her back down. "I don't believe that's all you came here for, not by a long shot."

Claire plopped back on the couch—and stared for a moment with her mouth hanging open. Then she found her voice. "Let me go!" She tried to jerk free, but he held on with a punishing grip. Her heart started to pound in her ears. She was frightened, but she kept her voice firm. "I mean it, Alan."

"You're one of those women who needs a little coaxing, that's all." He released her arm, but at the same time, with a quick, surprising move, he pressed his body against hers, craning over her and pinning her against the arm of the couch. He spoke right against her face. "I don't think you're willing to admit what you really want. Everyone in this two-bit town says you're in love with the local loser. But I don't buy that. I say the loser is just a convenience—an excuse to keep other men away, because you're a little afraid of men in general. But I've been watching you, and you've got a nice little setup here. I think we can get something good going between us, once you quit playing like you don't want what every woman wants..."

Claire stared at his distorted, too-close face, and wondered how she'd managed to walk right into this nightmare. She gave his shoulders a shove. "Get away from me!"

"Come on, Claire. Cut the crap." And then he did what she'd been fearing he'd do.

He smashed his mouth against hers. His tongue stabbed at her lips. Claire sat stunned and unbelieving beneath the onslaught for a moment—but only for a moment.

Then she began to struggle, demanding that he let her go. He muttered against her lips, "Relax, baby. Enjoy it..." And his soft, cool hand closed over her breast.

That did it. Somehow she wriggled around, reaching out, grasping desperately, until she touched his drink. She grabbed it up and popped him with it just above his ear. He swore, graphically, jerking back. She heard her silk camp shirt rip as he shoved her away without letting go of the material. Ice, Scotch, and broken glass rained down on them both.

Claire leapt to her feet and halfway across the room, while he brushed at the broken glass and loosed a score of invectives that should have turned the walls blue. Claire caught her own breath and waited for him to wind down, backing toward the door at the same time. She had it opened behind her and was ready to step out before he finally calmed enough to look at her.

"You bitch. What the hell's the matter with you?" He felt around beneath his hair, as if seeking some serious injury. She knew he'd find none. She'd hit him with the thin edge of the glass and it had broken like an eggshell. She'd surprised the daylights out of him, thank God. But he wasn't hurt.

From somewhere in the night, there came a long, sharp volley of detonating firecrackers. Claire said, "I want you out of here by noon tomorrow. Do you understand?"

He stopped cursing and looked at her. Then he smiled, a weak, smarmy kind of smile. Claire was struck by the chilling notion that she was seeing the true Alan Henson at last. "Sure, why not? Whatever you say." He actually winked. "And, hey. No hard feelings. Can't blame a guy for giving it one last shot, can you?"

Claire gaped at him, feeling suddenly nauseated. He'd virtually attacked her, and he expected her to just brush it off? She whirled on her heel and got out of there, because right then her instincts were murderous.

She didn't start shaking until she was halfway back to her cottage, passing the main building of the motel, which formed an L around the pool. Then it was as if the starch that had filled her veins had suddenly drained out of her. Her legs felt wobbly, her hands and arms quivered and she found she could barely stand up.

So she leaned against the two-story building, pressing her forehead to the wall, trying to take slow, deep breaths, until her composure returned.

Good Lord, she had almost been raped! There was no other word for it. If she hadn't had the presence of mind to grab that glass...

Should she call Sheriff Brawley? She shook her head. No, she had rescued herself, after all, and it hadn't gone far enough for her to really be certain that Henson had had rape on his mind. In fact, judging by the kind of character Alan Henson had turned out to be, he'd probably end up suing her for clobbering him with that glass. Malicious endangerment, or some such.

"Oh, Joe," Claire murmured to the wall. "How very right you were." For a moment more, she leaned against the building, picturing Joe's stern, beloved face, knowing the ever-present longing for what they'd never share—and yet feeling gratitude, too. He *was* her friend, no matter what he *wasn't*. And she'd always be thankful for his watchful care.

Soon enough, Claire found she was able to push herself away from the wall. The shock of what she'd just been through was passing, and her legs were willing to hold her upright once more. She was just lifting her head to aim her tired body toward her own cottage when she heard someone gasp.

"Oh, my God. Are you all right?" A woman and a man, guests of the motel, were rushing toward her.

Claire looked down at herself and saw that her blouse was gaping open and splotched with wet stains. Her face flaming, she clutched her torn blouse together and forced a smile. "Yes. I'm fine. Really."

"But what *happened?*"

"Nothing. Just a little...misunderstanding. It's all cleared up now."

The woman, who'd put a comforting arm around Claire's shoulder, looked doubtful. "You're sure? You're shaking all over."

Claire straightened and stepped back from the woman. "Yes. Positive. I'm fine. And it's only a few steps to the lobby. I live right behind it."

The man said, "We'll help you."

Claire gave a nervous laugh. "Really. There's no need. I can just go in the back door."

But they wouldn't let her make the short trip alone. They stood to either side of her and walked her around the cottage to the lobby door, insisting they must see that she had someone to look after her until she felt more herself.

Verna looked up when the woman led the way inside. "Good God, Claire. What happened to you?"

Claire forced a smile of reassurance. Then she thanked the couple again and sent them on their way.

Feeling as old as Methuselah, Claire tottered to the couch by the check-in desk and dropped into it with a sigh.

She rubbed her temples.

"Headache?" asked Verna.

"A doozy."

Calm, efficient Verna got the aspirin from a drawer behind the counter and the water from the cooler in the corner.

"Thanks." Claire chased the pills with the water.

Verna suggested in a soothing voice, "Tell me what happened. It's always better if you talk about it."

Claire shook her head. "No, I'd rather *not* talk about it—except to say that Alan Henson will be out of here in the morning. For good."

Verna frowned. "He . . . hurt you?"

"No, not really. He just scared about five years off my life, that's all." Claire looked up at Verna, who was still hovering beside her. Claire patted her hand. "Don't worry. It's nothing I won't get over. Really. I just want him out of here. And he'll *be* out. Tomorrow."

Verna wasn't completely convinced. "I think you ought to talk about it."

"I don't."

"You're sure, now?" Poor Verna. She wanted to help, but she didn't seem to quite know what to do.

"Positive," Claire promised, thinking she was getting tired of reassuring people—first that well-meaning couple and now Verna. She wanted to be alone, to collect her shattered nerves. And then to take the damn test that would probably shatter them all over again. "What I need is a good night's sleep. So you go on, Verna. And I'll lock up."

"But—"

"I'm serious." Claire dragged herself to her feet and got Verna's purse for her. "Out of here. Thanks for watching the desk tonight. I really appreciate it."

"Well, I—"

Claire herded the other woman toward the door. "Good night. And enjoy your holiday tomorrow." Though Verna usually worked Saturdays, Claire had given her a holiday with pay in exchange for Verna's promise to supervise the final touches on the Snow's Inn float for the parade tomorrow at noon.

"Well, okay, then," Verna allowed. "Good night."

When she was finally alone, Claire sagged back against the door for a moment and let out a long sigh. "At last," she murmured wearily.

* * *

Half an hour later, having taken off her ruined blouse and stained slacks and put on her summer pajamas, she stood in her bathroom and stared at the result window of the pregnancy test. She saw what the pamphlet had told her she'd see if she was pregnant: two pink lines.

Claire blinked, but the parallel pink lines were still there when she opened her eyes again. Her missed period and the new, subtle changes she'd felt lately in her body meant exactly what she'd feared they'd meant.

She was going to have Joe Tally's baby.

It was too much. Too much for one woman to take in one day. The confrontation with Joe, the harsh words with her mother, near-rape by a man she'd thought utterly harmless—and now this.

Claire looked around at her bright, spotless bathroom and truly understood what people meant when they said the walls were closing in on them. Her darting gaze found her own strained face in her bathroom mirror, and she knew that she had to get out of the cottage before she screamed those walls down.

She spared one brief thought for her duties as night clerk. Her business would survive an hour or two of her absence. Her machine would take calls. Anyone ringing the night bell outside the lobby in hopes of finding a room would be disappointed—but that would happen anyway. Every room was occupied. Yes, her motel would be fine.

But *she* wouldn't, unless she got out of there now.

Yanking off the pajamas as she went, Claire stalked into her bedroom and put on an old sweatshirt and some worn-out jeans. She shoved her feet into a pair of sneakers. Finally, after a little frantic fumbling in her purse for her keys, she fled to the kitchen and grabbed a flashlight. She slid out the back door, engaging the lock as she went.

Once out in the night, she circled around to the front of the motel, quickly moving to the far side of the street, where the cedar trees reached out their branches and wild blackberry vines grew in tangled profusion, and anyone wandering around on the motel grounds would be less likely to see her. At the end of the street, she took a path that ran roughly parallel with the river, under a thick cover of tall trees. She stumbled along for nearly an hour in the darkness, with only the thin beam of her flashlight to show the way. At last, by watching the terrain closely, she found the place she sought.

She started down a ridge to her right. The way was steep and rocky and she had to climb backward, carefully feeling with her toes for stable boulders, until she made it to the river's edge.

She paused, then, on the rocky promontory that she'd been seeking. She turned off her flashlight, and waited until her eyes adjusted to the night. As she waited, she listened.

Now and then she could hear a car whoosh past on the highway that curled around the mountain high above the opposite bank. And there were night birds calling, and frogs croaking—animal sounds. And the river, which ran deep here, lapped very gently at the rock where she stood. But that was all. No people, no bright lights, no firecrackers. She was alone under the stars.

She quickly stripped off every stitch she was wearing, and dived cleanly from the rock, tuning out completely her mother's chiding voice as it played in her head.

Swimming alone? Foolish, foolish girl. And naked, well, I never...

The water was cold and slick, liquid silk on her bare skin. She swam around the pool in circles, cleansing herself, clearing herself. Finally she pulled herself, shivering, back onto the rock. She dried herself with her sweatshirt.

Putting on her clothes once more, she sat on the rock and gathered her knees against her chest. Then, because it consoled as much as it grieved her, she let the memory of her one night with Joe Tally come into her mind....

Chapter Three

The moon had been on the wane that night. It provided little more than a sliver of light. The stars had seemed so far away, scattered across the heavens above the tall, dark trees.

Claire had wanted to hurry, but she'd forced herself to drive slowly on the twisting dirt roads, to watch carefully for each of the turns that would take her to the Tally Ranch. If she missed one, she knew, it could take hours to get back on the track.

Going slowly paid off. She found the entrance to the ranch with ease, though it was nothing more than a break in a barbed-wire fence with a rutted dirt driveway running through it.

Claire turned into the driveway, which made a loop in front of the weathered house. She drove into a yard of dust and weeds. Parked among the weeds were a tractor that had seen better days and two beat-up pickup trucks.

Behind the house, where the pasture land flowed away to timbered hills, the wild grass was still green that early in the year. It appeared silver, though, by moonlight. One lone horse grazed there, a swaybacked fellow, even to Claire's untrained eye.

It all looked so lonely. Claire knew a creeping apprehension. Under the mantle of darkness, the ranch seemed abandoned, a place where only ghosts might walk. She almost wished she hadn't come. Still, she didn't drive away.

She was worried about Joe. The word around town was that he was hiding out drunk here, only emerging long enough to buy more booze. She had tried to call him, but he wasn't answering his phone. Finally, she'd admitted to herself that she wouldn't rest until she found out for sure if he was all right.

So she'd called Verna and asked her to watch the desk. Verna had come right over, and Claire had set out to see if Joe was all right.

Claire pulled the van up in front of the house and turned the engine off. Then she opened her door, got down and peered into the shadows of the big front porch.

It was after she'd already closed the door of the van behind her that she heard the growling. She squinted harder at the shadows on the porch, trying to see who—or what—was snarling at her. Right then, as if in answer to a question she hadn't asked aloud, two big German shepherds materialized from the shadows by the front door.

Claire stood absolutely still. Her father, who'd loved big dogs, had once told her that sometimes stillness and lack of perceptible fear could give a person an edge with even the most attack-prone of animals.

The dogs approached her, sniffing, growling a little, but looking more wary than ready to attack. She let them smell her.

Then she said, firmly, "Sit." They both looked at her, measuring her. She snapped her fingers once, sharply, and pointed at the ground. "Sit. Now."

Both dogs dropped their hind ends to the ground and looked up at her with expectant, trusting interest.

She tried not to let them see her long sigh of relief. "Stay," she instructed with great gravity.

She calmly walked past them, and though she heard one of them whine hopefully, they stayed where they were. She went up to the porch, and when she got there she strode right up to the door and pounded on it decisively.

No one answered.

"Joe?" she called, her voice sounding eerie and strained in the silence. "Joe!"

Except for more whining from one of the dogs, no answer came. She tried the doorknob. It wouldn't turn.

About five feet to either side of the door were long double-hung windows, similar to the ones in her cottage at the motel. Claire inspected the one on the right, and saw that it was firmly latched from the inside. Curtains of some dark material were drawn across it, so she couldn't see in.

She approached the other window, her sneakers making the old porch boards squeak. It was screened, curtained and latched, like the first. She jiggled the frame of the screen, anyway, and saw that to remove it from the outside she would have to bend the frame.

Sighing, she turned toward the yard again, where the pair of dogs waited and her shiny, new van looked out of place among the derelict equipment Joe kept there.

Everything was locked up. No one answered her calls. She supposed there wasn't much else to do here.

But then she thought about the back entrance; maybe it would be unlocked. So she followed the porch around, jarring screens and checking for latches as she went, and finally trying the back door to find it securely bolted against her, too.

She was stymied. Short of breaking in, what more could she do? She descended the steps at the back of the house and walked around through the weeds to her van.

The dogs whined. She said, "Okay. Come." They wiggled over, like a pair of huge puppies, and gratefully received a few pats and strokes and gentle words.

From where she stood, she could see nothing of what went on behind the windows on either side of the front door. The shadows of the porch completely obscured them from her view. Still, she felt that Joe was watching her, that he was in there, though he wouldn't come to the door—just as he hadn't answered any of the number of messages she'd left on his answering machine in the past few days.

The dogs looked sleek and well fed. Someone was taking care of them. Who else could it be but Joe?

"Sit," she told the dogs again. They didn't even hesitate this time, but dropped to their haunches in the dirt at her feet.

She turned and opened the driver's door of her van, then felt under the seat for the heavy-duty flashlight. When she had it in her hand, she went to the back of the van, where she kept a little toolbox and a pair of work gloves. She pulled on the gloves, told the dogs once more to stay, and approached the steps to the porch again.

She melted into the shadows by the door, walked right up to the window on the left, and pried the screen out enough to bend it and then wrench it free of the sash. She lifted the flashlight—and shattered the glass of the bottom pane, grimacing a little at the way the splintering glass cut through the ghostly silence, which seemed to lie like a stifling blanket over the neglected house.

She took a few moments to carefully break off the shards that remained in the frame, so she wouldn't injure herself climbing in. Then, when no sharp fragments were left to cut her, she laid her gloves on the porch, lifted her leg over the sill and went in, shoving the dusty, dark curtain out of her way.

"Come on in, Claire. Don't let my dogs—or a locked door—stop you."

At the sound of Joe's taunting voice, Claire froze, straddling the window. She peered through the darkness at the room she'd half entered. But she couldn't see a thing. It was pitch black, except for what looked like the red glow of a lighted cigarette several feet away.

Joe helped her then, by flicking on a floor lamp. She blinked at the sudden brightness. But her eyes quickly adjusted, and she found herself staring at him.

He was stretched out on a frayed couch not ten feet away from her, wearing a faded flannel shirt and a pair of old black jeans with busted-out knees. The shirt was unbuttoned, and the lamplight gleamed on the washboard-hardness of his bare belly. She couldn't see his eyes; he'd shielded them from the glare of the lamp with the back of the hand that held the cigarette. But she didn't need to see them. She knew he was studying her as she hovered, half in, half out, of his living room. She watched, not sure what to do next, as the smoke from his cigarette trailed lazily toward the watermarked ceiling.

Feeling ridiculous, but too far down this particular road to turn back, she swung her other leg over the sill and faced him. "What's going on?" She dared to take a step toward him. "I called and called. Why didn't you answer the phone, or the door?"

He didn't bother to sit up, though he did grant her a slight shrug. "Well, gee, Claire. I guess you could say I just wasn't in the mood for company."

She ignored his sarcasm. "Why not?"

"None of your business." He gestured with a quick flick of his head toward the broken window behind her. "Now get lost. You can just . . . slip out the way you came."

She stood firm. "You've been alone long enough."

He chuckled, then, a sound so cold she shivered in response to it. "What are you up to, Claire? I hope you aren't here to tell me again how you can't live without me. I thought we'd settled all that the last time you begged me to take advantage of you."

She shook her head and kept her face calm. But down inside her she knew hurt. It was cruel of him to bring up her old foolishness after all this time. Six years ago, after the second time she'd humiliated herself and begged him to love her, she'd decided enough was enough. She'd come to grips with the fact that Joe Tally was never going to give her love a chance.

She'd stayed away from him for a couple of years. Then, slowly, they'd started coming into contact with each other again, sharing an occasional game of pool over at O'Donovan's, stopping to exchange greetings and personal news when they passed on the street. They'd developed a new kind of relationship; she thought they had become friends. And that was why she was here: to help a friend.

She decided it was necessary to make her true motive clear. "No, Joe. You don't have to worry." She forced a rueful chuckle of her own. "I'm over you. You're safe from me, I promise you."

He gave her a half grin, and she dared to hope he was relaxing his guard a little. "Glad to hear it," he muttered, and dragged on the cigarette.

"But I thought," she hurried on, "that over the last few years, we had become friends."

He exhaled, and flicked his ash on the scuffed hardwood floor. "You did, huh?"

"Yes. I did. I still do." She spoke more strongly, "I *am* your friend, and I'll always be your friend—no matter how hard you push me away."

He was quiet for a moment, watching her. And then he lazily sat up and stubbed out the cigarette in an ashtray on the coffee table in front of him. She stared at him, thinking that he looked grim, tired and rumpled, but in spite of the open beer can beside the ashtray, not drunk.

He swung his long legs to the floor and looked down at his bare feet for a moment. Then he looked at her again. He sighed. "I'm fine, okay? You've seen for yourself. Now you can go."

She bit her lip, reluctant after going so far with this, to leave without some understanding of why he'd chosen to withdraw from the world for a week. She asked, hesitantly, "Is it . . . about Mexico?"

He looked away. "Get lost. Go now."

She knew a little surge of triumph. At last she was getting somewhere. "It *is* Mexico, isn't it?" The last time she'd talked to him, a couple of weeks before, he'd mentioned that he was heading down to Mexico the next day to track some kid, barely eighteen, who'd skipped bail. "Oh, Joe," she coaxed. "What happened there? Is it . . . that boy you told me about?"

"Get out. I'm warning you."

"Oh, Joe, please . . ."

He looked at her again. And his eyes had changed. Now they were the eyes of a wolf as it measures its prey. "What is it with you, Claire? What's it always been with you?"

Claire stared at him, wondering what had gone wrong. She'd only wanted to help, but her questions about Mexico had triggered something ugly in Joe. Now the gloomy room seemed to vibrate with menace. She held her ground and insisted, "I'm your *friend*. I only want to help."

He shook his head, a grin worthy of the wolf he resembled curling the corner of his mouth. "You just won't get the message about me, will you?"

"Joe, I..."

He stood up.

"I..." Her throat closed up, and her mouth went dry as she watched him step around the coffee table and close the distance between them.

Oh, Lord. He was so... dangerously beautiful, with his whipcord-lean body and that sinuous way of moving he had. She tried not to stare at the hard muscles of his belly, which seemed to constitute a sort of sexual taunt, clearly displayed as they were between the open plackets of his shirt. Something inside her was shifting, going liquid.

"How many years," he was asking too softly as he came toward her, "have I protected you... from me?"

"Joe?" she asked his name, hoping for reassurance.

She got none. He demanded again, in a voice of velvet and steel, "How many?"

She stared into those eyes that burned her through the darkness, and she had to swallow before managing on a husky sigh, "About twenty."

He stopped coming toward her only when he stood so close she could feel his breath on her upturned face. She could smell him, the cigarettes and the beer, too, and his sweat. In another man, these things might have repelled her. But not in Joe. Never in Joe. She looked into those strange wolfish eyes and saw pure emptiness, flat deadness. At first. But then she looked harder, and beneath the emptiness, she saw despair.

"What happened in Mexico?" Somehow, in a hollow whisper, she got the question out.

"You're so innocent," he muttered, and his amber eyes seemed to devour her. "So damned naive, even after all these years."

"No."

"Yes."

She shook her head. It seemed very important right then that he see more of her than he was letting himself see. "No. I'm not innocent. I'm not."

"Then what?"

She swallowed and tried to explain. "I . . . try to keep trusting. I try to keep my faith, in the world, and in people. But nobody's innocent, except on the day that they're born."

He made a low, cynical noise in his throat. "You're innocent," he said again. "You're damned naive."

There was no convincing him. And it wasn't really important, anyway, she could see now. He'd accused her of naïveté to distract her. She was through being distracted. "Think what you want," she advised in a whisper. "But tell me about Mexico. Tell me, Joe. That boy—"

"You just won't let it go, will you?"

"No. Tell me."

"Fine." He gave her the truth then, never taking his eyes from hers. "He's dead."

"Oh, no. . ." She reached for him.

"Don't." He stepped back.

She dropped her arm. "What happened?"

His broad shoulders seemed to slump. He dropped into the one easy chair in the room, a brown corduroy chair as tattered and worn as the couch. Then, in a weary voice, he gave her the explanation she'd been seeking.

"He'd skipped his bail to run drugs, and then got in the way of a deal going down. I got there too late to do much good. The kid was gut shot, done for. I held his head in my lap and watched him die. I've been sitting in this house since I got back, wondering what the hell point there is to a world where a dumb kid gets murdered just because he's in the way. In a world like that, there's no damn room for innocence. All innocence can do is get you killed.'' Joe dropped his head on the backrest and stared at the ceiling.

Claire thought of the dead boy and wondered about the boy's family. She felt her eyes filling, though she knew that tears wouldn't help. ''Oh, Joe. I'm so sorry.''

He rolled his head enough to capture her gaze. ''Yeah. I know. You feel for all the idiots in the world, don't you, Claire?'' He chuckled, a tired, wry sound. ''You're something. Really something.'' He lifted his head then. And he stood up once more. He took the few steps to stand before her again.

Claire watched him, sensing another shift in him, but not quite sure what the shift would mean.

''You're good,'' he said, when he was so close that half a step would have brought their bodies into intimate contact. ''A good person, and maybe a strong one, too. A damn special thing.'' He raised his hand, then dropped it. ''Hell,'' he muttered darkly, and she understood his struggle with himself. He was trying not to touch her.

He lost the fight. He raised his hand again and very gently smoothed a strand of her hair back over her shoulder, his rough thumb whispering along her jawline in one achingly tender stroke.

The touch was all it took. The touch showed her everything. It put a cruel mirror up to her sacred, central lie, the lie she'd been faithfully telling herself for six years now.

She looked in the mirror his touch showed her and the lie faded away to mist and she was looking at the hard truth.

She loved Joe Tally. She had never stopped loving Joe Tally. She would always love Joe Tally. Until the day God took her breath for good.

He was watching her, his tawny eyes seeming to see it all. ''Tonight, I'm not up to protecting you.''

Her voice seemed to know what to say, though she had no awareness of framing the words. ''I know. It doesn't matter. I can take care of myself. I'm not as innocent as you keep saying.''

"Oh, no?''

"No. You need me. You need a...human touch. A woman's touch, to get past that dead boy. In the morning, you'll feel better. And you don't have to worry. In the morning, I'll go.''

"You don't know what you're saying.'' His voice was ragged. She heard the hope in it—and the raw need.

"Don't underestimate me, Joe. I know more than you think.''

"I have nothing for you. God, Claire. Tonight I don't even have what it takes to do the one favor I've always done you...to send you away.''

"You couldn't send me away tonight, anyway. I'm staying.''

He stared at her. "Damn, you, Claire. Go now or—''

"Shh.'' She dared to touch his lips. "It's okay.''

The touch did it. With a soft oath, he reached for her. She melted against him—and then felt his wince when she touched his shoulder.

She pulled back. "You're hurt....''

"Just a flesh wound.''

But she had to see. She carefully guided the open shirt off his shoulders to the floor, and found a clean gauze bandage, which looked white as snow against his tanned skin.

Joe looked at the bandage and then at her. "I swear. It's okay. The bullet passed right through the meat. I'm taking good care of it.''

"You're sure?''

"Absolutely.'' He took her head between his hands and tipped her face up to his. "But are *you* sure?''

"Yes.''

"Tonight.'' It was a rough vow, spoken sweet and low against her parted lips. "And never again. You'll go back to your nice, sane life tomorrow morning. We'll . . . stay away from each other, from now on. We'll cut it clean. Agreed?"

She stood on tiptoe, inviting his kiss. He nibbled on her parted lips a little, hungrily. But he insisted again, "Agreed?"

She nodded, as much as she could with her head cupped between his hands. "Agreed." A single tear escaped the corner of her eye. He caught it as it trickled back toward her hair, brushing it gently with his thumb.

And then, murmuring some dark, hot promise, he covered her lips with his own.

Chapter Four

The shock of knowing his mouth after all the years of yearning and denial held Claire utterly still for a moment.

She moaned in hungry joy and lifted her arms to clasp him as close as he was holding her. She ran her greedy hands all over his bare skin, feeling the hard beauty of lean muscle and the shape of the long bones beneath, cautious only of the bandage at his shoulder.

And as she touched him, he was touching her, burning her with his rough and tender hands, making urgent sounds, sounds of need and promise at the same time. He felt along her neck and down to the buttons of her shirt, fumbling with them, parting them, and pushing the shirt away to the floor to join his own.

He sighed and clasped her bare waist, as if learning the slim shape of it. She moaned in pleasure as his hand traveled up to cup the fullness of her breast, which was still bound by her bra.

He stood back from her, just a little, so he could work the front clasp. It came undone and fell away. He caressed her naked breasts, groaning a little, as she was, in discovery and delight. He held them, lifted them, and looked into her eyes. Then, slowly, he lowered his head.

She clutched him close as his mouth found her nipple and he sucked on it, bringing it to a peak of sweet sensitivity, then moving to the other one.

Claire let her head fall back, and felt his arm behind her waist, supporting her. She was glad for the support. If he hadn't provided it, she would have slid in boneless delight to the bare floor at their feet. He went on kissing her breasts for the sweetest eternity, and as he did, he worked at the fastening of her jeans, unsnapping and unzipping and then sliding the jeans down, along with her panties, to the floor at her feet. She kicked off her sneakers to aid him.

Then, feeling the cool air of the room touching her everywhere he wasn't, Claire realized she was naked. Naked in Joe Tally's arms. It was her oldest, most forbidden fantasy.

And for this one night of all nights, it was real.

She gasped as he slid his arm beneath her knees and lifted her up against his chest. But then she realized what he was doing, because he sat down with her across his lap in the big brown easy chair.

He kissed her mouth again for a long, sweet time. She reveled in it, feeling his desire for her, hard and ready, through the rough fabric of his jeans. He guided her head to his uninjured shoulder and his hand slid lower, to stroke down her belly to the place that was already wet and waiting for him.

Claire gasped and moaned. His fingers played gently at her entrance.

He whispered low and hoarse against her ear, "You *have* been with a man before, haven't you?"

She bit her lip, trying not to cry out at the pleasure his teasing fingers were giving. "There was a man. In college." She didn't tell him the rest—that it had been after the first time Joe had sent her away. She'd tried loving someone else. But it had been doomed from the beginning. Eventually, the man had realized her heart belonged to someone else. He'd been hurt, and Claire had been ashamed of herself.

"And it was ... all right?" Joe asked as his fingers, light as butterfly wings, continued their sweet, teasing play.

It took her pleasured mind a moment to make sense of his question; he was asking if she had any problems with sex. "It was ... fine, Joe."

"Good." His finger slid into her then. She gasped.

He began stroking her in earnest, and she felt her body instantly rising, readying itself for the high climb to the edge of ecstasy. "Oh, Joe," she sighed, and then moaned out loud.

He murmured yes, stroking faster. Her body responded, lost to anything but the command of his hand upon her.

She soared up and over the edge, crying out in blissful triumph. And then she went slack, cradled there in his lap.

For a time she just lay there, naked across him in the big brown chair. She rubbed her head against his chest, and sighed a little, and he lazily stroked her sweat-dampened hair back from her forehead. She gave a low chuckle.

"What's so funny?"

She sighed. "I was just thinking. I came here to comfort you, and it turns out you're the one who's giving the ... strokes."

He laughed then, a rumbling sound against her ear. "You'll get your chance. Very soon."

"Good." She cuddled against him some more. "Joe?"

"Um?"

She sat up a little, smiling knowingly when he winced; he was still very ready to go on with their loving. "I know you probably won't believe this, given the way I've always chased after you..."

He rolled his eyes a little and gave a short laugh but didn't say anything.

She went on. "But I really didn't expect...this to happen tonight. I, um, I'm not using anything. I mean, the pill, or anything..." She took in a bracing breath, and continued, "It should be my safe time, but, well..."

He was stroking her hair, his eyes soft and deep, as she'd never seen them before—and probably, she realized sadly, as she would never see them again. "I should have some condoms around here somewhere. Don't worry. We'll be careful."

She released the breath she'd taken. "Good."

He took her face in his hands again, and kissed her lips with soft, tender promise. Then he said, "Come on. We'll find them. And we'll put some fresh sheets on my bed. And I'll take a shower—" he glanced at his injured shoulder "—carefully."

He scooped her against his chest as he had earlier and stood up. This time she saw his slight wince when his hurt shoulder took half her weight. But before she could order him to put her down, he did it without coaxing, lowering her legs so she could stand.

He stepped back a little and looked at her, his eyes heavy and hot. "God," he breathed. "So beautiful. So soft." He touched her breast, just a brush of a touch, with the tip of a finger. Then he snared her hand. "Come on."

He led her down a dim hall to a bedroom sparsely furnished with an old, brass-framed double bed, a scarred dresser and a wooden rocking chair. From a hall closet, he produced clean sheets and they made the bed up fresh.

Then he took her to the bathroom, where he showered—carefully—as he'd said he would, and she sat waiting outside the tub with a towel to dry him off when he emerged. She did some looking herself, then, and found him as long and lean and tough as the wolf he sometimes made her think of.

She dried him—carefully—counting the scars on his hard body, kissing them, wondering how he'd acquired them, but not daring to ask.

At the back of a drawer in that same bathroom, he found two condoms. The packaging was wrinkled and marred, and Joe allowed that they'd probably been in the drawer for a couple of years.

"Even though my mother made her living on her back," he remarked dryly, "I guess I'm no Casanova."

She'd known about his mother, of course. Everyone in Pine Bluff knew. Still, she ached a little for him, hearing him say that hard truth out loud. At the same time, she felt gladness that he was "no Casanova."

He went on, "And I'm not so sure that these are still good."

She took one of the packages and studied it, without opening it. "I think it'll be okay. And I don't think I can get pregnant now, anyway."

They looked at each other, naked and unashamed in the harsh bathroom light. They both smiled and said in unison, "It'll be fine...."

She laughed, and he laughed back. And then they were reaching for each other, touching each other, eager as children for forbidden sweets.

He put his arms around her and waltzed her out of the bathroom and across the bedroom to the newly made bed. They fell across it.

He said, suddenly gruff, "I don't want to wait." He pressed himself against her. "I want to be inside you."

They had fallen facing each other. In answer, she rolled, guiding him over her, opening herself. He rose up between her knees, fumbling with the condom. She reached out, gentle and sure, to help him slide it on.

her knees, fumbling with the condom. She reached out, gentle and sure, to help him slide it on.

That accomplished, she lay back, looking at him, memorizing him above her—hard beauty and danger, cruel sweetness. Her love. He said something crude and poignant, something needful and real.

And he came down upon her, burying himself in her with one hard, certain thrust. She cried his name. He devoured the single word with a kiss, pushing himself so far up into her that the burning pleasure bordered on pain.

Then, having totally claimed her, he braced himself on his lean, strong arms and looked down at her, grimacing a little at the strain his own weight was putting on his bad shoulder. She reached up, to try to pull him down into her softness. But he shook his head and kept his elbows locked.

He looked at her—at her face, her soft breasts, and even lower—to the place where they were joined.

He pulled back. She whimpered. He pushed into her once more.

He muttered, "Claire. I wanted...to do this. To see this...you and me...."

And she moved, accepting and welcoming under him, taking the pain of his barren life, the horror of Mexico, all of it, any and everything that had ever hurt him and hardened him, into herself, holding it there, and finally giving it back as pure pleasure—as love.

Love unspoken. Because she didn't say the words. He didn't want the words. She would be his forever—but they would only share this one night.

She held him, moving with him, and this time they climbed to the stars together, hovered there, and cried out in unison as they careered back to earth.

They rested. Later, they made love once more, slowly and so sweetly, and she fell asleep with her head cradled in the crook of his unhurt shoulder.

She woke alone at dawn. She sat up in bed and looked around, and knew without having to search the rundown house that he had gone.

She didn't cry. She understood. They had an agreement. It was easier this way.

Now, six weeks later, seated on a rock by the river in the darkness, Claire laid her head on her gathered-up knees and allowed herself to cry.

She cried for her foolishness, for her irresponsibility on that starkly beautiful night. It was clear now that those condoms *had* been too old. She cried for her own desire, which had led her to this place and then left her to work out her fate on her own. She cried for the tiny baby growing within her. And she cried for her hopeless, unfulfilled love for Joe Tally.

Finally, no closer to a plan of action, but somewhat soothed by the release that tears bring, she wiped them away and stood up. She took in a long, deep breath.

The crying was over. Soon, she'd have to decide what to do. But not tonight. Tonight she'd be using all the energy she had left just to find her way back to her cottage and drop into bed.

Fighting growing exhaustion, she staggered back along the dark trail, sighing with relief when she at last came to the end of it and her sneakers touched paved road. When she reached Snow's Inn, most of the rooms were dark. As she slid around the side of her cottage, she spotted her casserole dish, waiting where she'd left it on the corner of the front porch what seemed like a lifetime ago. She scooped it up and carried it with her to the back door.

Once she attained the sanctuary of her cottage, she discovered it was later than she'd thought: almost one. She put her pajamas back on, and fell across her bed and slept deeply and without dreams until dawn.

Claire moved through the next morning by rote, forcing herself to eat breakfast, to take care of the check-in desk. Soon enough it was eleven, and Amelia Gennero, her relief housekeeper, arrived for work.

Claire left Amelia to take care of the desk, stepped out onto the porch—and heard the music coming from the other side of the river.

Lord, with all her own troubles, she'd forgotten that today was a holiday.

She walked across the bridge and found Main Street packed with tourists. The street was lined with makeshift booths, while the town loudspeaker system blared patriotic songs. Claire sent a grateful little prayer to heaven that this year Verna would be handling the Snow's Inn float for the parade at noon. Otherwise, Claire would be up in the schoolyard right now, taking instructions from her mother. For as long as Claire could remember, Ella Snow had orchestrated the Fourth of July parade.

Just as Claire reached the door to Mandy's Café, five "poppers"—tiny white firecrackers that were actually legal in Pine Bluff—exploded in quick succession at Claire's feet. A little girl laughed and shot off on swift bare feet, jostling tourists out of her way. Thinking that she'd be lucky to get through this day without murdering some firecracker-crazy kid, Claire went into the café and discovered she would have to wait to even get a seat at the counter.

Once she found a space, she ate her lunch with patient determination, forcing herself to smile and wave greetings whenever she saw someone she knew. Claire was just polishing off the last of her bacon-and-tomato sandwich when Sheriff Dan Brawley slid his ample bulk onto the stool next to hers.

"Hey, Short Stuff. Where's my smile?" The sheriff had always called her Short Stuff. He and her father had been close friends. When Claire was a child, Sheriff Dan and his wife, Ardette, often came over for Sunday dinner at the Snows' house. "Hey, Short Stuff!" Sheriff Dan would shout, and then he'd pick Claire up and toss her, giggling, toward the ceiling. Since then, Claire had grown to an above-average height, but Dan Brawley had never relinquished his pet name for her.

Claire pasted on a smile for him. "Hi, Sheriff Dan." She looked into his crinkly blue eyes. He'd been the sheriff for as long as Claire could remember. He was levelheaded and kind, and yet everyone in town knew that he could be tough when he had to be. Every four years, they voted him back in like clockwork.

Seeing him made her think of last night, when Alan Henson had attacked her and she'd considered calling her old family friend in his professional capacity.

"Claire?" the sheriff was asking, "are you okay?"

She nodded. "Fine." She realized she must have looked very strange right then, or Sheriff Brawley would never have called her by her real name. Claire shrugged, thinking it was no wonder if she looked strange. The past twenty-four hours had been nothing short of grueling, as far as she was concerned. "Just having...one of those days, that's all," she told him feebly. She glanced at the big clock on the wall.

It was three minutes to twelve. She'd told Henson to be out by noon—and then forgotten all about him once she'd seen the results of the pregnancy test. She should get back. If he hadn't checked out by now, she was going to have to deal with him.

She put her money on the counter and signaled to Mandy, who gave her a nod. "Gotta go," she told the sheriff. "See ya."

"Take care, Short Stuff."

"You bet."

Back at the motel, Claire took over from Amelia and asked if Alan Henson had checked out during the past hour.

Amelia, eighteen years old and under strict instructions not to chew bubble gum while working the desk, now unwrapped a piece. "Uh-uh." She stuck the gum in her mouth. "Was he supposed to?"

"Yes." Claire picked up the desk phone and punched Henson's extension. It began to ring. Amelia was already turning for the door, on her way to begin cleaning the rooms. "Amelia?"

Chomping Bazooka, Amelia looked back. "Yeah?"

Claire put the mouthpiece below her chin and asked, "Could you wait? Just a minute?"

"Sure." Amelia sat down in a straight chair by the door and stared at Claire, her jaw working industriously at the pink wad of gum.

Alan Henson's phone went on ringing.

Finally, Claire gave up. She put the phone down. "Amelia, would you come with me to Mr. Henson's bungalow, please?"

Amelia cracked her gum and looked at Claire with wide eyes. "What's going on?"

Claire explained carefully, "It's nothing terrible, really. Mr. Henson and I had a . . . disagreement last night. I asked him to be out by noon today. Since he's not, I'll have to talk to him again. And since he doesn't seem to be answering the phone, I'm going to have to do it face-to-face. I'd just feel better if someone went with me. However, if you feel uncomfortable about it . . ."

Amelia didn't need to hear more. She sucked the bubble she'd been blowing back into her mouth and stood up. "Nah, I don't mind. Let's go."

Claire left the lobby open, and they went out the back way, through her apartment and across the thick lawn that was still damp from its morning watering. Amelia walked slightly behind, cracking her gùm all the way.

"Hey, look at that," Amelia said when they reached the short steps that led up to the bungalow's miniature porch. "The door's open a crack. You think maybe he's gone?"

Claire shook her head. "His car's still there." She pointed at the silver Mercedes parked on Pine Court, the street that ran behind the bungalow.

Claire mounted the steps. "Alan? Mr. Henson?"

Henson gave no answer. So Claire squared her shoulders and marched up to the door. She knocked, an awkward knock, since she was trying not to push the door open at the same time.

And then she realized that all this hesitancy was getting her nowhere. If he was in there, he was hiding, and if he was hiding she was going to have to do more than tap politely and wait until he felt like answering.

She laid her palm on the door and gave it a push. It slid open on silent hinges.

"Mr. Henson!" she called.

But then she realized that calling would do no good, because Alan Henson couldn't hear her. He was lying on his side on the floor over by the credenza. He was utterly still. And the dark stain that had ruined the braided rug beneath him looked very much like drying blood.

Chapter Five

Amelia started shrieking. "Omigod! Oh, gross! He's dead!"

Claire tuned her out. Slowly, pressing back the eerie feeling of unreality that seemed to have settled over the whole world like a shroud, Claire stepped through the open door.

"Claire! Don't go in there! Oh, God. Somebody killed him!"

Ignoring Amelia's babbled pleas, Claire approached the still figure. She bent, and laid two fingers on his neck. The skin was cool but not cold. Against the pads of her fingers, she felt the faintest fluttering.

She looked up through the doorway at Amelia, who'd stopped squawking and was now simply staring, making little whimpering noises, her mouth half open, the pink wad of gum forgotten on her tongue.

"I think he's still alive," Claire said.

But this was all too much for Amelia, who only stared uncomprehending, shaking her head.

Claire stood up again. "Come on, we have to get the ambulance." She started to reach for the phone, and then realized there was no one at the desk to channel the call. So she rushed out, around the still-staring Amelia, and flew down the steps and across the grass.

She was in the lobby within seconds, calling 9-1-1.

The ambulance was there in minutes. And Sheriff Brawley arrived a few minutes after that.

Four hours later Alan Henson was in the hospital in Grass Valley, fifty miles away. He was alive, but still unconscious.

Sheriff Brawley, who had taken a statement from Claire right away, knocked on the back door of her cottage at a little after four and said he needed to ask her "just a few more questions."

Claire's mother was there by then. She had hurried right over as soon as she'd heard the awful news from Dinah Richter, who had heard it from Lolly Beals over at the grocery store, who had heard it from a number of reliable sources. Truth to tell, the whole town was abuzz.

Claire had no doubt that by the time Sheriff Brawley asked her for a second interview, there wasn't a soul in Pine Bluff who didn't know about the horrible thing that had happened at Snow's Inn.

And now they had more questions for her. Claire said, "Of course, anything you need to know," and Sheriff Dan said he would be right back. For this interview, there would be two police officers present, himself and his undersheriff, Wayne Leven.

At about four-twenty, Sheriff Brawley and Undersheriff Wayne Leven arrived together at Claire's back door. Claire showed them to the living room, and they each took one of the twin wing chairs opposite the couch. Claire sat on the couch, and a moment later, Ella came in from the kitchen carrying a coffee service on a tray. She slid in next to her daughter.

"Dan, Mr. Leven? Coffee?"

The men shared uncomfortable glances, and then both agreed that would be nice. There was an uneasy silence as Ella poured and passed the cups around.

Finally, they began talking of the subject that was most on all their minds. Claire asked if they had been able to determine how long Henson had lain injured on the bungalow floor before she had discovered him.

"To tell the truth," the sheriff explained between sips at the coffee, "with all the firecrackers going off all night, no one we've talked to can identify when the shot that injured Henson was fired."

"Yes, well," Ella said unnecessarily. "That makes sense, of course."

A silence ensued, where Brawley and Leven looked ill-at-ease, and Ella's apprehension was painful to see.

Then Ella said to Sheriff Brawley, "Dan, have a cookie. I know you love pralines."

"Why, thanks, Ella. Don't mind if I do." Sheriff Brawley took the praline and bit into it, and was careful to catch the crumbs in his napkin.

As Dan Brawley chewed slowly and thoroughly, his undersheriff, who was not from an old Pine Bluff family as were Brawley and the Snows, shifted impatiently in his chair. Finally, Leven said, "We've got to get on with this, Dan."

"I know, I know."

Leven turned to Claire. "Ms. Snow, we've already talked to a few people who are staying here at your motel. And by the time we're through, we'll interview everyone. And of course, we need to ask you some questions, too."

Ella said, "But you talked to her right after she found that poor man, didn't you?"

"Yes, but only about what happened today, about how she found Henson in his bungalow. Now we need to find out everything anybody can tell us about Henson himself—and about the last few days before he was shot."

Ella was shaking her head, looking doubtful. "I don't know. It seems to me that—"

"It's all right," Claire said. She could see no escape from this interview. At least they weren't asking her to go over to the sheriff's office behind the courthouse. "What did you want to know?"

"Let's see." Leven produced a little notepad and scrutinized it for a moment. He flipped it back a page. Then he looked at Claire again. "You've been dating Alan Henson, is that correct?"

Ella piped right up. "She has not. She absolutely has not. Why, only last evening, she told me—"

Claire put her hand on her mother's arm. "I can answer the questions myself, Mother."

"Fine. Of course. Fine." Ella smoothed her hair. Her face looked very pinched. In spite of her conflicts with her mother, Claire loved Ella deeply. And never so much as now, seeing the way Ella rushed to her defense, a mother hen protecting her endangered only chick.

Sheriff Brawley took another praline.

Undersheriff Leven commented flatly, "We've contacted Henson's wife in San Francisco." Ella gasped. Leven shot her a sharp, triumphant look. "So. You didn't know he had a wife?"

"No," Ella answered. "I certainly did not."

Claire said, "He never mentioned a wife to me, either."

"I'm sure he didn't." Leven scribbled himself a little note on the pad, then he asked Claire again, "*Have* you been dating Alan Henson?"

"No."

"You've been seen with him repeatedly."

Claire refused to be intimidated; she reminded herself that she had done nothing wrong. "We never had a date," she said quietly. "I ran into him over at Mandy's a few times, and we sat together for lunch. And he bought me a drink at O'Donovan's one night. And last night, my mother had him over to her house for a barbecue. When dinner was over, he walked me home."

Leven smiled. "He walked you home."

"Yes."

"And after that, what happened?"

Claire took in a breath. The truth was going to sound bad. Very bad. But lying would do her no good. If they hadn't already done so, they would talk to the couple who'd found her outside, leaning against the main building after Henson had attacked her. And they'd talk to Verna and Amelia, both of whom would have to tell them that she'd had some kind of conflict with Alan Henson last night. In the end, Claire realized, the truth was all she had.

So she told it. Slowly and clearly. Right up to the moment when she sent Verna home.

After she was done, her mother looked as if she might pass out, Sheriff Dan reached for yet another praline and Undersheriff Leven still wore that unpleasant smile.

Leven pressed a little, "Are you *sure* Henson was unhurt when you left him?"

"Yes. I'm positive."

Leven did not look convinced, but he evidently decided to move along anyway. He asked the question Claire had been dreading more than all the others. "After Verna Higgins left you alone, what did you do next?"

Even though she had known this moment was coming, she still was not fully prepared for it. Her mouth was very dry, suddenly. She took another sip of coffee.

How could she tell the rest? How could she say it?

I took a pregnancy test and found out I'm going to have a baby....

How could she just say that—in front of her poor mother and Sheriff Dan and the disapproving Leven?

Claire had hardly adjusted to the fact that she was pregnant herself. The thought of having her mother, Sheriff Dan and a virtual stranger know right now, before she'd even had a chance to think about what to do—no, she wouldn't do it. She *couldn't* do it. It was none of their business and it had nothing to do with Alan Henson, anyway....

"Ms. Snow?" Undersheriff Leven prompted. "I asked what you did next."

Claire set her coffee cup into its saucer. It made a scraping, clattering sound, a sure giveaway that she was rattled. She jerked her hands away from the betraying cup and folded them in her lap. The others were watching her, waiting. She knew she had to say something.

"Well, I . . ."

And the service bell out at the desk rang.

The other three tensed at the sound. For her part, Claire had never known such relief, even though she was fully aware that it was only a temporary reprieve.

She stood up. "Excuse me a moment. There's someone out in front. I'll be right back." Claire stepped around the coffee table and made a beeline for the foyer and the front desk beyond.

She came through the inner door to the lobby with a big, grateful smile on her face for whoever it was that had unwittingly interrupted her grim moment of truth. But the smile froze in place when she saw who her rescuer was.

Joe.

He stood there on the other side of the desk, looking hard and rangy and ready for anything. He was dressed in his usual faded jeans and a dark shirt.

Claire wanted to run to him and bury her face against his hard chest, and beg him to help her out of the trap she felt closing around her.

He didn't waste any time. "Brawley's back there now?" he asked quietly, tipping his head toward the door behind her.

She nodded. "And Wayne Leven, too. How did you know?"

"The word's out," he said cryptically. "You're in trouble."

"I know. Oh, Lord..."

"What did you tell them?"

Claire collected herself and explained as succinctly as she could. "I told the truth. Last night in his bungalow, Henson more or less attacked me. I hit him with a water glass and told him to get out by noon today."

"Was he hurt?"

"By the glass, you mean? No. It was a very thin glass, and he wasn't even cut that I could see. He was fine when I left him."

Joe's amber eyes bored through her. "What else?"

"At noon today, I went to order him out, and I found him unconscious on the floor of his bungalow. From what the sheriff told me a little while ago, he's been shot in the side, and he's in a coma from hitting his head on the credenza when he fell."

"And that's all?"

She caught her breath for a moment, thinking about the baby, before she realized he was referring only to her dealings with Henson. She nodded. "Yes, Joe. I swear it. I—" Claire cut herself off as she saw Joe's gaze shift to something behind her.

"Ms. Snow?"

Claire turned. Undersheriff Leven was standing in the door to her rooms.

Leven, who knew his town and everyone who lived near it, even if he wasn't from an old Pine Bluff family, demanded, "What do you want here, Tally?"

"I'm a friend of Claire's."

"Well—" Leven gestured at the lobby couch "—have a seat. We're just having a little talk with her. And when we're finished—"

Joe cut him off. "Is she under arrest?"

"Of course not, Joe." Sheriff Brawley, who had wasted little time following Leven out, spoke from the doorway to Claire's rooms. "We're taking her statement, that's all."

"From what she's just told me, you already have it."

"We're not quite through yet."

"Is she a suspect in the shooting of Henson?"

Though Joe had asked the question of the sheriff, it was Leven who hastily replied, "No, not at this point."

Joe looked from Leven to Brawley and back again. "Like I said, I think she's told you enough. She needs legal counsel before she says any more." Joe strode to the front door and held it open. "Have a nice day, gentlemen."

Leven looked red in the face. Claire assumed that he didn't like being one-upped by a bounty hunter. Joe had once told Claire that bounty hunters were considered little more than vultures by most legitimate policemen. "Damn you, Tally. Who the hell do you think you are?"

Brawley walked around the desk. "Never mind, Wayne. Let's go."

"But—"

"I said, let's go."

His face pinched and sour, Leven followed his boss to the door. But he couldn't resist one parting shot. "And where were *you* last night and early this morning, Tally?"

"Wayne," Brawley chided.

"It's all right, Dan." Joe turned to Leven. "I played poker in the back room of O'Donovan's until dawn. Then I walked with Rusty Farber over to Mandy's for breakfast. After that, Millie Jens came in and said they needed help with the parade floats up at the schoolyard. I was there until parade time."

Ella, who had followed the others out into the lobby, confirmed in regal tones, "That is correct, at least the last of it. Mr. Tally was at the school grounds all morning. As you know, I traditionally oversee the float lineup, and I did so this year. Mr. Tally was quite a help to us all." If one less thing had been wrong in her life right then, Claire would have smiled. Her mother considered Joe Tally far beneath her own lofty position on the social scale. But to Ella, even one's inferiors had a right to be supported when they told the truth.

Leven snorted and then said with a great show of irony to Joe, "Up all night, eh? You must be beat."

"You know, now you mention it, I am a little tired." Joe gestured once more toward the open door.

"This isn't the end of it," Wayne Leven said tightly. "One way or the other, it's our job to find out who shot Alan Henson. If Ms. Snow won't cooperate with us, then—"

"Enough," Sheriff Brawley said to his second-in-command. Then he spoke to Joe. "But he's right. Chances are, we will be back."

Joe said, "I understand."

Brawley and Leven went out the door.

When they were gone, Joe turned to Claire. "Are you okay?"

She nodded.

Her mother spoke up from right behind her. "Thank you for ending an . . . unpleasant interview, Joe Tally. And now my daughter and I would prefer to be alone."

Joe looked pained. Claire knew he'd always respected her mother, though Ella invariably played the high-and-mighty lady of the manor any time he came near. "Mrs. Snow, I don't think you realize the seriousness of this situation."

"Yes, I do. Of course, I do. I know exactly what's going on here. They suspect Claire of... shooting Alan Henson. But of course, since she *didn't* shoot him, everything will work out fine."

"Oh, will it?"

"Yes. Certainly. They will... investigate further and they'll discover who really did this awful thing, and everything will be as it should be."

"I'm glad you have such confidence in the system, Mrs. Snow."

"Don't be cynical with me, young man."

"I'm only pointing out that—"

Ella was waving her hand in that dismissive way of hers. "Never mind. We simply would like to be alone now. If you'll just... be on your way."

A rueful smile played on Joe's lips. "No," he said gently.

Ella gave a small start. "What did you say?"

"I said no. I'm staying here. With Claire."

"Don't be absurd. Claire doesn't need you! I'll be here."

Joe shook his head. "I'm sorry, Mrs. Snow. But she does need me right now. I don't think you've looked at all the sides of this situation. Though we all know Claire didn't shoot Henson, *somebody* did."

Ella was becoming indignant. "Well, of course, *somebody* did. I realize that. I'm not a fool."

"I just want to... hang around for a while, that's all. Until we know better what's going on."

"There is no need for you to 'hang around,'" Ella insisted. "I will be here."

"Mrs. Snow, in this situation, Claire could need more than her mother to watch out for her."

"This is ridiculous." Ella puffed out her already considerable bosom. "I suppose I'm going to have to be blunt with you. You are not wanted here. We want you to—"

"Mother."

Slowly, Ella turned to look at her daughter. "What is it, Claire?"

"Joe is staying." The words were out almost before Claire realized she was going to say them.

"What?"

Claire gathered herself and faced her mother. "I want him to stay."

After all, she told herself, Joe was right. Just watching him get rid of Brawley and Leven had made her realize how much she *didn't* know about what was happening to her. If he was willing to help her out now, she wasn't going to turn him down.

Ella was sputtering. "B-but, Claire! You simply cannot let him—"

"Yes, I can. I'm in trouble, Mother. The kind of trouble someone like Joe knows all about."

"I do not believe you're saying this."

"Believe it. It's true."

"I warn you, Claire. I will not stay here if he is here."

"I understand."

Ella looked hurt and bewildered. She also realized she'd just trapped herself with her own ultimatum. "Well, then, I . . . I suppose there is nothing more to say."

Claire reached out. "Mother, I—"

Ella jerked back. "No. Don't try to placate me. I am firm on this."

"So am I."

"Well. Humph. That's it, then." Gray head high, Ella strode to the open front door. "Call me when he leaves." And she was gone.

Claire went to the door and watched her mother until she disappeared at the turn to Sierra Street. She could hardly believe what she'd just done.

And she knew it could turn out to be a huge mistake. Her own motives were suspect. There was her own foolish love for Joe that simply refused to die—not to mention the baby he knew nothing about.

Yet he *was* her friend. He was willing to help, and he'd come to her side when she needed him—just as she had for him not too long ago.

Joe said from behind her, "She'll be back."

"I know." Claire turned to face him. He had moved away, toward the couch and chairs grouped tightly on one side of the wide lobby. "What now?"

"Got coffee?" He lifted a dark eyebrow at her. "I really didn't go to bed last night."

She nodded. "Come on. It's all made."

She led him back to her living room and got him a cup. He drank the coffee Ella had made for Sheriff Dan and Wayne Leven. Once he was on his second cup, Joe asked her to tell him the whole story of the night before.

She did, giving every last detail she could recall—until the point where she'd sent Verna home. Then she told a lie of omission, because she simply was not ready yet to tell Joe that their one night together had resulted in the most classic of consequences. She said only that she had felt cooped up in the cottage and had slipped out the back and gone for a walk in the dark, ending up at the river, where she went for a late-night swim. She told him she'd returned around one, which was the truth.

Joe watched her as she talked, and Claire couldn't tell whether he believed her or not. Then he asked her to tell how she'd discovered the unconscious Henson in the bungalow. Once again, she went through the whole thing in detail, from the call to Henson's room at noon, until the ambulance arrived.

Then he asked, "What about the gun that shot him?"

Claire was puzzled. "What about it?"

"Did they find it?"

Claire thought for a minute. "No. I didn't see a gun when I found him. And I don't think they found one, either."

Joe, who'd been sitting in one of the wing chairs, stood up. Claire jumped a little at the swiftness of the movement.

"Relax," he soothed. "I just want to check something."

He went out through the foyer and was back in minutes. "Where's the .38 I made you buy, Claire?"

Claire stared up at him. A couple of years ago, there had been a rash of night robberies in the county. Joe had come in one day and insisted Claire buy a gun and learn to shoot it. He'd been so adamant that she'd done as he ordered, though she didn't like guns at all. She kept it mounted where it was hard to see but easy to reach, beneath the counter.

She said just that. "It's behind the counter...isn't it?"

"No."

Fighting off a feeling that managed to be half numbness and half panic, Claire got up and went out to the lobby with Joe, where she saw for herself that the gun was not in its place.

"Are you sure you didn't move it?" he asked.

"Yes. I'm positive. It was there...yesterday, I think." Claire sank to the couch in the lobby. "Oh, Lord. In all the upset lately, I'm not really sure of anything. I *think* it was there yesterday...."

"What about last night?" Joe wanted to know. "Are you sure you locked the back door when you left for your walk?"

"Yes," she said firmly. She did remember that. She'd had to stick her flashlight under her arm to have both hands free to engage the deadbolt. "Yes, I'm sure I locked the back door."

"And what about the front? Did you lock it before you went back to your own rooms?"

"Of course I did. I *always* lock up."

"But what about last night specifically? Do you remember locking the front door last night?"

"Well, I..." Claire searched her memory. Locking up was a rote series of actions. She did them every night. As a result, in her mind, one night blended into another. She must have done it, mustn't she?

But then again, she'd been a wreck after what had happened with Henson, and the pregnancy test had been waiting. She couldn't be absolutely sure that she hadn't forgotten, with all that had been on her mind right then.

Joe was standing beside her. She looked up at him. "Oh, Joe. It was... a rough night." She shook her head slowly. "I can't be sure. Not absolutely." A feeling of true hopelessness washed over her.

Joe sat down beside her, and took her hand. His touch felt warm and rough and good. She'd never in her life been so grateful for another person's nearness.

She was terrified of this thing that was happening to her. It was like a nightmare, the worst kind of nightmare, one that seemed to become darker and more convoluted every minute. Right then, she longed to lean against him, to rest her head on his shoulder and drift off into forgetful sleep. She was sure that any real nightmares she might have while dreaming in Joe's arms could never compare to what was happening in her real, waking world.

He seemed to read her mind. "Scared?"

"God. Yes."

He guided her head onto his shoulder. She sighed, and rested there. "Don't be scared," he whispered. "We'll work this out. I swear it. It'll be okay."

He went on murmuring those soothing things she needed to hear, stroking her hair with one hand and holding her close with the other. His nearness was soothing for more than the soft words and the comfort of his touch. His nearness evoked memories—mostly of their one forbidden night—little, inconsequential thoughts that distracted her from her anxiety over what was going on right now.

She realized she hadn't seen him smoke since that night they'd shared. Had he quit? She could smell the faint taint of tobacco on him, but O'Donovan's back room was always smoky. If he'd been there all night, of course he'd smell of smoke.

"Did you quit smoking?"

He chuckled. The sound reverberated against her ear. "Leave it to you to notice something like that."

"Did you?"

"Yeah."

"How long ago?"

"About six weeks."

She smiled against his shoulder, and refused to wonder if the time coincided with their magical night together. "Good going, Tally."

"It was nothing, Snow."

She was quiet. Then, "How's your shoulder?"

"All better."

"That's good." She closed her eyes. And on the velvet darkness of her inner lids, she saw the snowy bandage against his tanned skin, remembered the hardness of his muscles beneath her hands, the rough, strong way he'd entered her body, thrusting so deep that she'd cried out in an agony of pleasure.

She couldn't stop her foolish heart from wondering what he would do now if she tipped her head up and begged for his kiss, if she turned enough to rub her breasts against him, if she—

Claire cut off the dangerous thoughts. Gently, so he wouldn't suspect what had been going through her mind, she lifted her head from the cradle of his shoulder.

Their eyes met. His were amber fire. She knew that he knew exactly what she had been imagining.

But all he said was, "Feel better?"

"Yes, thank you. Much better."

And she realized it was true. She felt stronger just from having rested against him for a few moments. Her mind felt clearer than it had since she'd pushed open the unlatched door to Henson's bungalow. She spoke with new spirit. "You know, my missing gun could be a coincidence."

He smiled. "You're right." He went on to suggest, "Why don't you call Amelia and Verna to make sure neither of them happened to move it?"

She stood up, full of fresh strength and purpose. "I will. I'll call them right now."

"Good. And while you're at it, has anyone else you can think of had the opportunity to take it?"

She thought over his question. Then, "Until yesterday, no."

"Okay, then. Let's start with first things first. Call Verna and Amelia."

Claire followed his instructions. She was lucky to reach both of her employees at their homes. Amelia, who still sounded somewhat hysterical, said she hadn't touched the gun, and couldn't remember the last time she'd noticed if it was where it should be. Verna, like Claire, thought she remembered seeing the gun in its place yesterday. Like Amelia, Verna claimed she hadn't so much as touched it.

Claire gritted her teeth and called her mother to ask her if she'd seen the gun. Ella did not take the news well. A man had been shot—and her daughter's gun was missing? Claire told her mother to settle down, and finally extracted the information that Ella hadn't even known Claire owned a gun—and she certainly hadn't moved it from behind the check-in desk.

When Claire had finished the call to Ella, she told Joe, "I can't think of anyone else to call . . . except the sheriff's office."

Joe, who was standing by the window, said nothing.

She explained, "I think I should report the gun missing, Joe. I really do. Because . . . Joe, I really am innocent. I really didn't shoot him. I swear it."

"All right," Joe said quietly. "Call the sheriff's office."

Claire dialed the number and spoke to Amanda Clark, one of the deputies. Deputy Clark took the information and told her to come in Monday and file a full report, if Brawley or Leven didn't contact her sooner. Claire hung up, feeling she'd made the right decision to tell the police about the gun.

"What next?" she asked Joe.

Before he could answer, the red light for room six blinked on.

Claire answered it. "Front Desk."

The man at the other end was distinctly annoyed. Was anybody going to clean his damned room today? Claire promised him prompt service and then hung up.

"What is it?" Joe asked.

Claire sighed. "Oh, I sent Amelia home after we found Henson. She was too upset to work. But she hadn't cleaned any of the rooms before she left. And now . . ."

Joe suggested, "Can you show me how to work the phones?"

She looked at him. "Oh, Joe. Thank you."

"Hell, don't thank me. All I'll be doing is sitting here punching buttons. You'll be the one up to the elbows in cleanser and dirty sheets."

After Claire showed Joe how to handle the desk, she tried calling Verna, just in case her head housekeeper might be willing to come in and help. But there was no answer, so Claire went about the business of cleaning eleven of the twelve units on her own. Henson's bungalow remained untouched; it had been taped off limits by the sheriff and his deputies.

She'd only begun when Joe appeared, announcing he'd turned on the answering machine. They devised a system; he'd help her for fifteen or twenty minutes, and then he'd return to the office to see if there were any calls to handle. She was pleased and grateful—and somewhat surprised to find that he could clean a bathroom with the best of them.

Two parties, in rooms five and one, had checked out during the commotion in the afternoon. By six o'clock, those two rooms were occupied once more. By seven, all the rooms save the back bungalow were clean and in use.

Claire wheeled the cleaning cart into the housekeeping closet and went to find Joe back at the desk. She noticed right away that his hair was wet and he was wearing a clean shirt.

He explained, "I had some clothes in my truck, so I took a quick shower. I hope that's okay."

"Of course. You found the towels all right, I guess?"

"Yeah. In the cabinet under the sink."

"Well, good."

They looked at each other. Claire tried not to think of that night when he'd showered and she'd waited with a towel, ready to help him dry off....

To distract herself from how much she'd enjoyed helping Joe dry off, she made a big show of flopping in a chair across from the lobby couch and demanding, "What's for dinner? I'm starved."

She'd thought she was teasing, but Joe didn't seem to realize that. "I ordered two steaks and baked potatoes, along with tossed salads and a bottle of red from Farina's. It'll be ready in ten minutes or so, so if you'll take over the desk, I'll go pick it up." Farina's was Pine Bluff's "nicer" restaurant. It was a step up from Mandy's, which catered to the short-order crowd.

Claire sat up straight. "Lord, Joe. Where have you been all my life?" She blushed as soon as she said it. Of course, he'd been around since she was ten. And he'd spent most of the time since they'd met telling her to get lost. "Never mind," she instructed tartly. "Forget I asked."

"Fair enough." He was hiding a smile; she knew it. He came out from behind the desk and strode to the door. She tried not to gape hungrily at his broad shoulders and lean hips. He turned, just before he left. "Back in twenty minutes. If anyone with a badge shows up, tell them nothing until I'm back here beside you."

She liked the sound of that. *Until I'm back here beside you...*

"Claire? Did you hear me?"

She wiped the dreamy smile off her face and snapped to attention. "Absolutely. I won't talk. Not a word."

"Good." And he left.

Claire sat there for a moment, thinking that the hard, honest work of making beds and scrubbing sinks had done her good. She was still very concerned about her situation, but she had a little more perspective on it now. Sheriff Brawley—and Leven, too—were working hard to discover what had really happened. The truth was bound to come out. And it was still possible that Henson would wake up and identify his assailant.

For the first time since she saw him lying so still in his own blood, Claire thought about Henson, the man. She would have been lying had she professed to like him after what he'd done the night before. But she did hope he recovered, for his own sake as well as so the truth could be known.

Sighing a little, she rested deeper into the chair and turned her head to gaze out the window at the lawn and the pool. This early in the evening, it was still in the high seventies outside, and one of her guests, svelte and tan in an electric-blue bikini, relaxed in a lounger near the deep end.

Lazily, Claire smoothed the damp tendrils of hair that had stuck to her nape. She'd haphazardly piled it all on top of her head when she started to clean the rooms, but much of it had fallen down, and the work had brought up a sweat.

Lord, it would be heaven to slip in a quick swim before Joe returned with their dinner. Claire glanced at her watch. She had fifteen minutes. If she hurried, she could manage it.

Claire switched on the answering machine once more and headed for her bedroom, shedding sweaty clothes as she went.

She was swimming a backstroke when she saw Joe's truck pull up in front of the lobby. She made for the edge, hefted herself out and grabbed her thigh-length terry beach jacket. She had it on and was darting across the grass as he emerged from the truck with the stack of white take-out cartons held carefully against his chest.

She beat him to the front door and held it open for him. "Allow me."

He stopped there in the gathering shadows of her porch, and he smiled a little, holding their dinner in conscientious hands. He looked down her legs, bare from mid-thigh, to her feet, and then back up over the fluffy robe to her face, which was pinkening now at the sweet brush of his regard.

"Have a nice swim?" he asked.

"Um. Yes. Fine." All at once, she was all awkwardness. It was silly. It made no sense. The question about her swim was as mundane as a question could get. All he'd really done was look at her.

But then, all he'd ever had to do was look at her. And, if she were honest, she'd have to admit that he didn't even have to *look*. Just having him near her was enough.

Suddenly she wondered, Did he mean to stay the night? He'd said he'd be beside her, until this bad time was through. And if he was at all concerned for her safety, then she knew he'd be nearby when darkness came.

He'd sleep on the couch, of course. Their agreement still held, suspended only to the degree that he was helping her through the trouble she was in. But not suspended enough that he'd let himself love her. They were friends; that was all.

Claire knew she must remember that, must not let her own longings have her hoping for things that would never be.

"Claire? Are you all right?"

She swallowed. She made herself smile. "Fine. I'm fine." She gave a mock bow in the direction of the door she held open. "After you."

Chapter Six

Claire insisted on putting their dinner on real plates, though she didn't change from her swimsuit because she didn't want to give the food any more time to get cold. They sat down to her table in the dining area, which was next to the kitchen and marked off from the living room by a wide arch.

The food was good, and Claire found she had a raging appetite. Neither of them spoke for a few minutes as they each attended to their steaks. Then Joe held the wine bottle over her glass, waiting for her signal to pour.

She thought of the baby. Alcohol was bad for babies.

"Half," she said.

He gave her what she'd asked for, and she was careful to take no more than a few sips, though she didn't know yet what she intended to do about the child. She wasn't making any decisions until her more immediate problem concerning the unconscious man in the Grass Valley hospital was cleared up.

Claire reconsidered. All right. Maybe she *did* know what she was going to do about the baby. But she just wasn't willing yet to face the myriad upheavals her decision was going to create.

"What is it?" Joe asked.

Claire looked up from her salad. "Hmm?"

"What's going on inside your head?"

She pushed a bite of salad into her mouth and chewed, mostly to give herself time before she answered.

Lord, what to say? If she kept the baby, of course he would have to know. Whatever did or did not exist between herself and Joe, it was his baby, too.

But what would he think when she told him?

That she was trying to trap him, most likely. She'd finally lured him into bed after years of begging him to give her love a chance. He'd spent one night with her—and guess what? She was *pregnant*. And after explaining so clearly that it was her safe time, too.

"Claire? What's wrong?"

Coward that she was, she just couldn't tell him yet. "Nothing, really. It's all just a little...overwhelming, I guess."

"Don't dwell on it," he advised.

She forced a brave smile. "I'll do my best not to."

Joe slept on the couch that night, as Claire had assumed he would. It was a rough night for her. Across the bridge, they held a street dance, and the music went on into the small hours. And there were even more fireworks exploding than the night before. But more than the noise, her own grim thoughts kept her eyes wide open and staring at the ceiling.

The next day, Sunday, Joe stayed with Claire all day except for a brief trip to his ranch in the early morning to feed the few animals and pick up more clothes. Both of them tried their best to be cheerful, but there was so much unspoken between them. And Claire found herself grimly sure each time the phone rang that it was going to be Undersheriff Leven asking her for another interview.

It was Amelia's regular workday. Claire was relieved when she showed up on time and appeared to be recovered from her hysteria of the day before. She chomped her gum and gave Joe the once-over but refrained from asking exactly what he was doing there.

Claire, who'd spent her sleepless night determining that adversity would not get the better of her, had also decided she wouldn't hide herself away. People would talk, of course, but she would not let the stares or the whispered comments interfere with her life in the least.

Every day, when Verna or Amelia relieved her, she went to lunch at Mandy's. Today would be no exception—except that she insisted Joe go with her. It would be her treat.

He gave her one of his most ironic smiles. "Are you sure you know what you're doing?"

"I know exactly what I'm doing. Amelia, no gum while you're at the desk." Amelia nodded. Claire turned for the door. "Let's go, Joe. I'm starving."

Mandy's was full, though not as packed as the day before. Ignoring the slight hush that settled over the room when they entered, Claire and Joe got a booth at the back. They ordered.

Before their food came, Eaton Slade, the local handyman, shuffled over. "Claire, you got a load for me?" He ran his fingers under the straps of his battered overalls. "Tomorrow morning, six-thirty sharp?" Pine Bluff had no garbage pickup. Every week, Eaton hauled the motel's trash to the dump for Claire.

"I'll have it ready," Claire promised.

"Good. You take care, now."

She smiled. "I will."

Eaton shuffled away, and Mandy brought their food. They ate quickly and without much talk. It was not a comfortable meal; Claire could feel the curiosity all around her, so strong that the air seemed too thick to breathe. She could easily guess what they all must be wondering. *Had* she shot the stranger from San Francisco? And why was Joe Tally sticking so close to her all of a sudden? They'd come in together. What might that mean?

She did her best to block out the feeling that everyone was watching them, and finished off her lunch.

"Want dessert?" she asked Joe as brightly as she could manage.

"I'll pass."

She paid the bill, and they went out together. Joe walked her to the post office, where she picked up the stacks of mail from the motel's box. In all the upheaval the day before, she'd forgotten all about the mail. Then they returned to Snow's Inn, where Amelia unwrapped a fresh hunk of bubble gum and headed out to get busy on the rooms.

Somehow, Claire got through the day. For dinner, she broiled some chops she had in the freezer. They watched a little TV. Then Joe stretched out on the couch and Claire went to her room to stare at the ceiling through the better part of another long night.

She was up at six. She took a shower in an effort to wash away the grim exhaustion from lack of sleep. Somewhat refreshed, she dried herself quickly and threw on her robe, then went back to her room to pull on slacks and a blouse and make her bed.

Joe was sitting at the tiny breakfast table in the kitchen, reading last Thursday's edition of the Pine Bluff *Sentinel* when Claire joined him a few minutes later. He'd pulled on his jeans, but his feet and chest were bare. His hair had that run-through-a-blender look, and his face wore a red seam down the side where a wrinkle in the pillowcase must have pressed most of the night. Claire had never seen anyone look so handsome in her entire life.

Deep inside, she knew the old ache, intensified now that she was forced to be close to him hour upon hour. The past two days, they did the things that married people did, shared food and the same roof. She'd seen him at times she'd never dared to hope she might see him: coming out of her bathroom, fresh from a shower, or now, in the morning, with the marks of sleep still pressed into his skin.

And she was finding that this was very difficult. It was too painful—to have him so near and yet be careful to keep the emotional distance that was part of their agreement. It was as difficult as wondering when Brawley or Leven would call on her again.

Since she'd found Henson unconscious, there hadn't been the slightest indication that his attacker was still around. It appeared that, if the assailant was still in town, he or she had no intention of bothering Claire. And Claire had yet to hear another word from the sheriff's office.

Joe's constant presence in her cottage began to seem less and less necessary.

Claire came to a decision, standing there in the door to her own kitchen, looking at Joe and feeling her heart ache with unfulfilled longing. Tomorrow, if nothing happened today or tonight, she'd tell Joe there was no sense to this. She'd thank him for his help and send him on his way.

And later, after she'd had time to collect her nerve, she'd decide how to go about telling him he was going to be a father *without* letting him even imagine she expected him to marry her.

And he *was* going to be a father. During the past two endless nights, Claire had had plenty of time to think. She'd admitted to herself that she'd already made her choice. It would not be easy, but she was fully capable of supporting and raising a child. She had a business that was adaptable and a lot of love to give. She would manage somehow.

Joe was watching her. "Rough night?"

She nodded. "Lately, I seem to have trouble falling asleep."

"I understand." He smiled at her, and raised his coffee mug. "I made the coffee."

She smiled back, thinking how lonely her house was going to feel when he was gone, now that she knew what it was like having him in it all the time. "Great," she said, and approached the pot.

But then she remembered that Eaton Slade was due any minute and she'd yet to put her own trash outside. She sighed and smiled a little. Life went on. Even unmarried pregnant women who were under suspicion for assault had to deal with getting the trash out on time.

She didn't have to worry about all the rooms of the motel, of course. Verna or Amelia took care of that every day. But Claire had to take her own trash out herself.

She bent and grabbed a big bag from under the sink.

Joe saw what she was doing. "Need some help?"

"Nope. I can handle it." Swiftly, she moved through her rooms, dumping the contents of each wastebasket in with the rest. When she was done, she sealed the bag and took it outside. Eaton drove up in his ancient Ford-auction pickup just as she was tossing the bag in with the rest. She waved at him, and then left him to his job.

Back in the house, she made pancakes for herself and Joe. Then she sat down across from him to eat, thinking that she was going to enjoy this last day they had together. Tomorrow they'd go back to life as it used to be.

They were just getting up together to clear off the dishes, when the night buzzer rang out in front.

"I'll get it," Joe said.

Claire let him go. She'd carried the plates and cups to the sink and started to put them in the dishwasher when she heard voices in the living room.

"Wait here," Joe said. "I'll get her."

"All right." It was Sheriff Dan's voice.

"Make it quick," Undersheriff Leven advised.

Claire, whose heart had started thudding painfully beneath her ribs, carefully took the towel off the rack and dried her hands. She watched as Joe came through the dining room to find her.

"Claire..." His voice was strange, husky. He looked as if it hurt him to even speak.

"What?" she asked. "What's the matter?"

"They found your gun, Claire. Yesterday. In Frenchman's Ravine, just outside of town."

"They did? So? Is that bad?"

"They ran some tests, and they found out..."

Claire realized that her knees felt funny. She braced herself against the counter so she wouldn't sink to the floor like a fool. "What?"

"Alan Henson was shot with your gun."

"No..." She pressed her knees harder into the solid resistance of the counter. It seemed terribly important right then to hold on to her dignity, to stand on her own two feet.

"Yes. Brawley and Leven are here."

"They...want to talk to me again?"

"They've got warrants, Claire."

"Warrants?" She said the word as if she didn't know what it meant.

"Yes. One to search this place—and one for your arrest."

Chapter Seven

The sheriff and the undersheriff drove Claire to the jail, though she could have easily walked there. Since Pine Bluff was also the county seat for Excelsior County, the sheriff's office and jail were built right on the back of the courthouse. It was five minutes on foot—to the end of her street, a right turn, and over to Courthouse Square, on the same side of the river as Snow's Inn.

Joe wasn't allowed to go with her, but the sheriff and Leven waited while Joe told her not to say anything until he got her a lawyer, which he swore he could manage within a few hours.

Sheriff Dan didn't handcuff her, for which she was grateful. He put her in the back of his 4X4 and drove her that absurdly short distance to the courthouse and then around to the back of it, where she entered the jail through the dispatcher's station.

Once inside, they took her valuables and put them in a manila bag with her name on it. Then she was fingerprinted, and they asked her an endless series of questions about her age and birthplace and parentage—questions that had nothing to do with Alan Henson. The answers to those questions were typed into a computer.

After that, Claire found herself listening to Sheriff Dan, who loved her mother's pralines, as he read her her Miranda rights.

"You have the right to remain silent, anything you say can and will..."

Claire thought, with a detached feeling of amusement, that it was just like those true-life police dramas on television. Reality programming taken one step further than any sane person would ever want it to go. It was reality programming that was happening to her.

Then Undersheriff Leven asked if she was ready to make a statement about her confrontation with Alan Henson.

As Joe had instructed, Claire said she'd wait to have her lawyer present.

After that she was taken to a long, gray room with one big cell and four little ones. There were several men she'd never seen before in the big cell. Someone she did know, Polly Flanders, was in one of the small ones. Polly was a big woman who was well-known for her violent streak. Claire assumed Polly's temper had gotten her in trouble again.

Deputy Amanda Clark locked Claire in the vacant cell next to Polly's. Claire sat down on the squeaky, single-spring bed that was bolted to one wall. As soon as Deputy Clark had left, Polly wanted to know what someone like Claire Snow was doing in the town jail.

Claire rubbed her eyes. "They think I shot a man."

"Did you?"

"No."

Polly let out a raspy cackle. "That's what they all say."

* * *

The big institutional clock on the wall outside the cell said it was ten forty-five when Deputy Clark returned and let Claire out of the cell. She was taken to another room where a powerfully built, tired-looking man in a gray suit waited.

"I'm Zack Ryder. A friend of Joe's. And your lawyer, if you want me." He held out a large, square hand. Claire shook it, thinking that his skin was warm and dry and his grip firm. When she looked into his eyes she saw they were kind.

She asked, "How much will you charge me?"

"Joe will be taking care of it," he said.

Claire shook her head. "No. I pay my own bills. How much?"

Reluctantly he quoted a figure and named an amount that he'd take as a retainer.

Claire considered, though she didn't really need to. If Joe thought Zack Ryder was a good lawyer, then he was fine with Claire.

"All right," she said. "You're hired."

"Good. Let's get to work."

They sat down across from each other in scratched plastic chairs, with a scarred institutional folding table between them. Zack Ryder explained the assault charges that had been filed against her, and what they would mean. Then he asked her to tell him of her relationship with Alan Henson and, step-by-step, everything she'd done from the time she left her mother's house on the night Henson was shot until she found Henson unconscious the next afternoon.

Claire told the story slowly and carefully. She told the absolute truth—except for the fact that she'd taken a pregnancy test and learned she was going to have a baby. When it came to that part, she told the same story she'd told Joe: that she'd felt cooped up and gone for a late-night walk.

In the hours in the cell next to Polly Flanders, she'd had time to think. And she could think of no way that the pregnancy test had a thing to do with Henson. It was her business, and her business alone. She felt wronged and invaded to be arrested for a crime she hadn't committed.

And as every hour of this nightmare passed, she found she was more and more bonded to the infinitesimal life within her. She would do anything to protect that life. Right now, that life was her secret. They could accuse her wrongly, lock her up and throw away the key. But she'd protect the truth of her baby from them for as long as it was possible. In this at least, blind circumstance was on her side. When they searched her cottage, they would find no trace of the test—Eaton Slade had seen to that this morning.

After she told him her story, Ryder advised her against giving a formal statement at this time. Claire was perfectly willing to listen to her lawyer on that point. She had not been looking forward to sitting in a dreary room like this one and being grilled by Undersheriff Leven.

Zack Ryder glanced at his watch. "Your preliminary hearing's set for today at two. Basically, we'll just sit there and let the prosecutor do all the talking. It'll be short and sweet. The judge will decide whether to bind you over to the grand jury for a more formal hearing of the charges against you. And, if the judge decides to send you to the grand jury for possible indictment, we'll get them to set your bail." He gave her a tired smile. "You'll be out of this place in time for dinner, I promise you."

Claire nodded, feeling dazed. Somehow, as the hours went by, it all became increasingly unreal—just more of her nightmare, unfolding before her. "Thank you," she murmured as Deputy Clark came to collect her once more.

She was taken back to her little cell to wait until two. They gave her lunch, which she could see had come from Mandy's. It was her favorite—bacon and tomato on whole wheat, light on the mayo. She knew that Sheriff Dan must have ordered it for her, a small kindness so she'd know he had not abandoned her. But she had no appetite. She took a few bites for form's sake, then pushed it away.

At one-thirty, she was led from the cell again. This time she was taken beyond the sheriff's office out into the court-house to a small holding room near the main courtroom, where her lawyer waited.

Ryder explained once more that she was not to worry. This wouldn't last too long, and they would learn a lot about how the prosecution saw the case should it go any farther. He went out before her, leaving her alone with Deputy Clark.

At last, she was led out into the courtroom and seated at the long table where Zack Ryder was already sitting. To her right was another long table where the county prosecutor, Buckly Fortin, was stationed. Up in the judge's seat sat Judge Willoughby, who just happened to be another of her mother's dear friends.

Claire glanced once over her shoulder at the observers' pews. She saw several people she knew, including Joe and her mother—sitting *together*. It was a testament to how numb and despondent she felt that such a sight did not even make her blink. Joe nodded and Ella telegraphed one of her most encouraging smiles.

Claire turned to face front again as Judge Willoughby began explaining how a preliminary hearing was only to make sure there was enough evidence that a crime had been committed to require a grand jury hearing. He asked Ryder if the defendant wished to waive the hearing.

"No, Your Honor. We wish to proceed with this hearing."

The judge then produced an affidavit sworn by Sheriff Brawley charging Claire with assault with a deadly weapon and battery.

Claire sat, silent and unmoving, as both Sheriff Brawley and Undersheriff Leven took the stand. They testified that Alan Henson was still in the hospital in Grass Valley. He was stable, but comatose. They reported what Claire had said to them in her interviews at the motel, and Buckly Fortin was careful to emphasize the times Claire had been seen in public with the injured man. They also produced sworn statements from Verna Higgins and the couple at the motel who had found Claire after Henson attacked her—statements attesting that Claire's clothing had been torn and she'd appeared in a state of shock. And of course, they had the ballistics report that proved Henson had been injured with Claire's gun.

When the prosecutor was done, Judge Willoughby asked if the defense had witnesses.

"None, Your Honor."

Claire listened, so numb she hardly registered her own disbelief, as Judge Willoughby declared, "The court finds there is sufficient evidence that the defendant could have committed the crimes of which she is charged. She must appear before the Excelsior County grand jury, which is scheduled to convene on Monday, July 13. At that time a more formal determination of whether she shall be tried for these crimes will be made. Is there anything else?"

Ryder stood up and requested that bond be set, listing the defendant's lack of any previous arrests and her strong ties to the community as proof that she could be trusted to walk free.

"Your Honor, I object," Buckly Fortin announced. "These are serious charges, and if the victim dies, there will be further—and even *more* serious—charges."

But Judge Willoughby overruled the prosecutor. He rapped his gavel, set the bail amount and stipulated that the accused was not to leave the county. Then he asked for the next case.

* * *

Both Joe and her mother were waiting for her when the sheriff's people gave her back her belongings and let her go home. Claire walked out into the late-afternoon sunlight and down the courthouse steps with Joe on one side and Ella on the other.

She tried to be grateful that she was free for a week at least, that the sun was shining and she could go about her life once again, for a time anyway, unconfined by bars and gray walls. But it didn't work. She was numb; she didn't want to feel. And beneath her numbness, anger burned.

She was *innocent*. She had done nothing, except fight off a man's unwanted advances. Yet in one week's time she would stand before a grand jury and find out if she would be going on trial for shooting that man.

It was so *wrong*. . . .

Also, she couldn't stop thinking about a tiny incident that had occurred in the courtroom. It was right after Judge Willoughby had set her bail. Ryder had been talking to her, telling her that Joe, whose business was working for bondsmen, would easily arrange her bond. She'd *felt* someone's eyes on her. Slowly, she'd turned.

Behind the prosecutor's table, in the front observer's row, sat an attractive blond woman in a trim maroon business suit. She was staring at Claire, her blue eyes icy cold. Claire felt the chill of the woman's hatred halfway across the courtroom.

She'd guessed immediately who the woman must be. But she turned to Ryder and asked in a whisper, anyway. "Do you know who that woman is, the one in the maroon suit?"

He'd nodded. "Mariah Henson. Alan Henson's wife."

Now, in the sunlight, Claire shivered a little. She had no doubt that Mariah Henson hated her.

"Honey, we've got the car right here," her mother said softly to her.

Claire looked down to the foot of the broad steps. Sure enough, her mother's big Chrysler was parked in the first space beyond the handicapped spot. Being a Snow and on the best of terms with all the officials in the county had its advantages.

"Thanks, Mother. But a car is ridiculous. It's just around the corner. I'll walk."

"But, dear. Surely you don't want to deal with all the responsibilities of the motel right now. Why don't you come home with me for awhile? Joe has volunteered to look after Snow's Inn for a few days." Ella actually managed a thankful smile for the man on the other side of her daughter. "Come on, honey. Let me spoil you for a while."

Claire shook her head. "Thanks, but no. I just want to go home."

They were at the foot of the steps now, beside Ella's car, beneath a big Japanese plane tree. A few people sat on the benches of the courthouse veranda, and one or two wandered up and down the steps.

Ella continued to keep her voice scrupulously low; this was family business and certainly no concern of hoi polloi. "Surely you aren't still angry about that foolish ultimatum I gave you Saturday. I take it back. I truly do. Both you and Joe know I don't feel he's...a suitable man for you. But these are special circumstances. If you feel safer having him watch over you, well, he's welcome to spend the nights at my house, too. Perhaps we can get Verna or Amelia to stay 'round the clock at Snow's Inn for a while. I'm sure either one of them would—"

"Thanks, Mother. But no. I want to go home. My own home. And that's that."

Joe said gently, "Claire, maybe you ought to listen to Ella."

Claire looked from her mother to Joe. The world had truly turned upside down. Joe Tally now called her mother by her first name and received no reprimand for it. Any other time in the past twenty years, Claire would have been ecstatic to witness such an event.

But right now it only seemed like more proof that nothing was as it should be, that nightmare was reality.

She said very levelly, "Thank you both for...everything. But right now I would like to be left alone to live my life, please. I am free for one week, and then all this...garbage starts all over again. For that week, I will live like an adult. I will take care of myself. That's how I want it, and that's how it will be."

With that, she moved from between the two of them and strode off down the street. She'd turned the corner onto Quartz Lane before she was really positive that neither one of them was going to follow her.

At the motel, she found Amelia manning the desk. Amelia jumped about a foot when she saw her boss stride in. The fanzine she was reading was whipped behind her back and she swallowed convulsively—ridding herself, no doubt, of a forbidden hunk of bubble gum.

"Claire! H-how are you?"

"Fine, Amelia. Thank you for looking after things."

"Hey. It's nothin'. Any time. Er, look...I really feel rotten about having to tell Wayne Leven that you said you'd kicked that Henson guy out the other night."

"Forget it," Claire told her, meaning it. "You told the truth, and that's all you can do." Claire bustled behind the counter, hoping this subject was done with.

But Amelia hadn't fully expunged her guilty feelings yet. "Well, I didn't like doing it," she insisted. "Because, no matter what they try to pin on you, everyone in town knows you'd never..." Amelia's voice faded as she registered the strained expression on her boss's face. "So, anyway, what's happened? In court?"

"They still think I shot Henson, and I have to go before the grand jury next week. But they let me out on bail until then."

"Gee, tough break," Amelia sympathized. "But at least you're out, right?"

"Right. That's what I keep trying to tell myself. Now what's the status of the rooms?"

Amelia puffed up her chest proudly. "I got all but number three and number seven done before Joe Tally had to leave for the courthouse."

"Great. What about the back bungalow?"

"It's still got the tape barriers around it."

Claire made a mental note. Tomorrow she would call the sheriff's office and demand to know when they'd be through collecting evidence—or whatever they were doing—from the bungalow. She wanted to get in there and clean it up.

And, yes, damn it, maybe she wanted to look around a little, too, see if she could find anything that the sheriff's investigators had missed—some tiny clue that might hint at who had stolen her gun and then shot a man with it.

"Er, should I get on back to work?" Amelia asked. She was looking at Claire nervously.

Claire knew she was scowling, and schooled herself to a calmer expression. "Yes, go ahead. And, Amelia?"

"Yeah?"

"Thanks again, for staying late."

Amelia's pretty face bloomed in a grin. "You're welcome. Really." She shoved the inevitable wad of gum into her mouth and went on her way.

Claire moved behind the desk and straightened up her work area. When the phone rang, she answered it pleasantly and took a five-day reservation for the middle bungalow for Thanksgiving week. She didn't even allow herself to think that by then she might be standing trial for the shooting of Henson—or worse, she might have been convicted, and be an inmate down at Folsom, or wherever it was they sent women who shot men and put them in comas.

After forty minutes or so, Amelia appeared to say she was done for the day.

"If you need me, you call me," Amelia said. Tomorrow was Tuesday, and Verna would be back.

"With all this . . . upheaval," Claire said, "I really *might* need you."

"Just call."

"Thanks. I will."

Claire sent her home and then locked the front door. If anyone came by, they could ring for service.

She went back to her rooms, and found them reasonably in order after the sheriff's people had searched them. Here and there, though, she noticed that her things had been moved slightly.

Her bed had been torn apart and on many of the smooth furniture surfaces there was a thin coating of chalky dust. She pondered the dust for a while, before she figured out that it must be the stuff they used to check for fingerprints. She stuck her finger in it and brought it to her nose to see if it had a smell. It was odorless, but to Claire, it *did* smell. It smelled of the violation of her home and her life.

She got out her cleaning bucket and spent two hours wiping away all the dust and putting her things back where they belonged. By then, it was nearly eight o'clock. She found a packaged pizza in the freezer and stuck it in the oven. Then she sat down at her little kitchen table and doggedly ate.

Just as she was cleaning up the dishes, her mother called. Claire reassured her she was fine and hung up as quickly as she could.

After that, she went into the living room and watched a little television, getting up when the lobby phone rang or, once, to answer the bell out front. Finally, it was nine-thirty—late enough that she could allow herself to go to bed without having to admit that she would be trying to escape this horrible day through sleep.

She showered and she put on her summer pajamas and she lay down on her bed. She did a little of her most recent nightly pastime, ceiling-staring. But then she sighed and curled herself into a ball on her side.

It was there, lying all tucked into herself, that she found the first comfort she'd found all day. She did it by allowing herself to imagine that the tight curl of her body cradled the tiny life within her, as much as it reassured her, its mother.

As soon as she discovered that imagining the baby brought solace, she let herself go farther, envisioning that tiny being—surely it was no bigger than her thumbnail now—swimming contentedly in its watery world.

She let her hand stray to her belly and she gently rubbed, pretending the baby could know her touch already, could sense the love she wanted it to feel. Her stomach, she noticed then, was as flat as it had ever been. She marveled about the changes that would come.

So far, the changes in her body were minimal: a certain sensitivity to her breasts, and a kind of knowing, blooming feeling that had made her sure in her deepest heart that she was pregnant long before she forced herself to take the test. At six weeks, she was experiencing no morning sickness, but maybe that was still to come. And even if she escaped the nausea and other unpleasant symptoms that plagued some women, soon enough her stomach would grow round, her breasts full. There would be no denying her condition.

And she'd have to tell Joe....

At that thought, all the warm, relaxing feelings faded away. She turned, fitfully, and tried to get comfortable on her other side.

Once more, she curled up in a ball and fiercely imagined her unborn child. But it didn't work. She felt too guilty about Joe, about this baby that she knew he'd feel responsible for, a baby he'd had no say in creating.

Joe himself was illegitimate. His parents had never married—either each other, or anyone else. Joe knew what it was to be called a bastard and have it be literally true. It was very possible that he was going to consider what Claire had done—foolishly letting herself get pregnant—as the worst kind of betrayal of his trust.

More than once over the years, he'd told her that he would never have children. He thought he'd make a lousy father, and he wasn't sure bringing a baby into a world such as this one was a good idea, anyway.

Claire turned over again. Suddenly it was impossible to find a comfortable place in her bed. And then, just as she was punching her pillow to make it fluffier, the outside bell rang. Groaning, she sat up. She shoved her feet into her slippers and pulled on her light robe and went to answer it.

She saw that it was Joe soon as she reached the lobby. He was clearly visible through the glass top of the door, gazing off toward the pool, waiting patiently for her to come and let him in.

But she didn't want to do it. She didn't want to talk to anyone tonight. No one she cared about, anyway. Strangers looking for a room, she could handle. But no one who mattered to her—and certainly not Joe.

She wanted to be alone to lick her wounds and—yes, all right, it was true—feel sorry for herself. And she would go mad right now if she had to look into eyes she loved and find pity and concern looking back at her.

Knowing she was being foolish, she ducked behind the desk and backed up until she was safely in her own rooms once more.

The bell rang again just as she reached the dim sanctuary of her bedroom. She climbed into bed and put her pillow over her head. Still, she heard the third ring. She ignored it.

After that, everything was quiet.

Until the small scraping sounds that told her the screen in the open window near her bed was being efficiently removed.

Claire sat up and gathered the sheet close, as if it might protect her. She watched as the shadowed figure climbed smoothly over the sill.

"What do you think you're doing?"

"Whatever it takes," he muttered wryly, "to make sure you're all right." He swung himself fully into her bedroom and stood tall.

"I'm fine. I want to be alone," she said.

"You've been alone long enough."

She stared at him, wanting to cry and laugh at the same time—but unable to do either. The irony of this situation was not lost on her. Six weeks ago, *he'd* been the one not answering his door, and *she'd* had to crawl in a window to get through to him.

"Go away," she snapped. Then, feeling hopeless and torn in two—wanting him to go, yet longing for him to stay—she found she couldn't look at him. She bowed her head and stared at her hands instead.

He took the two steps to the bed. "It's bad, huh?"

She didn't look up. "Just go. Please."

He said nothing. She felt the bed give as he sat on the edge.

Then he reached out, wrapped his arm around her shoulders and pulled her against his lean body. She went, resisting a little, but not enough to make him release her.

He cradled her against his chest and stroked her hair. She moved fitfully against him for a moment, and then she breathed deeply, finding that it felt good to have him hold her. Her body, of its own accord, began to relax. She sighed and allowed herself to listen to the reassuring sound of his heartbeat.

"Cry," he suggested softly. "Let yourself go. You'll feel better if you do."

"I can't, not now," she told him. "Right now, I just couldn't let down my guard that much." She took in a wobbly breath. "It's all so... *wrong,* Joe. I just can't believe that this could happen. It isn't fair. It isn't right...."

He made a low sound in his throat, one of agreement.

They sat there, in the warmth of the summer night, their arms wrapped around each other, saying nothing for a while.

The feel of him against her was better than words. The way he held her said he knew her numbness. The numbness that covered anger that, deeper down, covered fear at the way her own world had betrayed her.

She'd told him on that night six weeks ago that she was *not* innocent. But maybe he'd been right. She *had* been innocent. She'd been trusting, in the way that only a person to whom the world has always been fair can be trusting. She'd lived thirty years secure in her sheltered belief that good always won and truth set a person free....

And now, with a baby growing inside her, she was beginning to wonder if any of what she had so naively assumed was true. Lately the world seemed a cold and shadowed place. And it was into this place that her baby, within mere months, would be born.

Still, with Joe's arms around her, she felt a little stronger, a little more able to cope.

Joe stroked her hair gently. "Feel better?"

"Yes, Joe, I do."

"Good." He took her face in his hands. "Now listen. I've just come from talking to your mother."

For the first time in hours, Claire allowed herself a genuine smile. "You and my mother are getting to be real buddies lately."

"We both want the same thing," he told her. "For you to get through this without it breaking you."

She stiffened a little, thinking of the baby. For the baby's sake if nothing else, she couldn't afford to be broken. "It won't break me." Her voice was firm and clear.

"Good." He dropped his hands away and hitched a leg up onto the bed.

She bravely went on smiling, letting herself enjoy the humor in the idea of Joe Tally and Ella Snow putting their heads together over the problem of her own mental health. "And what brilliant plan have you and my mother cooked up now?"

"Well, it wasn't really your mother's idea. In fact, she's not at all thrilled about it." He looked unsure.

"What is it?" she demanded. "Joe?"

"Hell." He looked away.

"Joe?" She touched the side of his face to make him turn back to her again.

His skin felt rough, with a day's worth of beard. In her midsection, without warning, that familiar blooming sensation began.

Even now, she thought, with all that's happened in this miserable day, it's so easy to want him. So easy to remember that one glorious night . . .

He looked into her eyes once more and she saw that the touch had affected him, too. There was heat in his gaze. He wanted her, too.

In less than an instant, everything had changed. Their easy companionship had become something else. She was painfully aware of what she'd hardly considered before; they were sitting in her darkened bedroom, on her bed, in the middle of the night.

"Damn it, Claire." His voice was gruff. "Don't even think it. It's not a good idea."

She didn't want to hear him tell her what they shouldn't do. "Joe…" She touched his face again, tracing a slow trail along his strong jaw to his neck, and lower down, until she clasped his shoulder, felt the strength in it, through the fabric of his shirt.

"No," he said.

"Please…" She was shameless. She didn't care. Right then, there might never have been an agreement. It didn't exist. There was only herself and Joe and the hunger to be close to him, to take him inside her, and to move with him to a place beyond guilt or innocence, where only sensation reigned.

He clasped the hand that clutched his shoulder and his eyes burned into hers. "It would be a mistake."

"No." She shook her head for emphasis. "It would only be…what we both want. It would hurt no one. And it would give me…comfort, when I need it the most. Just like what I gave you six weeks ago. A fair exchange."

For a long moment they looked at each other. And then the miracle happened.

With a low groan, he reached out and pulled her against him. His hard arms encircled her and his mouth closed over her own.

The kiss went on forever, hot and carnal and weighted with the promise of what might come next. Claire reveled in the taste of him, after these long weeks of hunger and longing. She moaned and her lips parted. His tongue played with hers as she pressed herself against him. She let her hands roam freely over his broad back and shoulders, relearning every hard contour. Her senses swam; she was awash in a sweet and slightly frantic delight.

But then, out of nowhere, he pulled back.

She cried softly, "No!"

But he held her at arm's distance once more. "Claire." His tone was rough and husky. "This is not what I came here for."

She opened her heavy eyes and looked at him, so he would know this was a conscious choice for her. "It doesn't matter. It's what I want."

"You're sure?"

"Beyond a shadow of a doubt."

"You'll regret it. After all this is . . . worked out."

"Never. Not for a moment. As long as I live."

He was gripping her shoulders tightly, holding her carefully away. He stared at her so hard she felt as if his eyes seared twin holes in her own.

Then he said, "All right."

Chapter Eight

Her body, which had been straining for his, relaxed. She allowed herself a faint smile. "Gee, Joe. You don't have to sound so grim about it."

Now it was his turn to smile. "I'm not. Not really. I want you. I've always wanted you." He shifted uncomfortably on the edge of the bed. "And I don't seem to be able to hide it very well lately."

Claire's heart was pounding faster. It was a lovely thing to hear. Joe Tally desired her . . . had *always* desired her.

He went on before she could let her thoughts carry her away. "But not tonight."

She felt the disappointment a child feels when she's told she won't be going to the ice-cream shop after all. And then she smiled at herself. "Why not?" The question was good-natured.

"Hell. First off, I don't have anything for contraception. Do you have anything here?"

She looked at him and had to hold back a slightly hysterical laugh. He had no idea that the cow was already out of the barn on that score.

Her conscience spoke up clearly. *Tell him. Tell him now.*

But she just couldn't get her mouth around the words. Not yet. She couldn't see how he would be anything but angry when he found out. At the very least, he would withdraw from her, something for which she wouldn't blame him in the least.

Today had been rough enough. Its only bright spots were her thoughts about the baby and these past few minutes here in the dark with Joe. If he turned away from her now, it would hurt worse than it ever had before.

She *would* tell him. But not yet. Not for a little while longer...

"Claire?"

She realized he was waiting for her to answer his question about contraception. She shook her head. "No. I don't have anything here."

"Right." He seemed a little embarrassed. She loved him more than ever. "And besides that," he went on, "I'd just rather you...thought about this a little, considered how it would affect you, if you and I..."

"Oh, Joe." She touched him again, on the side of his face. She would never get enough of touching him. "Okay. Let's let it be for tonight. We'll both think about it. Fair enough?"

"Yeah. Fair enough."

There was a small silence. From outside somewhere, a mourning dove called. Claire shook herself and recalled what he'd been leading up to before desire carried them away.

"And now tell me, what did you and my mother decide?"

He stood up and went to look out at the night, perhaps seeking a sight of that lonely dove. Then he turned to face her. "Really," he hedged, "it was me. Ella doesn't like it, but she's willing to go along because she does agree that you need some time to regroup, some time away from everything, without the pressures of running this motel."

"What, Joe? What's the plan?"

"Well..."

"Come on. Spit it out."

At last he did. "She's willing to take over for you here for a few days, so that you can go out and stay at the ranch with me."

Claire just stared. "My mother *agreed* to that?"

Through the shadows, she could see his white teeth flash in a rueful smile. "I have to admit, I made a big deal about my *guest* bedroom. And I went on and on about how you and I are friends and nothing more. Now, after what we've just been doing, I guess what I told her wasn't much short of a bald-faced lie." He was quiet. Then, "So? What do you say?"

"Well, I—"

"Hey, think about it. Give yourself a minute. Or even two. Just realize I promised your mother I'd call her tonight with your decision—and it's getting pretty late."

Claire let out a little groan of protest at his railroading tactics. But then she thought about his proposition.

She decided immediately that it held definite appeal. In her confusion and pain right after her release that afternoon, she'd thought only of getting back to her everyday life. But maybe, for right now, everyday life wasn't what she needed.

She loved her business. However, it was a twenty-four-hour-a-day job. Maybe some time away would be good. Maybe she'd get a new perspective on her predicament in different surroundings.

Also, in the past few minutes, everything had changed between herself and Joe. After what they'd just agreed, she wouldn't have to spend all of her time denying her longing for him—and that put a new light on things. Given that she could touch him and hold him, it would be wonderful to be alone with him.

Perhaps, she thought with rising excitement, out of this, the worst ordeal of her life, there would at least come some memories that she could cherish in the years to come.

Joe started convincing her again. "I've been . . . cleaning things up a little at the ranch, I promise you," he said with an eagerness that did her heart good. "It's not the Ritz, but it's a hell of a lot more comfortable than the last time you were there."

She fiddled with the sheet hem a little, pleased as a girl with her first crush at having *him* be the eager one for once.

"Well, what do you say?"

"When would we go?"

"Tomorrow, in the morning. Ella will come in around nine, and you and I will take off."

"For how long?"

"A few days—the whole week until the grand jury hearing, if you want. Come on. It'll be the best thing, I'm sure of it."

She looked directly at him. "All right, Joe."

"Does that mean yes?"

She allowed herself a genuine, anticipatory smile. "Yes, it means yes. Let's do it. Tomorrow morning, let's . . . get away from it all."

As he had the two previous nights, Joe slept on the couch. Surprisingly, once she'd given him his blankets and pillow and settled back into her bed, Claire found she was drowsy. She drifted off into a deep and dreamless sleep.

The next thing she knew, it was eight-thirty in the morning. Her eyes came open and she was looking at the digital display of her bedside alarm clock. She lay there, staring at it lazily for a moment, thinking that she'd just enjoyed her first decent night's sleep in days. She felt ten years younger and ready for anything . . . almost anything.

And then she realized that her mother would be there at nine and she had half an hour to be packed and ready to go.

She fairly leapt from the bed. She showered in five minutes flat, and was dressed in jeans and a sleeveless shirt in ten. She'd just dragged her big suitcase out from under the bed and begun piling things into it, when the tap came at the door.

"Come in."

Joe pushed the door inward, and ventured a few steps into the room. He looked warily on as she tore through her drawers, tossing the chosen items halfway across the room to the bed.

She turned. "I forgot to set my alarm. Why didn't you wake me?"

"You needed the sleep." He held out a mug of coffee. "I figured you'd be ready for this about now."

She grinned at him thankfully and paused in her frantic preparations long enough to take a few sips.

He watched her as she drank. "There's no real hurry, you know. Your mom's coming to stay. It won't bother her if you're still packing when she arrives."

"Now that we're going, I don't intend to hang around one minute longer than necessary." Claire set the coffee on the bureau and turned to snap the suitcase shut. "There," she said. "Now I need to make my mother a list of the things she can't forget to do."

"She's helped you out before, hasn't she?"

"Yes, but it's better if it's written down." She dodged around Joe and went to the kitchen, where she found paper and pencil and set about writing down such things as *Pick up mail and sort daily* and *Verna in at eleven, off at five. She relieves you at desk for an hour for your lunch, any hour you prefer. . . . Checkbook in flat drawer directly beneath guest register.* She glanced up at Joe, who was wiping down the kitchen counter and rinsing out the coffeepot.

"Joe, what's the number at the ranch?"

He told her and she wrote it on the paper. When she'd jotted down all the salient points she could think of, she hurried out to the lobby to sign a few checks in the big checkbook, in case her mother had to pay anyone before Claire returned.

She was just shoving the checkbook back in its drawer when Ella arrived, appearing on the porch and waving cheerfully at Claire through the glass top of the door. Claire went to let her in.

The minute her mother was inside the door, Ella set down her small suitcase and reached out. Claire went into her mother's arms. Ella held her close and Claire remained compliant in the lengthy embrace.

At last, Ella pulled away and took her daughter by the shoulders. "How are you, dear?"

"I'm okay, Mother. Honestly."

Ella pursed her mouth. "I'm not really sure this is a wise idea."

"I know. Joe told me."

"But, well, I would like to see you have a little time to...get your bearings again, after all that's happened. And I do want to help. Any way I can."

"I know. And I'm grateful." Claire took Ella's hand. "Come on. Let me refresh you on how the phones work, and go over the list I just made out."

When she was through going over the list, she thought of one more thing, but she hesitated to bring it up. It seemed a lot to ask.

Her mother said, "I know that look. Go ahead and ask me. I can always say no."

"Well, it won't be a pleasant chore."

"Ask me."

"All right. There's still a tape barrier around the back bungalow—the one Henson stayed in. I want to know when the sheriff's people are going to let us get back in there."

"You want me to call Dan and ask for a time that the tape will be removed, is that it?"

"Exactly. And I want you to pin him down about it. Really, reasonably, it should be soon—in the next day or two, don't you think?"

"I certainly do," Ella answered staunchly. "And I'll be glad to have a word with Dan."

Claire hid her smile. Perhaps having such a formidable, overbearing mother had more advantages than she'd previously imagined.

Ella asked, "And once they let us in, shall I have Verna take care of it, clean it up and get it ready to rent out again?"

"No," Claire said. "Just lock it up, and call me."

Ella frowned. "Claire, dear, I'm sure by the time Dan and Wayne Leven are through in there, they'll have found out every...clue there is about who actually shot that man. They *are* the professionals, after all."

Claire just looked at her mother. She didn't need to say what she was thinking. *Some professionals. They've arrested an innocent woman.* All she said aloud was, "I mean it, Mother. I want you to leave it alone and call me right away. I want your word."

"Oh, honestly," Ella groused. "All right. You have my word. I'll lock the bungalow and call you immediately when the sheriff's office lets us in there."

* * *

Ten minutes later, Claire and Joe were up in the cab of his pickup, waving goodbye to Ella as they pulled out of the space in front of the cottage.

They were trundling across the bridge when Claire thought about breakfast—and about her determination, made before her arrest, not to hide herself away from anyone or anything.

"Joe?"

"Yeah?"

"In all the rush, I forgot to eat breakfast."

"Don't worry. I haven't got much food at the ranch, but I do have eggs and bacon. Can you last half an hour without starving?"

"I could. But I'd rather stop and eat at Mandy's."

They'd reached the stop sign at Main Street. A left turn would take them out of town. With his foot on the brake, Joe gave her a look. "You always did have more guts than sense."

"I'm going away with you, Joe. But, no matter what a rush I might be in to get out of here, I'm not *running* away. I have nothing at all to hide."

Joe, who seemed to realize that arguing over this particular issue would be a waste of time, turned right and looked for a place to park.

Mandy's was not the loud, bustling place it had been over the holiday weekend. At nine-thirty on a Tuesday morning, the counter was only half occupied and one or two of the booths were empty. There were few serious eaters at this time of the day. But Mandy's was a town gathering place, so there were still plenty of people drinking coffee and discussing the latest issues of local interest.

When Claire and Joe walked in, the hush was so sudden and total, it echoed.

Claire was not surprised—it was exactly what she'd expected. She knew very well that after yesterday's courtroom hearing, *she* was currently the main issue of local interest in Pine Bluff. She scrupulously ignored both the stares and the furtive glances as she and Joe walked the length of the room to take the same booth they'd claimed on Sunday.

Mandy, who usually took her sweet time about providing service when the place wasn't packed, was there with a full coffeepot and an order pad almost before they sat down.

"Good to see you, Claire." Mandy was famous for her saturnine expression, but now she actually trotted out a smile. She turned to Joe. "Joe."

Claire and Joe said good morning.

Mandy asked, "So what'll you have?"

They asked for eggs and bacon and toast, and turned their cups up so Mandy could fill them. And then, as they sat sipping coffee and waiting for their food, Claire was reminded of the other reason—her hopeless love for Joe Tally being the first—that she had come back to Pine Bluff after college. She'd come back because, though people here knew way too much about each other's business, they also stood by their own.

First, it was Brenda Tyler. Brenda clerked in the school administration office and, on Sundays, she played the organ up at the community church. She was sitting in the booth behind Claire's, and she tapped Claire on the shoulder. Claire turned.

Brenda asked with great gentility, "How are you doing, Claire?"

"Just fine."

"'Lo, Joe."

"Miss Tyler."

"Claire..." Brenda tactfully lowered her voice. "I want you to know that you are in my thoughts. You are in my prayers. And if there is anything—anything—that I can do for you, then you just let me know."

"Thank you, Brenda. Thanks a lot."

"Stay strong," Brenda advised, reaching a pale, veined hand over the seat of the booth to give Claire's shoulder an awkward pat.

"I will," Claire promised. Brenda gave Claire's shoulder a quick squeeze and then returned to her coffee and her crescent roll.

After Brenda came Bo Sims, who owned the local garage. He stood beside their booth, carefully clasping his own grease-stained hands together, and told her everyone was thinking of her. After that, Lolly Beals, the clerk at Pine Bluff Grocery, strolled over.

Lolly said, "Don't you worry. Things'll work out."

Even Mandy, who usually tossed the plates of food down and turned away almost before they hit the table, paused to give Claire a pat on the hand when she delivered the food. All the time Joe and Claire ate, people dropped by the booth and said quiet, kindly words.

Claire's predicament was never referred to directly; under such public circumstances that would have been presumptuous. But the people of her town wanted her to know that they were thinking of her. And if she needed them, they were there.

When Joe and Claire got up to leave, Mandy said the check had already been paid.

Since they'd eaten, they decided to drive on to Grass Valley and buy groceries right away. That whole process took a few hours, so they didn't arrive at the ranch until early afternoon.

The dogs came bounding down out of the shadows of the porch to greet them when they pulled into the yard.

"Gonzo! Relay!" Joe commanded. "Sit!" The dogs whined but did as their master bid.

Claire got down and gave them the pats and kind words they'd been seeking. Then she stood for a moment in the bright sun to note that Joe had laid gravel in the driveway and chopped down the weeds since her last midnight visit. Also, the derelict tractor had been moved, probably to the barn in the pasture behind the house. One of the two beat-up trucks was gone; the other, of course, had been their transportation out here.

In the shadow of the barn, she could see the swaybacked horse.

Beside her, Joe chuckled as he noticed the direction of her gaze. "That's Demon. A has-been if there ever was one. My old man loved that damn horse. So I've never had the nerve to ship him off to the glue factory where there is no doubt he belongs."

Claire shaded her eyes so she could look at Joe, because the harsh sun was a burning ball just above his head. She was thinking about his father, a recluse, whom no one in Pine Bluff had ever really known, and she was touched that Joe would keep his father's aging horse. She gently teased, "Aw, come on. You're just a softy, admit it."

"I don't admit a damn thing—except it's good to see you smiling again." The hot breeze blew a loose strand of hair across her mouth. He brushed it away, guiding it back behind an ear.

She caught his hand, and she turned it over and then laid his open palm against her cheek. "Thanks, Joe. I think this little 'vacation' you've arranged is going to turn out to be exactly what I need."

"Good." His thumb caressed her, gently rubbing at the side of her mouth. She sighed a little, enjoying the way, down inside her, desire was stirring and wakening....

Then one of the dogs whined.

Joe's hand dropped away.

Claire forced herself to think practical thoughts. "Guess what? We've got a truck bed full of groceries, and it's ninety degrees out here."

"You said it, I didn't."

"So let's get to it."

She turned and marched to the back of the pickup. After a moment, he joined her there. Together they unloaded the groceries and her suitcase and took them inside.

Claire was more than a little surprised when she stepped beyond the threshold into the cool interior of the old house. Outside, he hadn't done much but lay the gravel drive, cut the weeds, repair the window she'd broken—and add a wooden glider on the porch, something she'd complimented when they passed it on the way in.

But inside, he had painted and bought new furniture, so that it seemed as if she was in a different house than the dreary one she'd broken into weeks before. In a side window, a new air conditioner hummed.

Joe explained, "I left it on yesterday. So it would be comfortable in here, just in case you came." His voice was hesitant, almost shy.

"I see." She felt shy herself, suddenly. She looked up, remembering the watermark that had been on the ceiling. Now there was no sign of it beneath a fresh coat of paint.

He seemed to read her question in the direction of her gaze. "I patched the roof, so it should be okay. If not—" he shrugged "—I'll find out I've got problems when we get the next good rain.... Now, come on. Let's get these groceries to the kitchen." He led the way through the hall, and then together they set about putting the food away.

When they were done, she turned to him. "Joe, I really am impressed," she said of the changes in the house. "You must have been working at this pretty steadily since..."

He gently finished for her. "The last time you were here?"

She swallowed. "Yes."

"I guess I have, now that you mention it."

"All this—" she made a gesture that encompassed the whole house and the weedless yard "—couldn't have left you much time for chasing bad guys."

"It hasn't."

"You've been taking some time off?"

"Yeah, I guess so." He leaned back against the counter and folded his arms. "Truth is, I'm considering a career change. Hunting down bail jumpers isn't doing it for me anymore." His voice was as casual as the way he leaned against the counter, but Claire sensed this subject troubled him more than he wanted to let on.

"Since Mexico?" she dared to ask.

She was pleased to see he didn't tense when she mentioned the place where he'd watched a boy die. "Yeah, since then," he answered without heat. "And probably before that. Skip tracing..." He paused at the use of the more current name for the business of bounty hunting, "Well, it's a rough life. You're out on your own with no one on your side. A lot of bounty hunters aren't much more than borderline crooks themselves. I'd like to...maybe do more with my life."

She put a hand on his arm. "Like what?"

Beneath her hand, she felt him stiffen. He chuckled, but his golden eyes turned hard. "Hell. Maybe I'll run for president. Who knows?"

She felt a little hurt—and left out of the harsh joke. "Joe, I didn't mean to—"

"Right. Sure."

"All I asked was what you might do instead. Is there something wrong with my asking that? It seemed like a logical question." She tried to pull her hand away.

He snared it so quickly she hardly saw him move. "Yeah. A logical question. And you said it so politely."

She was bewildered. One minute they'd been having a nice conversation, and then suddenly he'd turned defensive on her. "And just how else would I say it?"

"How about a little honesty? How about just saying what you're thinking. You know, 'Joe, are you *crazy*? What *else* will you do? You barely made it through high school. How are you going to *eat*?'"

"That is *not* what I was thinking, and it's unfair of you to assume it was." She tried to jerk her hand from his grasp.

He held on. He said nothing for a moment as his hand held hers prisoner, and his eyes branded her. Then his expression softened. He spoke gently, regretfully. "I know."

She was still hurt. "You know you were being unfair?"

"Yeah."

"Then why did you do it? Why did you . . . attack me like that?"

"I'm thin-skinned about this. To be honest, I don't know what the hell I'm going to do for work if I give up what I know."

Claire studied his lean face and then suggested, "Maybe we could just kick some ideas around. Explore the options. Talk about what you know and what you can do, and see what kind of jobs you might be able to apply your experience to."

He was rolling his eyes. "Okay, okay. But later."

"When?"

"Sometime in the next few days, all right?"

"Deal," she said, pleased, hoping that when they did talk about this, she could be of help to him. He had done so much for her lately, she was beginning to feel there was no way she could repay him.

She relaxed, and felt his hand relax around her own. They smiled at each other.

And then he reeled her in by her captured hand, so she came up against him. Her breasts brushed his chest. She hitched in a breath and stared up at him.

"Claire?"

She moistened her lips. "Yes?"

He watched her mouth. "To tell the truth, there's something else I'd rather do now than talk..."

He didn't have to say more. She knew what was on his mind. It was clear in his amber eyes. Still, she wanted him to say more. She wanted him to say that he wanted her here as much as she wanted to be here, that he desired her as much as she desired him. She wanted all the beautiful words that lovers always want, including the words *I love you*, though she'd long ago accepted that she would never hear those words from Joe Tally's lips.

"Hell, I..."

"Yes?"

"I...put your suitcase in the guest room, like I promised your mother."

She smiled, knowing that what she and Joe wanted of each other was something mothers, in spite of all their righteous efforts, are rarely able to prevent. Still smiling, she touched his collar with her free hand and let her fingers trail up to caress his neck and the side of his jaw. His skin felt almost smooth. She realized he must have showered and shaved early this morning while she still slept.

Gruffly, he went on. "I also... took care of the contraception problem when we were in Grass Valley."

She glanced away, and then back. From somewhere far off, her conscience chattered at her, insisting that it was dishonest not to tell him that contraception was totally unnecessary.

Claire shut the chatter out. She'd said nothing when he made the brief stop at the drugstore, though she'd known what he would buy there. She would say nothing now. This time with Joe was a lifeline for her. She would neither say nor do anything to endanger it.

Her life was coming apart. Was it so wrong, for a little while at least, to want the chance to simply *feel* and *be*?

Unaware of the battle her conscience was trying to put up, Joe released her hand and tenderly cupped her face. Then he began combing her hair in lingering strokes with his fingers.

The chatter of her conscience faded away to nothing as Claire clutched his strong shoulders and pressed closer against him.

"Claire, I want you." He lowered his mouth and kissed her, and Claire forgot what the word *conscience* meant. Then his hands were sliding down her neck and over her shoulders. He began rubbing her back. "And I want to make love with you," he said. "I want to make love with you now."

She couldn't find words. So she nodded instead.

Chapter Nine

Joe Tally looked down at Claire's upturned, inviting face. Her lips were soft; they waited for his kisses. Her body leaned eagerly into his, as sweet and compliant as his was hard and hungry. Her dark eyes were shining.

He knew that what they were about to do was probably one massive mistake for everyone. It was not good for Claire, who had never been anything but kind and generous to him. It was dishonest to her mother, who had only gone along with his bringing Claire here because he had sworn that he and Claire were nothing more than friends.

And for himself, it was plain stupid. He'd always been careful to keep away from Claire—until that night several weeks ago, anyway. But that night he'd broken his own rule about her. He'd put his hands on her, he'd been inside her. And he'd spent too damn much time since then thinking about being inside her some more—and reminding himself how he'd sworn to both of them that he wouldn't do a thing like that again.

Yet here he was, with her in his arms. And nothing was going to stop him. He would do it again.

Plain stupid. Because, in the end, for her sake, he would have to give her up. And that was going to be grim.

"Joe?" Her sweet, flushed face showed concern. "What is it? Is something wrong?"

He put his hands on the curve of her back and pulled her so snugly into him that her breasts swelled full against his chest and he could feel the warm cove between her thighs, that hot and welcoming place where he most wanted to be.

"Nothing's wrong," he muttered. "Not a damn thing..." And he took her soft, waiting mouth with his own.

She sighed and opened for him. With his tongue, eager and knowing, he explored the moist place beyond her lips, starved for the taste of her, as he'd been since that first taste, all those weeks ago.

He kissed her for a long time, tasting her at his leisure, as they stood there against the kitchen counter. And then his hands found the buttons of her shirt and he slipped them quickly from their holes. With a hungry moan, he pushed the thing off her shoulders, revealing the sweet swells beneath, protected now only by her ivory-colored bra.

He cupped her breasts, and squeezed them, feeling for the response of her nipples, which rose and hardened like dark pearls in their lacy nest. And then, a little roughly, he fumbled for the clasp of the bra, found it, at last felt it give. He then slid the straps down her arms, so that her breasts were bare for him.

She let out a little sigh, as if she liked being bare for him. He sipped that sigh from her willing mouth in another extended, thoroughly arousing kiss.

Then he kissed his way downward, so he could get his mouth on her breasts, too, take the nipples beyond his hungry lips. As he suckled her, he felt her body yearning back and up, offering him everything, eager and so achingly, innocently carnal, that the taste of her was everything sexual—and everything pure.

He nuzzled his way over, so he could taste the other breast. And she offered it the same as she had the first, pushing herself so sweetly up against his mouth, sighing and holding his head to help him keep his hold.

As he had the last time, that night when she had come and brought her light and goodness into this darkened house, he wanted to touch her in that most intimate of places. He wanted her completely naked, at the command of his hands.

So he worked at her jeans, unhooking, unzipping, and finally sliding them and her panties down her slim legs. She helped him toward his goal, kicking off her shoes, kneeling to push off her socks and then rising again, stepping free of the hindering jeans. He pulled her close again and his hand slipped into that nest of curls, until he found the center of her desire. She was wet and eager, and he loved the way she stood on tiptoe, holding herself up for him, so he could love her body and make her moan.

But then she was pushing at his shoulders, murmuring half protests, and though he didn't want to stop or even pause in what he did to her, he forced himself to pull back a little.

The minute he hesitated, he knew what she was up to. She wasn't satisfied with being the only one without clothes on. Eagerly, like a child with a large present, she began to unwrap him. She yanked his shirt from his pants and, with little urgings and cooings, she slid it up and away. She knelt— he stared, aroused as hell, at the beautiful curve of her back—and she pulled off his boots and then his socks. Slowly, rubbing herself along his legs and body, she stood once more to unsnap his jeans, parting the plackets with an adorable little sigh, and then slithering them down his hips and off, taking his briefs along, too.

Then she took a step back. "It does look like it's healing well," she said huskily.

He stared at her, uncomprehending, until she placed her lips on the red, puckered scar at his shoulder where that bullet he'd got in Mexico had gone clean through.

"Yes, it's fine." He heard himself groan. And he gathered her close, feeling the whole nude length of her against him and thinking that it was worth it to live thirty-two grim and dreary years for this moment and the few like it they might share in the next brief days alone together.

He held her tighter, as if he could squeeze out the thought that their days here were numbered, that what they were doing would have an end. Now was not the time to think of endings.

She squirmed a little. "Joe?" she asked, sensing his dark thoughts. He made soothing noises and loosened his hold.

As soon as he did that, she slipped around him. Laughing, she disappeared into the hall.

He followed where she led him: to his own bedroom, pausing only for a detour to the bathroom, where he found the condoms he'd put away when he carried her suitcase to the guest room.

With the needed protection in hand, he went into his own room and stood in the doorway. She was stretched out on her side across the bed, smiling, her eyes dreamy, her body pale and pure as her name: Snow. Softly, in that polite voice bred into her as a Snow and a *somebody* in her community, she complimented the new easy chair in the corner as well as the king-size bed on which she lay.

Never taking his eyes from her, he approached the bed. He wanted her so much, it hurt. His manhood stood out, hard and ready. She watched him come, her eyes meeting his. And when he reached her, she held out her hand.

After seeing that she was protected from pregnancy, he set the rest of the condoms aside, and took the hand she offered. He went down, beside her, and then, at her tender urging, he kissed her and rose over her.

She wrapped her beautiful legs around him, and she pulled him down again, this time into the sweet heart of her softness. He went willingly, sighing, holding himself back enough that she could fully take him at her own pace. He found he was more in control this time than that other time, when his need for her had been the need of a drowning man for air.

He held his weight on his hands and thighs enough that she could set the rhythm, and when he felt it and knew it, he moved with her, a slow, heating build of sensation, one that he was able to sustain for an eternity of ever-mounting ecstasy.

But then the rhythm changed. Her movements became hard and frantic. He allowed himself to surrender to the insistence of her hips meeting his. His need grew in tandem with hers. They moved together, rolling, from one side of the big bed to the other, until, finally, he was on top once more.

He drove into her. She took all of him. She cried out, and her body closed around him with her completion, tight and so sweet he thought he might die. She held him so hard, forever it seemed, and then, with a long sigh, she began to relax.

Her sudden total softness, her utter surrender, was the finish of him. His climax came like something sucked out of him. He pushed into her. She opened fully. His mind spun away as his body knew an utter, numbing release.

He collapsed on top of her. She wrapped her arms around him and held him to her heart.

He lay there, thinking what he knew he shouldn't, what he was going to have to be very careful never to say aloud to her: that she had shown him twice now what beauty and wonder there could be in this troubled, hurtful world. That in her arms, however briefly, he'd found something he'd never thought to know.

She breathed his name against his skin. Gently he rolled away and then gathered her into his body. She sighed. With a cherishing hand, he brushed damp tendrils of hair from her forehead.

"Oh, Joe. I feel so peaceful. I could just drift off to sleep right here...."

He murmured his agreement and closed his eyes.

A while later, they got up and showered together and went out to the kitchen looking for something to eat. They made fat sandwiches, poured milk, and sat at the table together.

As they ate, she asked him questions—about his mother, and his father, and what growing up was like for him. Joe found it wasn't hard at all to answer any question she asked.

He talked for hours, and she listened to every damn word. He told her how his father brought his mother to the ranch to live, and then kicked her out when he found out what she was. He talked of the years he lived with his mother, about all the men, in and out all hours of the night—until she finally found a man she thought she loved. He was a mean sonofabitch, and Joe had the scars to prove it. In the end, partly to keep from losing that man and partly to protect her son, Belinda Sweeney dropped Joe off with John Tally.

Joe told Claire, "My father was...a quiet man. He didn't know how to...show himself to other people. I think he took one chance, with my mother. And when he walked in on her with someone else, he never took a chance like that again. Folks thought he was crazy, because he would come into town and turn away, mumbling and looking freaked when people would try to talk to him. But...contact just scared him, I think. Hell, I guess I don't really know. He came here from Kansas alone. If I've got other family, I don't know who they are.

"I could never get through to him. He wouldn't *talk,* you know? But the day he came and stuttered out that he wanted to make me his legal son, I knew what I meant to him. And that was enough."

Claire asked softly, "Where is your mother now?"

"She's dead, too. I got a letter from one of her girl-friends. About six years ago now. Lung cancer. She never would give up those smokes."

"Did you hate her?"

He smiled. "Nah. I loved her. She was so damn beauti-ful."

Evidently, Claire had heard that before. She nodded. "That's what they all say. In town. That she was beautiful and bad."

He shook his head. "I think she was lost, more than bad. It was like she was looking desperately for something, and she just never could find it. Maybe, finally, she did find it. I hope so."

They were lying across his bed together at this point, looking at the few pictures in his father's one dog-eared al-bum. She pointed at a studio portrait of a wide-eyed little boy. "That's you. It is, isn't it?"

"Yeah. I couldn't have been more than three. My mother had it taken, I guess. She sent a bunch of old pictures of me in the mail, after she left me with my dad. I think this was one of them."

Claire stroked the picture's plump face. "Oh, Joe. You look so innocent. . . ."

He shrugged, watching her, realizing that he wanted her again. "I was born innocent, like everybody else in this world," he told her as he flipped the album closed and set it on the nightstand. "I just saw too much, too soon, to stay that way."

He pulled her toward him. She came with a soft, willing sigh.

That evening, after dinner, they wandered out to the porch and sat in the glider, with the dogs snoozing at their feet. Not bothering or really needing to talk, they watched the stars grow brighter as night claimed the world.

Claire, who was experiencing pure happiness at that moment, and grateful beyond measure for the feeling, leaned her head on Joe's shoulder. Then she discovered she did want to talk.

"Joe?"

"Umm?" He had his arm around her. He pulled her a little closer and brushed a kiss against her hair.

"Tell me some more."

"About what?"

"About you."

"What?"

"I don't know. Something that's not about the past. Something about you right now."

"Like what?"

"Well, if I knew, I wouldn't be asking." She lifted her head enough to kiss his cheek, then she rested against him once more. "I know what. Tell me who you'd be, if you could be anyone—anyone in the world."

He was quiet. The glider silently rocked them. She almost wondered if he'd chosen not to answer. Then he said, "Sheriff Brawley."

She sat up and peered at him, to see what he was getting at. "Sheriff Dan?"

"Yeah. If I could be anyone in the world, I'd be Dan Brawley."

Claire gaped, and then realized gaping was not a way to get him to tell her more. She closed her mouth and tried to look interested instead of stunned. "Why Dan Brawley?"

Joe laughed. It was a good, deep laugh. When the laugh faded, he said, "Claire. You're like looking through a window sometimes. My answer surprised the hell out of you, huh?"

She sighed and shrugged. "Well, it wasn't what I expected, I'll admit. I love Sheriff Dan, I really do, even with... everything that's happened to me lately. But the man is past sixty, Joe. And if he doesn't cut back on the pralines, he's heading for a heart attack." She punched his arm playfully. "Now tell me why you'd like to be him."

Joe looked off toward the dirt road beyond the break in the fence. "He's a good man, with a job that matters. He does what he has to do, and *I* think he makes a difference. When I was a kid, he used to... stick up for me with the other kids."

Claire hadn't known that. "He did?"

Joe nodded. "Yeah. And he always did it with class." He glanced at Claire, and then looked out again, past the dirt road this time, to the pine-covered mountains beyond. "You know how, when I first came here, I had my mother's name?"

"Mmm-hmm."

He grunted. "It took my old man a while to get used to having me. My mother never told him I existed until she dropped me off on him. Oh, he believed I was his, all right. It was kind of hard to dispute that, since I looked so much like him—and I had his weird, yellowish eyes. But he didn't rush right over to the courthouse and demand I be declared his legal son. That came later. So, for two years I was walking around looking just like him, and yet named Sweeney. Even the dim bulbs knew I was a bastard."

Claire winced a little at the bluntness of the word but was careful not to interrupt. It was so wonderful to be sitting here on Joe's porch and listening to him talk to her so easily about who he was and how he'd become that way.

He went on. "And kids can be mean. A couple of them, Ben Brown and Filo Morris, used to try to get me after school and mess me up a little, just to let me know that I was . . . well, you know, trash."

Claire had to bite her lip to keep from announcing her outrage. During their growing-up years, Ben and Filo had truly been a couple of bullying creeps. But Claire knew that to speak right then could mean Joe would decide he'd said enough. She said nothing.

Joe didn't stop. "Anyway, it wasn't too bad. I got a few licks of my own in, and Ben and Filo stopped trying to take me on two-on-one. Instead they got into heckling—yelling things at me in the middle of town. Or throwing rocks when they knew I probably couldn't catch up with them and get them back. Stuff like that.

"More than once, during school, they'd set things up so *I'd* be the one to get caught retaliating for something they'd started. One day, they were following me down School Street on the way to the bus stop after school let out. They were being real subtle, whispering and snickering behind their hands, saying certain words loud enough that I would hear them. *Bastard, whore, crazy old man.* I knew who they were whispering about—me, my mother and my dad.

"The point finally came that I'd had enough. I was ready, I swear. I was going to turn around and take them on and then I was going to be the one who ended up in detention for it. And I didn't give a good damn."

"So what happened?"

"Sheriff Brawley, that's what. Right then, he appeared, to me it seemed like it was right out of nowhere, in his big white sheriff's 4X4. Hot damn, you should have seen him. A knight in shining armor never looked so strong and righteous. He must have assessed the situation at a single glance. He leaned out the window, real casual, and he called, 'Hey, boys. Hold on there just a minute.'

"Well, me and Ben and Filo, we just froze right in our tracks. Very slowly, like he had the rest of his life to do it, Sheriff Dan climbed down from that truck. And then, even slower, he strolled over to the three of us.

"He put an arm around Filo, and one around me, and he asked us how we were doing, if we'd got all our homework done. And the three of us, we bobbed our heads. 'Yes, sir. You bet, sir,' like our lives depended on it.

"And then, he stepped back. He put his hand on that nine millimeter he always carries, and he said how he'd hate to see any one of us end up in trouble. 'Trouble's a problem,' he told us. 'Once it gets started, it's got a habit of following a guy around. Understand?'

"Ben and Filo and me nodded so hard, we were lucky our heads didn't break off. Then the sheriff smiled and got back in his 4X4 and drove away." Joe allowed himself a low chuckle. "Those two didn't bother me for a week after that, at least." He turned to grin at Claire. "And that is why I'd like to be Sheriff Dan."

All at once, looking at Joe as he talked about the sheriff, Claire realized what he was trying to tell her. "You want to work for the sheriff's office, don't you? You'd like to be a deputy, and someday sheriff, right? You want to be a cop." She sat up straighter, proud of what she'd deduced. "I'm right, aren't I?"

For a moment he said nothing. Then, "Yeah." His voice dripped sarcasm. "Wouldn't that be a kick in the pants? Bad Joe Tally as your local law enforcement officer."

Claire pulled away from him enough to let him know she would not be brushed off about this. "Admit it. Someday you'd like to run for Sheriff of Excelsior County. What's wrong with that? It's an admirable ambition. If I were you, I'd be proud of it."

"You would, huh?"

"You bet I would."

Suddenly Joe seemed unable to sit still. He stood up, nudging Gonzo, who gave him an injured doggy whine. "These damn dogs," he muttered. "You can't take a step around here without falling on one of them...."

"You're not changing the subject on me, Joe." Claire was determined. "Not this time."

He strode to the porch rail and turned on her. "It's an insane idea. I'd have to go back to school."

"Do you have any money?"

"Yeah." He looked at his boots. "Some."

"You'd manage. If you really wanted to manage."

"Come on. They're not going to hire me over at the sheriff's office."

"You won't know until you apply."

He refused to be convinced. "And, besides that, who the hell is going to vote for me for sheriff, anyway?"

Claire stood up, too. "Joe Tally, this is your major problem in life. You think too little of yourself. You always have. You've got to look at this logically. If anybody has prior experience suitable for a career in law enforcement, it's you. And would you please give the people of Excelsior County a little credit? Who's to say they aren't smart enough to realize that you're exactly the man to take over when Sheriff Dan retires? And in case you never noticed, lots of people in their thirties go to school." She realized Joe was smiling at her. "What is so funny?"

"You. You're all ... het up."

"Well, I have a right to be het up. You get me het up when you talk that defeatist baloney."

"Yes, ma'am."

"I'll tell you what you should do, and I just pray you have sense enough to take my advice."

"I'm listening."

"Good. This is it. You should...follow your dream, that's what you should do. I don't care if it's corny. It's what a person has to do. You can't just sit around and let things happen to you, you have to *make* them happen, you have to..." Claire's voice trailed off. Her zeal deserted her as suddenly as it had come. She sank to the glider, feeling utterly foolish.

Who was she to talk about *making* things happen? She was sitting here, powerless, doing nothing at all, when next Monday she very well might be indicted for shooting a man.

"Claire?" Joe's voice was so tender.

She looked down at her hands. "I guess it's always easier to tell someone else what they should do," she murmured. "Too bad I don't have any answers for myself."

"Give it time," he suggested, and came to sit by her again. His hand closed over hers. "The answers will come."

Chapter Ten

Claire woke the next morning feeling wonderful, though she didn't really know why right at first. Then she reached out a toe and felt Joe's hairy leg and remembered that she was in his bed. She had slept there the whole night—well, they hadn't really done a lot of sleeping. She blushed at the ceiling and grinned fatuously to herself. Then she stretched and yawned and rolled over to kiss Joe awake.

Right then, the phone rang.

In spite of her little moan of protest, he reached across her and answered it on the third ring.

"This is Joe Tally."

The voice on the other end, a male voice, said something.

Suddenly, Joe was all business. "How many are there?" He listened. Then, "Nah. The one fax machine in town is an iffy proposition. I'd rather just copy them down, okay? Let me get a piece of paper. Hold on." He shoved back the light cover and was out of the bed in an instant.

He was so beautiful, so lean and lithe and yet powerful-looking, too, that Claire caught her breath at the sight of him standing by the bed.

He asked, "Hang this up for me, would you, when you hear me pick up in the kitchen?" She nodded, thinking that she'd gladly walk off a cliff for him if he asked her. She figured she could manage to hang up the phone. He handed her the handset and brushed a quick kiss on her lips. "This won't take long," he promised, only mouthing the words, so the man on the other end of the line couldn't hear. "Keep the bed warm."

She nodded again, a little vacantly, a woman already anticipating the return of her man to their bed, and not really caring about much else. And then she remembered that Joe had said he was taking some time off from chasing bail jumpers.

"Joe, is this about a job?"

He had already pulled on his jeans and was halfway across the room. He paused. "Don't worry about it, okay?"

She was on the alert now. "Joe—?"

"Will you please just hang up when I get it." And he left her sitting there.

She stared at the spot in the doorway from which he'd disappeared, until she heard his voice on the extension. Then she quietly did as he'd asked.

She sat there in the bed for a moment, then tossed the covers back and found her robe. Belting it, she followed him into the kitchen and stood in the doorway, watching him as he wrote himself notes on a yellow legal pad. He glanced up right away and saw her. He eyed her for a moment, then gave a quick, fatalistic shrug, and went back to his phone call.

His side of the conversation was cryptic. "Yes, okay. Go on.... I've got that one. She's what?"

Slowly, Claire approached him and gazed over his shoulder. He was making a list of names, addresses and phone numbers. On the top, he'd written *All alibis airtight... described financial planner... lawsuits pending*.

Beside some of the names, he'd also jotted notes. *Took her for fifty thou... retired, college professor, housewife*. All of the addresses were in the Bay Area. The last one was the address of Henson's wife.

Claire had seen enough to have a general idea of what the call was about. She went to the cupboard and got down a can of coffee and began setting up the maker to brew.

Within minutes, Joe said, "Thanks, Ted. I owe you one. Yeah. You take care." He hung up.

Claire pushed the coffeemaker back to its spot against the wall and flipped the switch on. She felt rather than heard Joe's approach.

And then his arms were around her waist and he was brushing kisses along her neck. She sighed, in spite of the fact that she had a few questions that demanded immediate answers.

His warm, rough hands cupped her breasts through the thin fabric of her robe. Her nipples grew instantly jutting and hard, and she knew in a moment she would forget all the questions she needed to ask.

Firmly, though her body cried *don't,* she put her hands on his and straightened her spine. "What's going on, Joe?"

He teased her nipples with his thumbs. They ached to be unconfined, completely exposed to his tender ministrations.

Somehow she managed to demand, "I mean it, Joe. I want to know."

He let out a long breath, and rested his chin on the top of her head. Then, his regret as palpable as her own, his teasing hands left her breasts and settled on the curve of her waist. "All right. That was Ted Hanks, a private investigator I know in San Francisco. He's been doing some checking around for me."

She turned to face him. "And?"

"And he's found out some things about Henson."

"Like?"

"Like he's a real sonofabitch. Calls himself a 'financial planner,' when what he really does is convince people what a trustworthy guy he is and then take them for everything they're worth."

Claire thought, rather grimly, of her mother. "Lord. The night he was shot, he told me just what you said—that he was a financial planner. He was setting up my mother to give her a few pointers."

Joe gestured at the yellow pad on the table. "Your mother's lucky. Those are mostly the names of people with lawsuits for fraud and theft pending against him. From what I've pieced together so far, it looks like he was laying low in Pine Bluff, trying to decide what to do about all the people who were suing him—and probably wondering when the San Francisco police would step in with criminal charges."

"So there are a lot of people who might have wanted to shoot him?" She couldn't keep the sudden elation from her voice.

"Claire, don't get carried away...."

She brushed around Joe and strode to the table. "Someone on this list could have shot him, couldn't they, Joe? The person who really shot him could be right here on this list!" She stared down at the list, her spirits rising, her heart beating faster in her chest. She felt on the brink of something—of vindication, of final proof that she was innocent beyond all doubt.

"Probably not."

She jerked her head up and glared at him, angry at him, though she knew she was not being fair. But fairness had nothing to do with it; his words dealt a blow to her hope. She needed that hope, and so did the baby. "What do you mean? You just said—"

"I said all those people were bilked by Henson. But every one of them has an airtight alibi for the night he was attacked."

"No..."

Slowly, he approached her. "Claire. Listen. I understand how betrayed you must feel, but Leven and Brawley do know their jobs. They never would have gone after you unless everyone else with a possible motive had been eliminated. From San Francisco to Pine Bluff is a good four-hour ride. Each one of these people, including the wife Henson apparently ran out on, can prove that they couldn't have been both in Pine Bluff in time to shoot Alan Henson and also at the other locations where witnesses place them."

Claire slowly sank to a chair. Her heart settled down. Now it felt dead in her chest.

Joe put a hand on her shoulder. She knew it was a gesture of support—to let her know he was there for her. "Look. I'm sorry."

She tipped her head back and forced a smile for him. And then she put her hand on his and gave it a reassuring squeeze. "It's not your fault. I'm sorry I jumped on you."

He hooked her chair with his foot and pulled it around, until she was facing him. He then knelt in front of her. His eyes were softer, full of more emotion and promise than she'd ever seen in them in all the years she'd longed for him and been denied.

"I swear to you," he told her. "I'll do every damn thing I can to find out what really happened. I'll pull in every marker I've got out there—and I've got a few. But the best bet to find out who really did this thing is still the police.

They are the experts, and they have resources we can't even get near.''

"But, Joe, they believe *I* did it. They've stopped looking. How are they going to find out anything, if they consider the case closed?''

Claire was looking right into Joe's eyes or she wouldn't have seen the way they changed. She saw beyond his impassioned reassurances to his secret concern. He was thinking she was right. Her arrest meant the police had stopped looking for other suspects. If things went on as they were, Claire could be convicted of shooting Henson—and the real culprit might never be found.

As she read Joe's thoughts in his eyes, a wave of true hopelessness washed over her. She reached out. "Oh, Joe. Hold me. Please.''

She fell against him, almost toppling them both to the floor as he surged to his feet and took her in his arms.

She buried her head against his bare, warm chest. "Joe. You know about me. In spite of the awful things that can happen in life, I've always thought the world was a fair place. A good place, overall. But now, I'm not so sure.... That's the worst thing in all this, to think that I live in a world where the bad guys get away, and the innocent ones pay.'' She clutched him closer. "I can't stand to believe that. I hate that I'm beginning to believe that.''

He held her tight, and stroked her back, murmuring soothing words that they both knew did little to change the trouble she was in.

For several minutes, she let herself lean on him. Then she pulled back. She looked him in the eye, and told him what she wanted to do. "I want to go to San Francisco and talk to those people, Joe. I think we should leave right away.''

Joe was quiet for a moment, and she knew his silence was not a good sign. Finally he said gently, "Claire, you can't do that.''

She stiffened, and pushed herself away from him a little more. "What do you mean, I can't?"

"I mean, you can't leave the county. And it's pointless anyway. They've all been interviewed by the police already. If the police had learned anything that led to another suspect, they would never have arrested you."

Claire felt her shoulders slumping. She drew them up square. "Then why did you even bother to take down the list?"

He had his answer ready. "It's information. Gathering information is part of the process of trying to figure out what really happened."

"Fine. That makes sense." He looked relieved, until she went on, "And so does this—you fully intend to talk to these people. On your own. As soon as you think you've got me settled down enough you can leave me alone for a few days without me having a nervous breakdown."

"Claire . . ."

"Just tell me. Am I right?"

"Claire, you're having a rough time right now, and—"

She cut him off. "Joe, I'm a little freaky lately, I'll grant you that. But I have not lost the ability to reason. Unless a miracle happens Monday and the grand jury lets me off, you plan to talk to the people on that list. Admit it."

"Damn it." He dropped his arms from around her waist.

"Just tell me the truth."

He gave in. "All right. Yes, I'll probably talk to them."

"Good." She smiled. Then she went to the cupboard, got two mugs, and poured their coffee. She returned and handed his to him. "I want to go with you. We can leave today."

He set the cup she'd handed him on the table in a gesture impatient enough that some of it sloshed over the rim. "Claire, you can't just take off for San Francisco."

"Because I'm under arrest for a felony?"

"You got it."

"It's okay. I'm not leaving the state, and we can call Sheriff Dan and leave him a phone number for wherever we're staying. It'll be strictly aboveboard. He can call and get us back here any time he wants."

"Dan's a good man. But he's got a job to do. The judge stipulated that you're not to leave the county. Dan will only tell you that you can't go."

Claire slid into a seat at the table, sipped her coffee and considered. For the first time since her nightmare had begun, she saw a real possibility for action on her part. If she could *do* something to help herself, despair could be kept at bay. She wasn't giving up on this, no way.

She told Joe, "Then we won't tell Sheriff Dan. We'll just go. And we'll get back here as soon as we can."

Joe dropped to a chair across from her. "Claire, it won't work. If you get caught, your bail will be revoked. And you don't understand what you want to do, anyway. Tracking down people to talk to them about a subject they'd rather forget is not fun work. Most of it's plain boring, and then, occasionally, you get to put up with some verbal abuse, not to mention the possibility that someone will get violent on you."

"I don't care." She reached across the table and grabbed his hand. "I have to do something, Joe. Don't you see? I *have* to."

For the longest time he said nothing. Then he sighed. "Look. You think about it. Give it a couple of days."

"I don't have a couple of days."

"Until tomorrow, then. Maybe something will happen between now and then. In the meantime, you can really think this over."

"I *have* thought it over."

"Fine. Wait one more day. Agreed?"

"And tomorrow, when I still want to go, you'll take me?"

He slipped his hand out from under hers and stood up. "Let's get some damn breakfast. I'm starving." He marched to the cupboard and got down a box of pancake mix.

"Joe. Be straight." She picked up the yellow pad and shook it at him. "Say you'll take me, or I will go by myself."

Joe slammed the cupboard door and turned to face her. "All right. I'll take you. I think it's a major waste of your time and a bad idea. But I'll take you."

"Tomorrow."

"Yeah. Right. Now get off that cute butt of yours and help me make some pancakes."

After breakfast, they found their way back to Joe's wide bed. For a time, once more, Joe made Claire forget everything but the magic that happened when he touched her.

They were still lingering beneath the sheets when Ella called at a little past nine. Joe answered, then held the phone away from Claire for a full minute, so that Ella would think he'd had to fetch her in the guest room. Claire rolled her eyes and tried to tickle him while he made her wait, but he remained impervious to her attempts to undermine his little subterfuge.

Finally he let her have the phone.

"Claire? Is that you?"

"Yes, Mother. I'm right here."

Her mother sighed. "How are you feeling?"

Claire rubbed her foot slowly up Joe's hard thigh. "Much, much better. I think this was really a good idea." Joe jerked his thigh away and shook a finger at her. She put her hand over the mouthpiece and whispered, "Okay, okay..."

"Claire. I can't hear you. I think our connection's going bad."

"No, it's only me, Mother. Really. I wasn't talking into the phone. Now tell me, how are *you* doing at the motel?"

"Just fine. I have a few things you'll probably want to know about."

"Such as?"

"It looks like the story about Alan Henson will be in the newspapers. Did you know that man is more-or-less a crook?"

"Yes. I've . . . heard that. Who told you?"

"Reporters. I spoke with three yesterday—one from Sacramento, one from San Francisco, and also Eppie Salts from the Pine Bluff *Register*. They were looking for you, but I told them you were unavailable for comment."

"Good. What else did they say?"

"Oh, a few things that were totally untrue, of course." Ella's tone was too offhand.

"Such as?"

"Claire, dear . . ."

"I want to know, Mother." It was always possible the reporters knew something she didn't.

"It will only upset you."

"I'll live, I promise you."

Ella stalled a moment more.

"Mother."

"Oh, all right. They wanted to know if you were in love with Henson. I told them the very idea was ridiculous. You hardly knew the man."

"And?"

"They wanted to know if he'd managed to con you out of any money. I told them absolutely not."

"Did you tell them that he had been planning to give *you* a little financial advice?"

"Claire Lorraine Snow, you bite your tongue. It's bad enough that I was such a fool. I'd prefer not to read about it in the Sacramento *Bee*."

"Don't be too hard on yourself, Mother. Henson charmed the wallets out of a lot of people's pockets. You wouldn't have been alone."

"So you've heard that, too? Who told *you*?"

Claire grinned at Joe over the mouthpiece of the phone. "I have my sources."

"Well," Ella sounded philosophical, "I was fortunate. He didn't get a chance to take advantage of me."

"Exactly. Count your blessings."

Ella actually chuckled. "You know, I do believe Joe was right about getting you off to that ranch. You seem a thousand percent more cheerful. It does my heart good."

"Yes, it was a wise idea. Now what else did the reporters ask?"

"Dear..."

"Just tell me, Mother."

There was a pause. Then, "The one from San Francisco asked if you shot Alan Henson because he was your...lover and you found out he was a married man."

Claire fiddled with the phone cord a little before responding. "I see. Did they ask anything else?"

"No, actually, that's it. Claire, are you—?"

"I'm fine, really."

Ella's voice turned brisk. "Well, you know your mother. I just *had* to get my two cents in. I told them you had never had the slightest interest in Alan Henson, and that you most definitely did not shoot the man." Ella paused again, then asked, touchingly unsure, "Did I do the right thing?"

"Thanks, Mother," Claire told her. "You did just fine."

"Good." Ella's relief was clear. Then she went on. "Also, the main reason I called is that Wayne Leven just left. I managed to get out of him that Alan Henson's condition is the same—and the bungalow is no longer off-limits."

Claire had drooped a little at the news that there was no change in Henson's condition, but she perked up when she heard about the bungalow. "I can get in there now?"

"Yes, but I still think you ought to just take it easy and let me have Verna—"

"Did you lock it up?"

Ella sighed. "Yes, dear. I followed your instructions exactly."

"Good. I'll be there in forty-five minutes."

Claire reached across Joe to hang up the phone.

"What now?" he asked, looking wary.

She paused, stretched across him, to place a swift kiss on his lips. Then she sat up and reached for her robe. "I need to get back to the motel right away. Will you take me into town?"

She was half off the bed, thinking about fitting in a quick shower, when he snared her hand. "What's going on?"

She sat back down and turned to him. "Leven said we can get in the bungalow now. I want to have a look around in there."

"What's the point?" He held tight to her hand. "All you're going to find in there is detection powder and a bloodstain on the rug."

"I still want to look."

"You're wasting your time."

"It's my time to waste."

"Claire . . ."

"I'm going, Joe. Please come with me."

He muttered something low and crude.

After that, there was a silence. They gauged each other. Both of them were naked, and neither of them cared. Claire thought how quickly she'd become accustomed to being naked around Joe. It seemed so right, so utterly natural.

They had come a long way with each other. In a strange way, her tragedy had bonded them. And now, her intention to help herself out of this trap she was in had made her stronger than she'd been in days. She felt that she was his equal again. She felt ready to do anything to learn more about what had really happened to Henson. It was a good feeling, and she was glad for it.

"Damn," Joe remarked.

"Does that mean you'll come with me?"

He released her hand, only to haul her against him and put his mouth on hers. He kissed her long and hard. And then, when she felt her bones going to butter, he released her.

"All right," he said. "Let's get ready to go."

Forty minutes later, Claire and Joe entered the bungalow where Alan Henson had been shot. Claire had a clipboard in one hand and a flashlight in the other. On the clipboard was the housekeeping list of everything that was supposed to be in the small cabin: from the few dishes and pans in the tiny kitchen, to the television and the toiletry supplies.

"Okay, Sherlock, what now?" Joe asked wryly.

Claire shot him a narrow look—and then found herself staring at the rust-colored stain on the braided rug. It was a big stain; she couldn't help picturing the unconscious Henson as she'd found him, lying there. It was not a pleasant memory.

"Well?" Joe prompted.

"Now, I look at everything," she said with more authority than she felt. "*Everything.*"

And that was exactly what she did.

She crept through the living room, bedroom, bathroom and efficiency kitchen at a snail's pace, peering into every cupboard, feeling along every sill and crevice, shining her flashlight into corners and under furniture. She shook out the curtains and pulled the linens off the bed. She moved cushions and turned chairs upside down, beating at them in hopes they would disgorge some small object that might provide a single clue.

She found a gouge in the wall where the bullet had likely hit after it went through Henson. Of course, the bullet wasn't there. The sheriff's office had that.

She discovered that one glass of the eight the motel provided was gone. She knew which glass it was: the one she had broken trying to get Henson to let go of her. But there wasn't a glass shard in sight; she had no doubt that the bits of glass were in a bag down at the courthouse, marked as evidence against her.

Nothing else that belonged to Snow's Inn was gone. Even the complimentary shampoo, half-used, was sitting on the edge of the tub in the bathroom.

All of Henson's things had been removed, no doubt for his wife to collect from the courthouse at her leisure. Except for the bloodstain and the chip on the wall, there was nothing—nothing—that shouldn't have been there.

As Joe had warned, the police had been thorough. If Henson's attacker had left a cigarette in the ashtray or lost a button that rolled under the couch, the sheriff's office had it now.

At a quarter to eleven, Claire finally gave up. She stood up from a last look under the couch, rubbed her back, and told Joe she'd seen enough.

He came to her and put his arms around her. She rested against him for a moment. Then she lifted her head for a quick kiss. "Okay. I give up. Let's blow this joint."

They locked up and went back to the office, where she told her mother to go ahead and have Verna clean the bungalow and throw the ruined rug away.

"Then shall I go ahead and rent it to guests?" Ella asked.

"No. Just lock it up. The floor has to be stripped and re-waxed." Henson's blood had seeped right through the rug and into the floor, but Claire decided not to go into detail about that to her mother. "I'll take care of it when I come back to work."

"Certainly, dear. I'll do just as you say." Her mother glanced from Claire to Joe and then back at Claire. "And I'm so glad you're feeling better. You do look much more . . . relaxed, dear. I must say."

"I *am* more relaxed," Claire said, thinking naughtily about just how relaxing being with Joe could be. Joe, over by the window, cleared his throat, and she knew it was a signal that she was looking downright dreamy-eyed. Swiftly she added, "Getting away to somewhere . . . neutral, like the ranch, has been a godsend. I really do feel a thousand times better than I did yesterday when we left."

"I'm so glad," Ella beamed. "And I don't want you to worry about a thing. Honestly. I am managing just fine here."

"I know you are, Mother. That's why, if it's okay with you, we've decided to take a trip to San Francisco tomorrow."

Ella's beaming face went slack. "What?"

Over by the window, Joe coughed again. Claire shot him a glance, and he gave her a warning frown. Claire smiled back sweetly. Of course, he was still hoping that between now and time to leave, he could convince her to give up on the trip.

Well, they were going. He could just get used to it. She would hold him to his word. And if he broke his word, she really would go alone.

"We're going to San Francisco," she repeated, since her mother was still staring at her as if she'd lost her mind. "Just for a day or two. The ranch has been so good for me, I think an even more *total* change of scene will be even better."

"But, dear, I don't think you can go that far away, can you?"

"We'll leave a number with you, of course. So if the sheriff's office needs us, we'll come right back home." Claire waved a dismissing hand. "I'll work all that out, Mother. Don't worry. I just want to know if you can take care of things here."

"Well, of course I can. I planned to do just that, but I don't understand—"

Claire cut her mother off with a hug and a kiss on the cheek. "I know I've said it before, but I am so grateful to you. We'll call you with the number of our hotel, as soon as we have it. And I'm going to take my car, okay? I'll leave you the motel van, in case you need it. Now, I just want to get a nice dinner dress from my room, and we'll be on our way."

Claire, behind the wheel of her car, followed Joe back to the ranch. He drove a little faster than necessary. Claire knew he was miffed because she'd one-upped him about San Francisco.

Well, she decided, he could just go ahead and be miffed. He *had* promised to take her, after all. So making plans with her mother had not been out of line in the least. He was only mad because he'd still intended to discourage her, and now he was less likely than ever to succeed.

They pulled in between the break in the fence, and Joe parked in front of the house. Claire stopped her car right behind him. She got out and went around to the back seat to get the dress she'd collected from her closet at the motel.

She heard Joe order the dogs away and then, from behind her, he demanded, "What the hell do you need with a fancy dress? It's not going to be any party, it's not going to be any damn fun at all."

She brought out the dress she'd hung on the hook in the back seat, closed the door, and turned to face him.

Now that she was looking right at him, she had to admit he looked more than a little miffed. His eyes had that wolfish gleam. She was reminded—as she hadn't been in days—of the dangerous side of him. Joe Tally was not a man to cross. But she kept her shoulders back and stared him square in the eye.

"No, it's not going to be a party," she told him. "But my mother thinks it is." She waved the dress under his nose. "I took this to allay her suspicions. If I went without something to wear to a nice restaurant, she would have been sure we were up to no good."

He made a low noise in his throat, a scoffing sound. "Something to wear to a nice restaurant, huh?"

"Yes."

"You've just got every damn thing under control, haven't you?"

"Joe, you agreed we could go tomorrow."

He took the step that backed her up against the car. "You just don't get it. You've got a few days to...take it easy. And then things could get pretty bad for you. What the hell do you want to go chasing all over creation for nothing for? I'll do that. I'll handle it. Just trust me, okay?"

"I do trust you. I swear. But it's my life, Joe. My freedom, and my good name. I have to do what I can. Please. Try to understand."

"No. You understand." His eyes were hot with frustration. He took her by the upper arms, hurting her a little. Her pretty dressed was wrinkled between them as he spoke right into her upturned face. "If you go, you're disobeying Judge Willoughby's direct orders. Also, chances are ninety-nine to one that we'll get nowhere with anyone on that list. For me, that's okay. I'll take it one step at a time, and I'll find out what I can and go on from there. But you're pinning your hopes on it, I can tell. And when we're through trying to talk to those people, you'll feel worse than you did when you found out you could end up on trial for criminal assault.''

''No,'' she said firmly. ''I won't feel worse. Even if nothing comes of it, at least I'll know I did everything I could. I'll know I didn't just sit here, waiting for the ax to fall. Now, please let go of me, Joe. You're hurting my arms.''

He released her immediately, and stepped back. Then he swore under his breath. And he turned and strode into the house.

Chapter Eleven

Fifteen minutes later, Claire was in the kitchen making sandwiches for a lunch she hoped she could convince Joe to share with her, when he came up behind her.

"Claire?"

She stopped in mid-motion, still clutching a half-open loaf of bread, as he tenderly brushed her hair aside and placed his lips on the nape of her neck. His hands strayed to her shoulders. He rubbed them a little, and then he massaged her arms, too, as if to banish any discomfort he'd caused earlier when he'd clutched them so hard.

Then he reached over her and gently took the loaf of bread from her hands. He turned her to face him, tipping her chin up with a coaxing finger to get her to look in his eyes.

"Sorry," he said.

"It's okay."

He dragged in a long breath. "Well, at least you know exactly how I feel about this trip."

"Do I ever."

"Sure you won't change your mind?"

Claire bit her lip and shook her head.

He shrugged. "Okay."

Her heart lifted a little. "Okay, what?"

"Okay, then I think we should go ahead and leave today. We'll get into San Francisco and get settled by this evening, and we might even be able to get started on the list tonight."

Claire looked at him, wary yet still hopeful. "You mean it? We're leaving today?"

"Yeah. As soon as we pack and call your mom."

Joe knew of a nice hotel near Union Square and called to reserve them two adjoining rooms for that night and the next. Claire clucked at the extra expense; they would end up only using one room. But Joe seemed determined to protect Ella from the knowledge that bad Joe Tally and her daughter were much more than friends.

As soon as their rooms were reserved, Claire called Ella and told her they were leaving a little earlier than originally planned. Ella still didn't really understand why they were going, but she seemed to have decided that she trusted Joe. After a brief exchange, she took the phone number of the hotel and told her daughter to "Have a lovely time. Everything will be just fine here."

Next, Joe called a neighbor who lived on twenty acres adjoining the ranch and asked if he would feed Demon and the dogs for a few days. The neighbor said he'd be glad to.

"Okay, then," Claire said when he'd hung up. "Let's get going."

"Your eyes are shining." He shook his head. "Such a pity you're so damned naive."

He was sitting on the edge of the bed. She bent down and kissed him. "Don't bet on it."

He grabbed her arm and gave a tug. She landed neatly on his lap. "You are. A total innocent."

She glanced heavenward. "Haven't we had this argument before?"

He chuckled. "Yeah. And you lost."

"I did not. We . . . reached no conclusion."

He wrapped his arms around her and nuzzled her neck. "That's right. We ended up making love."

Though she knew they should be on their way to San Francisco, she couldn't resist. She turned her mouth to his. His mouth was warm—and so inviting.

She allowed her lips to part, and the kiss deepened as he lifted her and lay her on her back across the bed. He came down on top of her. His hard body felt so good pressing into hers. She began to think that perhaps a little later start wouldn't hurt anything.

But just as her hands inched downward, to caress the hard curves of his back and buttocks, he relinquished her mouth and rose on his knees above her.

He grinned down at her. He looked very smug, she thought, in spite of the obvious bulge in his jeans.

"You see?" he pointed out in a voice that was a little more husky than perhaps he intended. "You see what we *could* be doing, if you didn't have to go out and chase down the bad guys?"

Claire sighed and smiled. "I'm willing to put the bad guys on hold for, say, twenty minutes or so."

He faked a thoroughly offended look. "Twenty minutes? *Twenty minutes!* Twenty minutes isn't half—hell, it isn't a *quarter*—of the time I need to do all the things I'm going to do to you."

She couldn't help but ask, "What things?"

He shook his head. "Uh-uh. You'll just have to wait."

She blushed. She was *not* going to ask him "Till when?"

And he wouldn't tell her. He stretched out over her once more, and taunted her with a last, bone-melting kiss. And then he stood and announced they had to be on their way.

Luckily, there was a pillow within easy reach. She hit him in the back of the head with it as he strode toward the door.

They checked into the Sir Walter Raleigh Hotel at a little after five and, since both of them were hungry, went out into chilly late-afternoon San Francisco looking for a quick bite to eat.

Two blocks down and around the corner, they found a sports bar and deli, where they got thick turkey sandwiches and tall bottles of beer. While they ate, they scanned the newspapers they'd bought at a stand on the way. The brief stories about Henson—and Claire—told them nothing they didn't already know.

They talked about Henson's wife, Mariah, for a while. Ted Hanks had learned that she was a very wealthy woman, and that her money was her own. She was the CEO of a large cosmetics firm based in San Francisco, and she'd married Henson five years before.

"A very smart lady," Joe said. "It's a mystery why she married a shyster like Henson, but she's been no fool about him when it comes to her fortune. She's kept him far, far away from her money and her work."

Claire took the list of names from Joe and found Mariah Henson's address. "She lives right here in the city limits. We could start with her."

Joe was shaking his head. "She's still in Grass Valley, with Henson at the hospital, or at least she was this morning. I've got Ted keeping an eye on her place. He'll contact us if she comes back to town."

Claire swallowed her disappointment. She was a little anxious about trying to talk to Henson's wife. After all, the way the woman had looked at her had turned her blood cold. But the woman was more likely than anyone to have some kind of clue to this whole mess. And, as far as Claire could see, a betrayed wife would have the best motive of all to steal Claire's gun and shoot the man she thought was fooling around on her. No matter how airtight Mariah Henson's alibi, Claire longed to try to talk to her.

But it looked as if the talk would have to wait.

"Okay," Claire conceded. "Then what?"

"There are three other names with addresses right here in town. We'll see how far we can get with them tonight."

"Sounds good."

"Okay. Now listen up. . ."

Joe explained how they would proceed with the list. They were going to try to catch the people face-to-face. He said that, in his experience, calling first rarely worked; it was so easy for people to just say no and hang up.

"Sometimes, surprise is everything in getting people to open up," he said. "It keeps you on your toes. Keeps you ahead of the other guy."

"I don't quite follow."

"You'll see." He tipped his beer at her. "Just try to. . . follow along, whatever I do. Take a hint."

"You mean, if you act strangely, I should play along."

"You got it." He finished the beer.

Twenty-five minutes later, they were on their way.

They took a cable car partway to the first address they'd chosen, then walked. Claire, who'd always loved the crammed-together buildings and steep streets of San Francisco, found the walking exhilarating, though after half an hour of it, she was glad she had worn appropriate shoes.

Finally, on a rundown street where the buildings looked dingy rather than charming and the characters lurking near the corner bar were the kind a person wouldn't want to meet after dark, they found the residence hotel they sought. Inside, there were dirty, off-white walls and lonely-looking men sitting in threadbare chairs.

The front desk was a hole in the wall with bars over it. Inside the hole, a surprisingly pretty young woman sat chewing gum. Claire couldn't help smiling—she was reminded of Amelia.

"Yeah? Whaddaya want?" the young woman asked.

"Professor Whitling, 3B," Joe said.

"Whaddabout 'im?"

"We'd like to talk to him," Claire explained.

"Justaminute." The young woman called the room. Apparently the professor was in, because she lowered her voice and shared a short exchange with someone on the other end. She looked up. "Yabillcollectors?"

Claire blinked. The woman was looking right at her, and Claire hadn't understood a word she said.

Behind her, Joe said, "No, we're not bill collectors."

"'Kay. Gwanup."

Minutes later, they stood in a dim hall and knocked on the door to 3B. It was pulled back almost immediately, leaving Claire to suspect that the tenant had been waiting behind it for their knock.

"Yes?" A man of late middle age stood in the doorway and looked up at them. He was short, thin, and balding like a monk—the crown of his head was bare, but there remained a fuzzy fringe above his large ears.

Joe asked, "Professor Lionel Whitling?"

"Yes. What is it you want?"

"A few minutes of your time. We'd like to ask you some questions about Alan Henson."

Professor Whitling's soft gray eyes went flat. "I've already told the police all I know." He started to close the door.

Joe stuck his boot in it.

Professor Whitling made a small, shocked sound, and looked down. "Kindly remove your foot from my door."

"You know he was shot?"

"I told you—"

"Shot by some sneaky bastard who won't admit to the crime?"

"Please—"

"See this woman here?" Claire gasped as Joe took her by the shoulders and pushed her right up against the door. "She's the one they're blaming. Look at that face."

Whitling blinked and sputtered. "I assure you, I—"

"*Look* at that face. This is a good woman, and she's probably going to prison—unless somebody helps her. Unless everyone who knows anything about that two-bit chiseler, Henson, tells us everything they know."

"I don't know anything," Whitling insisted. "I—I was here, the whole time. Ask Ladonna down at the desk...."

"But you *have* filed a lawsuit against him, haven't you?"

Joe gave Claire a little shake. She remembered he'd warned her she was supposed to pick up any hint he dropped. Was this a hint? She imagined so.

She tried to sound just as pitiful as she probably looked, caught between Joe's leg and the door, held by the scruff of the neck. "Please, sir. Please. If we could just ask you a few questions. I would really appreciate it so much... Ouch, you big bully," she whined at Joe.

Whitling, who seemed totally confused by then, decided to become protective of a lady in distress. "See here, young man. I think you're hurting her...."

"He's very... passionate, about this," Claire explained in a voice made thin by the slight constriction of her windpipe. Joe held her by her collar and she was dangling above the ground. "He gets... carried away. If you would just agree to talk to us... Oh, easy, ouch..."

"All right, all right. Release her, and I will speak with you."

Joe let go of Claire, but didn't remove his foot from the door. "Thanks, Professor. We really appreciate this."

"Oh, yes!" Claire gushed. "I can't tell you how much this means..."

"Well, ahem." The little professor now seemed quite proud of himself. And why shouldn't he be? He'd saved an innocent woman from her overbearing companion. And perhaps, in the end, he could save her from much worse. "I suppose you might as well come in," he allowed. He stepped back and gestured at the small room beyond, a room that seemed, at first glance, to be literally made of books.

Professor Whitling told them about himself. It was not a happy tale. He'd lost his job teaching English at a local state university after cutbacks—right after he put his life savings in Alan Henson's slippery hands. He'd lost his house; he had no family. His lawyer was costing him the last of the money he had.

"All I've got left is my books," he told them, gesturing at the hundreds of volumes stacked nearly to the ceiling along every wall.

He moved a few of the numberless heaps of books out of the way so they could sit down, made them tea on a hot plate, and answered all their questions. Unfortunately, beyond his own sad story, nothing he could tell them gave the slightest clue to the mystery they sought to solve.

When they got up to go, he seemed reluctant to see them leave. "More tea?"

Out the one dirty window on the side wall, Claire could see that dark was coming. "Thanks, Professor. But we really do have to go."

When they were out on the street once more, Joe complimented her on her "performance" in getting them into

Whitling's room. Then he asked if she was game to try another name.

She forced herself not to look up at the lonely professor's window—and not to think how many other sad stories she might have to hear before they'd seen this thing through.

"You bet," she told Joe. "Who's next?"

But no one was home at the neat little brick row house halfway across town that they tried next. Joe said they'd come back if they had time. Otherwise, they'd have to try calling.

Next, they found themselves at a big apartment complex near Golden Gate Park. They used the intercom buzzer over the mailbox to ring the woman in 219.

"Who is it?" The voice sounded young and breathily feminine.

Joe nudged Claire. She read the name off the list. "Ms. Tetley? Andrea Tetley?"

"Yes. Who is it?"

Claire shrugged and simply answered the question. "It's Claire."

"Who?"

"Claire Snow. May I talk with you?"

"What about?"

"Alan Henson."

There was a pause. The intercom crackled a little. Then, "I'll come down."

Two minutes later, the type of young woman who causes traffic accidents appeared at the top of the stairs beyond the iron gate that protected the building proper from the open lobby. She wore short-shorts and a tank top, in spite of the cold night air. Her beautifully manicured feet were bare. If she was chilly, she wasn't letting it show. She had full lips, even fuller breasts, and more hair than a sheepdog. The woman posed there on the landing, as if expecting someone to snap her picture. When no one did, she placed one hand on the railing and proceeded down the wide stairs that ended at the iron gate.

Claire and Joe watched her progress. Halfway down, she paused and made eye contact with Claire. "Are you Claire?"

Claire nodded. One sweep of thick, black lashes, and Claire was dismissed; the woman had laid eyes on Joe.

She kept on coming, until she stood just on the other side of the protective gate. She crooked a finger at Joe.

Joe eyed the woman doubtfully, but Claire, who wasn't forgetting the way he'd held *her* by the scruff of the neck to prey on the poor professor's latent chivalrous streak, decided Joe would have to do his bit for their cause, as well.

Claire gave Joe a poke with her elbow. He took a step toward the gate.

The woman made a big show of batting the eyelashes she'd just used to dismiss Claire. "I'm Andrea. And who are *you?*"

Claire volunteered, "Andrea, this is Joe. Joe Tally."

"What can I do for you, Joe?" She spoke in a slow, steamy-sounding drawl, which Claire thought rather miraculous. The poor woman should be freezing, after all.

Joe cleared his throat. "You can answer a few questions."

"Like what?"

"Like what's your relationship with Alan Henson?"

Andrea's melting chocolate-colored eyes narrowed. "Are you reporters?"

"No."

"I already talked to the police. You're not police?"

"No."

"Then what?"

Joe evaded the question with a provocative statement. "Since you've talked to the police, you must know that someone shot him."

Andrea clucked her tongue, a very pink tongue. "Yeah, I heard. Poor Alan. What an idiot. I could have told him this would happen.... You detectives or something?"

"Yeah, that's right."

"Who are you working for?"

Claire cheerfully volunteered, "We're working for me. I'm the one they think shot him."

Andrea licked her lips and smiled at Joe. "Wow, tough break."

Joe prompted, "You were going to tell us how you knew Alan Henson."

"I was?"

"Yeah."

Andrea put a long crimson fingernail in her mouth and nibbled it very gently, considering. Then she wrapped her hands around the bars of the fence and sighed. "You know, Joe. You are really...hot. You have got this really...hot way about you. Oo-oh, and those eyes... Maybe you and your...client would like to come up to my place for a drink."

Joe glanced over his shoulder at Claire. His look said everything. *Is this one absolutely necessary?*

Claire smiled. "We'd love to, Andrea."

Andrea made a big show of discovering a key between her incredible breasts. She unlocked the iron gate. *"Entrez-vous."*

It took them well over an hour to escape Andrea's clutches. She made margaritas that tasted like straight tequila, and she kept asking if they were hot—and turning up her air conditioner.

Each time she plunked herself down beside him, Joe scooted away from her, and asked her another question about Alan Henson.

Andrea quickly explained that she'd been down in Los Angeles on a modeling assignment over the Fourth of July weekend—and only returned late Sunday afternoon.

Then she backtracked to tell all about how she had met Alan Henson at her health club. She'd felt a little sorry for him; he seemed such a quiet, shy kind of guy. They'd had drinks together a few times—and, well, you know how it goes....

He'd told her he was down on his luck. She'd lent him money. Though, of course, ordinarily, it was *men* who gave Andrea Tetley money.

But Alan was just so sweet and, surprisingly, he was a real devil in bed.

"I was just a sucker for that man, I tell you," Andrea told Joe. "And I really wouldn't have sued him if that little devil hadn't gone and proposed to me. I mean, I *believed* him. My *pride* was hurt when I found out he was already *married.* What's a girl to do, I ask you ... ? But, when I heard he got shot, and could end up a *vegetable,* I felt bad about it, I did. Maybe I was hasty, hiring a lawyer and filing suit and all. I just don't know." She sat next to Joe again and put her slim hand on his thigh. "Tell me, Joe. What do *you* think I should have done?"

"Exactly what you did," Joe answered. He stood and grabbed Claire's arm. "And now, Ms. Tetley, we really do have to go."

"So. What did we learn from our visit with Andrea?" Claire asked brightly once they'd returned to the hotel for the night.

Joe, who was sitting at the little round table by the window and scribbling something on a steno pad, gave her a dark look. Clearly playing sex object was not his cup of tea. But he did volunteer, "That the woman actually has air conditioning, even though San Francisco rarely gets above eighty degrees year-round."

"Very funny. But seriously."

Joe snorted. "Okay. I'd say that Henson does seem to have a way with women."

Claire nodded, thinking of her mother, who'd been so taken with him, too. "You're right. Obviously he could charm men, too, or there wouldn't be any men on the list. But a sweet, naive man like Professor Whitling would be a pretty easy target for any smooth talker. However, Andrea didn't strike me as the kind of woman to ordinarily waste her time on a guy without money *or* looks. I think she requires one or the other from most men."

Joe nodded. "Good point." He went back to his steno pad.

"What are you writing?" she asked.

"Notes."

"About what?"

"Just random stuff. It helps me put things together."

"Random stuff like what?"

"Like things we've heard and found out. Whatever sticks in my mind. Things like what you said just a minute ago, about Henson being charming to women even without looks or money. Disjointed stuff—like Andrea Tetley's air conditioner—or all those books Whitling had about some guy named Oscar Wilde."

Claire laughed. "Oscar Wilde was a writer, Joe."

"Oh, yeah? What'd he write?"

She dug around in her memory of English Lit 1A. "Let's see. How 'bout...'The Book of Life begins with a man and a woman in a garden ... It ends with Revelations.' "

Joe grunted. "Don't flaunt your college education at me." But she could see the amusement in his eyes. He went back to his notes.

Claire sat on the bed, watching him, thinking how much she enjoyed looking at him.

Eventually she slipped off her shoes and hoisted her feet onto the bed. She closed her eyes, feeling marvelously content right then in spite of everything. She could hear Joe's pencil as it scratched across the paper, and inside her, the baby they had made was safe—for the time being, at least.

Thoughts of the baby brought on the thought that she had yet to tell Joe there *was* a baby. As guilt chased her peaceful feelings away, Claire turned onto her side, away from Joe, where he sat at the round table.

Lord. She *should* tell him. It was wrong—especially now that she was sure she would keep the baby—*not* to tell Joe about the child. And it seemed even more wrong to keep quiet after all he was doing for her, after the amount of trust that had bloomed between them lately.

It would hurt to lose his trust. Something inside her died a little at the thought. Yet it was very likely she *would* lose it, as soon as he knew that she'd managed to get herself pregnant during her "safe" time.

Well, her conscience chided, if she lost his trust, it would be her own fault. And the truth was that no matter what he might think of her once she told him, he deserved to know that he was going to be a father. If she had any integrity at all, she'd open her eyes and say his name, and when he looked at her and said "Yeah?" she'd simply begin.

We made a baby that night six weeks ago. I thought it was safe but it wasn't. And I've decided not to have an abortion, so I...

Claire sighed and shifted again on the bed. She found it difficult to even imagine how she was going to put the words together. The careful speeches she tried to make up in her mind always sounded awful, even inside her head.

She had no doubt they'd sound ten times worse once she actually uttered them aloud.

And beyond the difficulty of telling him, there was her determination to accomplish her goal here in San Francisco. She'd had a hard enough time getting him to go along as it was. Though so far they'd had no trouble, he'd said that sometimes the kind of thing they were doing could turn out to be dangerous. There was no way he'd let her continue with this if he knew she was going to have a baby.

And that was why, beyond everything else, it was impossible to tell Joe now.

She *must* find out who really shot Henson, or the baby could be born in prison. He—or she—would end up getting the same kind of rocky start in life that Joe had had. Born innocent, as Joe had been, but destined not to stay that way for long.

No, she couldn't let that happen. The baby must have what Claire's parents had given her, what Joe had never had—the chance to grow up unafraid to love and be loved.

"Claire?" Joe sounded concerned.

She turned her head and opened her eyes. He was still sitting at the table, with his pencil in his hand, but now he was looking at her instead of his steno pad.

"Umm?"

"You okay?"

"Fine. Why?"

"You were tossing around. Something bothering you?"

She forced a weary smile. "Nothing more than the usual." He set his pencil down and stood up. She lied some more. "Really, Joe. I'm fine."

He stretched, his long body strong and lithe in the shadowed light from the little lamp over the table. Then he came and sat on the edge of the bed. "Fine, are you?"

"Yes." She went on smiling. "Really. I am."

"Okay, you can stop convincing me."

"It's not working, huh?"

"No, so give it up." He bent and placed a kiss on the bridge of her nose. "You were great tonight."

"I was?" His praise warmed her. She brushed his hair back where it had fallen over his forehead.

"Yeah. Terrific," he said. "If you ever get tired of the hotel business, we could go into partnership in a detective agency."

She could tell by his grin that he was joking. Still it was an appealing fantasy. "I can see it now . . ." He put his hands up, as if picturing the sign over the door. *"Tally and Snow."*

"Almost. Except you've got it backward."

"Oh, no . . ."

"Oh, yes. It should be *Snow and Tally.*" She closed her eyes, briefly, as if listening to the sound of the title in her mind. Then, "Yes, that's much better."

"Snow and Tally, huh?"

"You bet. After all, besides sounding better, it's also alphabetical."

"Alphabetical? The *alphabet* decides it?"

"You can think of a fairer way?"

"How about the guy with the most experience goes first?"

She shook her head, and then took hold of his shirt and pulled him down, so his lips were only a fraction from hers. "Uh-uh. Alphabetical."

"Experience."

"Alpha—"

He interrupted her in mid-syllable. "For an innocent, you learn fast."

"I have to. It's a rough world."

Very lightly, with his tongue, he traced the shape of her lips. Then he suggested, "We could forget the world—and how rough it is—for a while...."

"We could?"

"Mmm-hmm."

"Okay. Show me how."

"Glad to..."

And he kissed her, slowly and sweetly. She let go of his shirt and wrapped arms around his neck, drawing him down.

All her shadowed, anxious thoughts began to fade.

In a leisurely manner that set her senses aflame, he kissed his way down her body, unbuttoning and unhooking and sliding everything she was wearing out of the way and then off.

She kissed him back and did a little unbuttoning and un-zipping of her own. Soon enough, they both wore nothing.

"Have I ever told you?" he wondered in a voice both gruff and tender.

"What?"

"How much I like—"

"Yes?"

"Being naked with you."

She made a sound of agreement, of feminine under-standing.

"What does that mean?"

"It means—"

"Yeah?"

"That I feel exactly the same."

"Good." He took her hand. "Come on."

He pulled her off the bed. She went without reluctance. He led her to the bathroom, where he turned on the taps in the huge tub, poured in some foaming bath oil provided courtesy of the Sir Walter Raleigh Hotel, and led her down into the steaming, bubbling water.

"Is this the time?" she asked on a sigh.

"The time for what?"

"When you do all those things you mentioned this afternoon?"

"What things?"

"You know, the things that take more than twenty minutes."

He chuckled.

She asked again, "Well, is this the time—or not?"

He assured her that it was.

Beneath the froth of bubbles, under the hot, soothing water, she felt his hand on her thigh.

With a long, yearning sigh, Claire let her head relax against the rim of the tub. Joe's hand moved higher.

Claire forgot everything, as she knew he intended her to. She forgot the man who now lay unconscious in the hospital, and the unknown person who'd shot him and left her to take the blame. She forgot her hopes that she might learn what had really happened from one of the people on Joe's list. She even forgot that there was a secret she was keeping from Joe—a secret that, once revealed, could destroy his trust in her, and shatter the wonder they now shared.

For a long, long time, she thought of nothing but Joe's hands, and the pleasure they were giving her. And once his hands were through, there was his mouth, and after his mouth, there was the best part of all. . . .

Sometime later he carried her to the bed, and he made love to her some more.

After that, as soft as a baby's blanket, sleep settled over her. She woke, but only partway, when she felt Joe cover her and pull her close.

He kissed her, a breath of a kiss, and smoothed her hair back with his callused hand. "Shh. Sleep now."

The next thing she knew, it was morning.

* * *

The desk called them at six, as Joe had requested. They quickly showered, and room service was knocking on the door just as Claire finished dressing. She ushered in the bellman, who had their breakfast, and told him to wheel the cart over by the round table.

"Breakfast!" she called to Joe in the bathroom as soon as the bellman had left. He came out right away, smelling of after-shave, with a towel around his waist and water droplets still gleaming in the triangle of hair on his chest.

He leaned across the cart and kissed her. They sat down. She poured the coffee. As they ate, they planned the busy day ahead.

Chapter Twelve

Before noon, they'd been cursed at and threatened with two lawsuits. They'd put fifty miles on her car driving around Alameda and Oakland.

Three people on the list had agreed to talk to them, and from them they'd only learned more of the same about Alan Henson. He charmed people and took their money, and he seemed to have no conscience about the personal destruction he left in his wake.

They took a break for lunch, during which they decided on their next moves and talked about the few things they'd learned.

After lunch, they went further south, to Daly City, San Bruno and Burlingame. They learned from a fortyish, exhausted-looking housewife that, thanks to Alan Henson, her children would be paying for their own college educations—if they could find jobs that made that much. They talked to a retired couple with nothing left of their life savings. The couple lived in a painfully tidy trailer that their children had chipped in to buy for them after Alan Henson had cleaned them out.

By four o'clock, they began moving back toward San Francisco, trying again to reach the people who hadn't been available on their first pass through the area. They were lucky—at least in the sense that they found the two people they'd missed before. But the first one, an older woman, yelled at them to leave her alone, she'd done nothing, and she'd already told the police as much. She marched into her small house and slammed the door.

Joe said, "I have a feeling that's all we're going to get from Mrs. Yamamoto."

Claire sighed and agreed.

The second one, Titus Paley by name, ran a dry-cleaning business in Daly City. Since he hadn't been at his house or the dry-cleaning shop earlier, they decided to give both locations one more try.

They found him at the dry-cleaning shop. When they told him they wanted to talk to him about Alan Henson, Titus Paley pulled a .45 out from behind the counter and pointed it at them.

"Alan Henson cost me two of my three shops and my cabin in Tahoe," Titus explained in an extremely level voice. "I didn't shoot him—if I had, you can be damn sure he'd be dead now. I got nothing else to say to anyone 'cept my lawyer, so get out."

Both Claire and Joe thought it wisest not to argue. They backed out of the shop and got in the car and speedily drove away.

After that, they took a break for dinner.

As dark drew on, they tried the little row house not that far from Union Square. Again, there was no one there.

They drove across the Golden Gate Bridge to Sausalito that night. Two of the names listed addresses there. But they struck out on both counts that time.

Finally, they went back to the hotel for the night, no closer to finding out who shot Alan Henson than they had been when Claire had insisted they come here.

When they lay down together in bed, Joe reached for her. She went into his arms. He loved her as tenderly and thoroughly as he had the night before. Claire tried to give herself up to the beauty of his touch, but time pressed in on her. She couldn't entirely forget how close they were to the end of the list—and how little they'd learned.

At last, when he settled her against his body, she tried her best to simply close her eyes and forget everything. She succeeded, eventually. For a few brief hours she knew nothing except the soothing oblivion of a dreamless sleep.

The next morning, Claire woke to the sound of the phone ringing. Joe answered it.

"Yeah?" he said. Then, "Great. Thanks, Ted." He hung up.

Claire opened an eye and groggily demanded, "That was your detective friend?"

Joe yawned and stretched. "Yeah."

Claire sat up in bed. All her grogginess had fled. "So? Don't hold out. What did he say?"

Joe yawned again. "Well, you know how he's been keeping an eye on Mariah Henson's apartment?"

"Yes? And?"

Joe reached out and wrapped his hand around the back of her neck. He pulled her close and kissed her, a lovely, lingering kiss. Then he told her, "It looks like she's in town, maybe taking a break from sitting by her husband's bedside."

Claire shivered a little, partly at the memory of the hatred in the woman's blue eyes the one time Claire had seen her, and partly with anticipation. She'd almost given up hope that she might get a chance to talk to Henson's wife.

She asked, "Did your friend see her?"

Joe shook his head. "I said, *it looks like she's in town.* Ted came off an all-night surveillance job and decided to stop by there on his way home. He managed to get into the parking garage."

"And?"

"Her car's there."

Claire was already halfway to the bathroom. "Don't just lie there, Joe Tally. We have to get going, talk to her while we have the chance. Order breakfast. We don't have all day."

"Yes, ma'am." He was laughing at her enthusiasm as he picked up the phone again.

Mariah Henson's apartment house wasn't that far from Professor Lionel Whitling's run-down residence hotel. It would have taken less than half an hour to walk from one place to the other.

But the two places were universes apart in every other way. The professor lived in a dreary room in a drab building on a narrow street.

On Mariah Henson's street, the charming turn-of-the-century architecture that usually distinguished San Francisco had been swept away. In its place were modern buildings of marble, steel and glass, structures that looked more like places to do business than somewhere anyone would want to live. The buildings weren't skyscrapers by any means, but they seemed to loom and intimidate nonetheless.

The street was spotless, and the sea wind swept in off the bay, smelling assertively clean and crisp. Trees were contained in big stone planters along the sidewalk, and security guards waited just beyond front entrances to quickly discourage anyone who had no business there.

The guard in Mariah Henson's building stopped them the moment they stepped beyond the big smoked-glass doors. "Good morning. How can I help you?" He stood behind a stone desk in front of a polished stone wall opposite the main door.

Claire cast Joe a quick glance, to let him know she wanted first crack at this one. His response was a nod so brief that only she could have seen it.

She said, "We'd like to speak with Mariah Henson, please."

"Is Mrs. Henson expecting you?"

"I'm sure."

The guard's dark brows drew together over his large nose. Claire's evasive response had gotten nowhere with him. He demanded, "Is she expecting you or not?"

Claire drew herself up and decided that the best defense was to get pushy. "No, she's not expecting us. Ring her apartment and tell her Claire Snow would like to speak with her, please."

The guard grunted. "Fine. Just a minute."

He punched some buttons behind his stone podium and made the call Claire had told him to make. As he waited for someone to pick up on the other end, Claire tried not to look worried. After all, it was highly unlikely that Henson's wife would actually consent to speak to them.

In a moment, she knew, she and Joe would be told to leave. She wondered if they should try finding their own way into the parking garage and lurking near Mariah Henson's car until she showed up to claim it.

So sure was she that they would be turned away, she had to stifle a gasp of surprise when the guard said, "You can go up. The elevator is down that hall. Tenth floor. Number D."

The tenth floor was also the top floor, it turned out. Claire and Joe got in the glass-walled elevator and stared at their own reflections as they smoothly ascended the floors.

At the top of the building, they stepped out into a hallway. At one end of the hallway there was a huge round window that offered a breathtaking view of the bay. At the other end, there was a marble wall with brass letters on it: 10A and B were to the left, C and D to the right.

Joe and Claire approached the marble wall and turned right. They walked to the end of that hall, where they could choose between C and D. They turned right, and at last came to a pair of tall double doors. The brass plaque beside the doors informed them that they had reached apartment 10D.

A maid straight out of a B movie let them in. She wore a black dress with white apron, collar and cuffs. She was tall and Swedish-looking, her hair pulled back in a French roll.

"This way, please. Mrs. Henson expects you." She led the way from the high-ceilinged, skylit foyer to a high-ceilinged, skylit sitting room. "Sit down, please." She gestured at the plush modular couches and chairs arranged around a black marble fireplace.

Claire sat down in one of the chairs. Joe went and stood by the fireplace. The maid left them.

As she and Joe exchanged a telling glance, Claire had to stifle a laugh. Mariah Henson's apartment was so aggressively luxurious, it almost didn't seem real. It was a palace of areca palms and leather and polished stone and glass. The view of the bay out the one window wall was stunning in its splendor. A huge crystal nautilus shell displayed on an ebony pillar drew the eye back in disbelief time and again—the thing was four feet in diameter, at least.

Mariah Henson kept them waiting for several minutes. She was giving them time to be intimidated by the sheer opulence of her living room, Claire had no doubt.

But at last she appeared, looking calm and aloof, wearing a silk jumpsuit the same maroon color as the business suit she'd worn to Claire's preliminary hearing four days before. She swept into the room and took the big leather chair across from the smaller one Claire had chosen.

She rested her hands on the chair arms, and she looked slowly from Claire to Joe. Her blue eyes were flat. "You'll excuse me if I don't offer you coffee. I don't imagine this is a social call."

"No," Claire answered evenly. "It's not."

"What do you want, then?"

Claire decided to cut right to the point. She leaned forward. "Mrs. Henson, we're trying to find out who shot your husband."

Mariah Henson's maroon fingernails dug into the butter-soft leather of her chair. "Don't insult my intelligence. He was shot in *your* little bungalow, with *your* gun, after having some kind of a fight with *you*. If you really want to know who shot him, the best place to look is in a mirror."

Claire said simply, "But I didn't do it."

Mariah Henson loosed a delicate but quite audible *humph*. "You seem to think I actually might believe you. Well, you can give that up. I am not a fool."

"No, Mrs. Henson, you're not a fool." Joe spoke up from his post by the black fireplace. "And that's why we think that you are aware of all the people who hate your husband—all the people who have very good reasons to wish your husband was dead."

The woman glared at Joe. "The police have been thorough, in case you weren't aware. There is no one else who had both a reason to shoot Alan—and the opportunity."

Claire said, "You're wrong. I may have had the opportunity, but I had no reason to shoot him. We had a...disagreement, and it was settled without having to resort to—"

Mariah Henson groaned aloud. "Oh, please. Let's be specific here—because I *am* curious. Just exactly what kind of disagreement did you have with my husband?"

Claire swallowed. "What do you mean?"

"Just what, exactly, was going on between you and Alan? That's what I want to know."

"Nothing was going on between your husband and me."

Mariah Henson gave another of her delicate little *humphs*.

Claire stared at the woman. Things were becoming uncomfortably clear. Claire could see now why the woman had agreed to talk to them—because she had a few questions of her own. Questions that, when answered, would give Mariah Henson all the reason she needed to call the guard down in the lobby and order them thrown out. They'd end up learning nothing, and in the meantime, Mariah Henson could enjoy making Claire squirm.

"Well?" Alan Henson's wife inquired. Her sculpted brows lifted a fraction.

Joe said, "He tried to rape her."

Mariah Henson gasped.

Joe went on as if he hadn't heard the sound. "But Claire is smart and quick. She grabbed a glass and broke it on the side of his head. It was a thin glass, so it shattered on impact, causing no harm to your husband, but scaring him enough that he let her go. She ordered him to get out of her motel. And that is the last she saw of him, until she found him unconscious the next day." He casually readjusted a cloisonné egg on the black marble mantel. "Does that answer your question? Or would you like to hear more? We've gathered a lot of information about the other people in your husband's life. You know, all those poor folks your husband has ripped off in his brilliant career as a *financial planner,* not to mention all the women he—"

"Enough! That is it, that is enough...." Mariah Henson sputtered. Joe shrugged and said no more. In the deadly silence that followed, Mariah Henson rose to her feet. When next she spoke, her voice vibrated with righteous wrath. "That...what you just told me...is a rotten lie. And that woman—" she pointed a finger at Claire "—knows it. Alan would never force a woman. Alan is a lot of things, but a rapist is not one of them. Deep down, he's a good and gentle man, a man no one—except for me, of course—understands. He has a...weakness for other women, and a few professional problems of late, but when he regains consciousness and is well once again, we'll work everything out."

"If you feel that way," Joe asked pleasantly, "then why did you steal Claire's gun and shoot the sonofabitch?"

That did it. Mariah Henson's face turned the same color as her jumpsuit. "Out!" she shouted. "Out of my home!"

"Sorry," Joe said a little sheepishly, once the security guard had shown them the street.

"For what? You were great. We were getting nowhere being nice, so you made the right move to go for broke."

He chuckled and put his arm around her. "You do catch on quick."

She shivered a little. It was still early in the morning, and the wind off the bay had a real chill in it. "Come on. Let's go somewhere warm for a few minutes. I'm freezing."

They walked a few blocks until they found a coffee shop. They went in, took a booth, and ordered hot cocoa. Then they discussed the encounter with Henson's wife, and Joe jotted down notes.

"Okay, Snow, so what did we find out?"

Claire sipped her cocoa and savored the heat of it. "This is just an opinion..."

"Opinions are allowed."

"I think Mariah Henson's got her eyes open about her husband. It looks to me as if she's known exactly what he is all along, and, in her own way at least, she loves him, anyway. She keeps him away from her money—and she blames the other woman whenever he gets into trouble with one." Claire fell silent. She stared out the window by their booth at the gray buildings and the windswept street.

"What else?" Joe asked.

"Nothing. That's all, really."

"There's something. You're holding back."

She sighed. "Oh, I suppose it's just that, after talking to her, I feel let down."

"Why?" Joe raised his eyebrows at her over the rim of his own cocoa mug.

"Because now, I just don't think she shot him."

"You're saying that until now, you *did* think she did it."

"Yes, I guess I did. Even though she supposedly can prove she couldn't have been in Pine Bluff, I thought she'd set up an alibi—or hired someone to do it. After all, she certainly has the money to pay for something like that."

Joe grunted. "If she paid someone to kill him, she got taken. After all, that job was left undone."

Claire lifted her mug again. "Yeah. I guess so." She drank the rest of the sweet, warm chocolate.

Joe reached across the table and chucked her under the chin. "Hey. Chin up."

She set down her cup. "I can't help it, Joe. I really don't think she had anything to do with shooting Henson. After all, she *knows* what he is. It looks to me like she's *always* known just what he is, and she doesn't care. If she stole my gun, she'd have come after me, not him. We're getting nowhere, Joe. Worse than nowhere. Before we talked to Mariah Henson, I still suspected that she was the one. Now, I don't even have that."

Her hand was lying on the table. Joe covered it with his own. He gave it a squeeze, and smiled into her eyes, and said nothing—not even "I told you so," which he certainly had a right to say. She turned her hand and squeezed back, forcing a smile to match his.

Lord, he was a wonderful man. She didn't think, in all her years of hopelessly loving him, that she had ever loved him as much as this moment, when he held her hand across the table of this little booth, and smiled into her eyes and didn't say "I told you so."

He suggested, "We could take a break from this. Sometimes a break helps to put things in perspective. We could do a few touristy things—go to Fisherman's Wharf, visit Ghirardelli Square . . ."

She shook her head and gave his hand one more squeeze. "Thanks, but I'm okay." Gently, she pulled her hand from his. "Now who's next?"

He didn't speak for a moment. Then he shrugged. "We'll give the Radners another try." The Radners were the owners of the row house in town. "And then we've got the two addresses in Sausalito and a Dr. Simonsen in Berkeley—and that lady in Oakland we didn't reach yesterday."

And that's all, she thought but didn't say. She kept her smile in place. "Let's get moving, then."

The row house was, as before, deserted. This time they tried knocking on the doors to either side of the house and across the street, but the neighbors either didn't come to the door or claimed ignorance of the whereabouts of Mr. and Mrs. Radner.

Joe decided, "All right. When we get back to the hotel, we'll try calling. And if that gets us nowhere—"

"I know. It's time to give up on the Radners."

"That's about the size of it, at least for this trip."

They went back to the hotel, but only to get the car; they didn't even bother stopping in the room. They drove across the bridge to Sausalito and found that no one answered the doors at either of the addresses they had there, either.

They had lunch, and then backtracked over the Golden Gate, to the Bay Bridge and up to Berkeley. They found Dr. Simonsen at his office; he was a pediatrician. He agreed to talk to them, and led them to a small consulting office with a window on the parking lot and stuffed animals on top of the file cabinets.

He explained that he'd met Alan Henson at a small art gallery opening. He'd liked the man right off, and they'd become friendly acquaintances. When Henson called to offer him some very special business opportunities, naturally he'd listened. And he'd bought in.

He'd lost thirty-five thousand dollars before he realized he was being had. He'd hired a lawyer, and that was that. Henson had not ruined him, which was more, he understood, than some of the people the man had "advised" could say. He'd spent all last weekend, when Henson was shot, in Oregon visiting his mother and father on their small ranch.

"Anything else?" The doctor smiled politely at them across his desk.

Joe asked if he knew of anyone else who might have reason to want to cause Alan Henson pain. Dr. Simonsen could think of no one.

Claire and Joe thanked him and left, driving south to the Bay Bridge and then returning to the hotel.

It was after six when they reached their rooms—and the red light was blinking on the telephone, letting them know someone had left a message while they were gone.

Claire immediately thought of Ella, and imagined some crisis had probably arisen at Snow's Inn. Joe called the desk right away.

"Ella did call," he said after getting the messages. "But so did Sheriff Brawley. He called a little after noon, and said we were to call right back. He's tried to reach us twice since then."

Claire's spirits sank another notch. She reached to take the phone from Joe. "I'll do it. We both know it's about me."

"I don't mind," he told her gently.

She looked at him and knew she should insist; their being here was her doing, after all. "Joe, I should do it."

He saw her indecision and took over, punching up the number of the sheriff's office without discussing it further.

The sheriff wasn't near the phone. The dispatcher told them to wait at that number. He would reach the sheriff and have him call them back.

Fifteen minutes later, the phone rang again. Joe answered. His side of the conversation was cryptic.

"Yes, Dan. I understand.... But I want to tell you that she did invite us up.... All right. Don't worry. I know. I understand, but this is a tough time for her. You have to realize.... All right. Yes. Tomorrow noon, you have my word." He hung up.

Claire knew what he would tell her before he began. She said it for him. "Mariah Henson called in a complaint."

Joe nodded. "The sheriff says we're lucky. She called and insisted on talking to him personally. He was able to settle her down pretty much. He called your mother, and got the number here from her. And he's giving us the rest of the night here, with the understanding that we're to talk to no one else about Alan Henson. We have to report to him at the Excelsior County sheriff's office at noon tomorrow—or else."

Claire thought about the Radners, and the two people in Sausalito... and the woman in Oakland. They represented her last tiny hope of helping herself out of what was happening to her. And now, with a phone call, Sheriff Brawley had snatched her hope away from her.

"You want me to go ahead and call Ella?" Joe asked.

"No." She'd let Joe handle the toughest call. The least she could do was take care of her own mother. "I'll do it." She took the phone and dialed Snow's Inn.

"Dear, I've been worried sick," Ella said as soon as Claire identified herself. "Dan Brawley called here and—"

"I know, Mother. Don't worry. Everything's all right."

"I didn't know what else to do, so I gave him—"

"You did the right thing. Don't worry."

"What will you do now?"

"We'll probably go back to the ranch." Claire tried not to sound as low as she felt. "Look. Don't worry. Nothing is wrong. I have to see Sheriff Dan tomorrow. I'll stop in after that. Now, are there any other problems?"

Ella assured Claire that everything was going smoothly at Snow's Inn, so Claire said goodbye.

Once she'd hung up, Claire wished she could just lie down on the bed and close her eyes. Suddenly, she felt so exhausted. And yet she couldn't bear the thought of sitting still.

"Let's pack up, then," she muttered, and marched into the big walk-in closet area to begin collecting her things. "We might as well go on home tonight."

"Hey, wait a minute." Joe followed after her.

She began grabbing things off hangers. "What?"

He took the blouse she was folding out of her hands and laid it across her open suitcase. Then he clasped her arms and made her look at him. "What's the matter with you?"

She squirmed a little in his grip, but she wasn't really fighting him. She wasn't fighting anything right then.

"Nothing's the matter," she answered with a total lack of conviction. "I just...I don't feel like hanging around here, that's all."

He stared at her measuringly. And then he seemed to come to some sort of decision. He asked, "What do you mean, hanging around? We've still got some work to do, don't we?"

She blinked. "Excuse me?"

"You know, the reason we came here. Sausalito. The Radners. And the lady in Oakland. What else would I mean?"

"But you said Sheriff Dan said—"

"Hell. What he doesn't know won't hurt him. As long as we're there to check in on time tomorrow, what's he going to know about what we were doing tonight? Because we'll be real gentlemen about this. There will be no more complaints. Besides, what's he going to do if he *does* find out— arrest you?"

"Very funny."

"Oh, really? I didn't mean to be funny. I'm dead serious here."

"But you promised we wouldn't talk to anyone else. If we do, we'll be breaking our word...."

"Okay, fine." He released her. "Get packed and we'll head home."

She didn't move. "We shouldn't—"

"You're right. It's a bad idea." He turned and started reaching for his own clothes.

"But..."

He stopped. "Yeah?"

"Well, I mean, if we were really polite, and *nice* about it..."

"Yeah?" His tawny eyes were gleaming.

"I mean, who could it hurt?"

"Exactly." He gave up any pretense of packing his clothes. "I'll call the Radners now. And then it's back across the Golden Gate to Sausalito. And how about if we try the Oakland address tomorrow on the way out of town?"

Claire nodded, then followed him into the main part of the room, where she waited to see what the phone call would yield.

It yielded nothing but an answering machine that explained how the Radners weren't near the phone right now, but would love to get back to them soon. Joe left a brief message, just his name and the hotel's phone number, at the beep.

After that, they headed for Sausalito one more time.

They had no luck with the first of the two people, a man named Ed Farnsworth. They tried the second, Alexandra Brock, who lived in a graceful Spanish Revival house, which was perched with attractive precariousness on one of the famous Sausalito hills.

When they rang the bell, a moon-faced woman of perhaps forty-five peeked warily around the mahogany door at them, not unlatching the chain. "Yes?"

"Ms. Brock?" Claire spoke right up.

"Yes. What is it?"

"I'm Claire Snow and—"

"Claire Snow?" Alexandra Brock's hazel eyes widened. "You're the one who shot Alan, aren't you?"

Claire backed up on the narrow step. Already, she was picturing another scene like the one with Henson's wife.

But she was wrong. Alexandra Brock was fiddling with the chain. She finally succeeded in unlatching it, and pulled the door back. "Come in, come in. I saw your name in the paper . . . as the *suspect* in the shooting. I'm just thrilled to get to meet you."

Joe and Claire barely had time to exchange stupefied glances before Alexandra Brock ushered them into her lovely home.

She took them to her living room, a warm place of hardwood floors and dhurrie rugs, and fat, soft couches with lots of bright pillows strewn around. She clucked over them as she made them comfortable and offered drinks, which Joe and Claire politely declined.

Then Alexandra talked. Nonstop.

"Oh, I was just so *thrilled*, when I saw it in the paper. I suppose I should feel bad. He is a human being, after all. But, then, he's not, really, is he? In reality, he is pond scum. He told me he loved me, can you believe it? *Loved* me. And I don't know. He was such a sweet man, he seemed like the most *harmless* man. How could a man like that tell anything but the truth, is what I thought at the time? Oh, I was a fool. A *fool.* Walking around with stars in my eyes. Forty-nine thousand. That's what he ended up costing me, can you feature it? I went to my savings and loan and I cashed in my certificates of deposit and I was singing love songs while I did it. I wrote him several large checks with a dreamy smile on my face. Go figure it. How did he do it? I don't imagine I will ever know. Oh, but after I woke up from my romantic daydream, I had other, darker dreams. I dreamed of doing just what you did, Claire." Claire started to protest that she hadn't done the shooting, but said nothing, because she doubted Alexandra would have heard, anyway. Alexandra rhapsodized on. "I dreamed of pointing a gun at him and pulling the trigger. Oh, Lord, I admire you so. I wish it had been me."

A girlish giggle escaped her. "But I suppose, I'm glad it wasn't me. Who wants to go to jail for trying to kill a weasel, after all? And I'll tell you, I mentioned to more than one person that I would love to kill that piece of flotsam. So you can be sure that I was relieved that I had two houseguests last weekend who will testify in court that I was never out of their sight long enough to drive to that little town of yours and do the deed." Alexandra giggled again. "A murderous woman like me needs an alibi." She twinkled at Claire. "But I'm sure you understand."

Claire nodded. "I have to admit I do."

"Now." Alexandra took a sip of the glass of wine she'd poured herself when her guests declined. "What can I do for you? Anything, just ask . . . within reason, of course . . ."

Claire and Joe asked the usual questions. Did Alexandra know of anyone else who might want to harm Henson? She didn't. Had he been in touch with her since he left for Pine Bluff? No, she hadn't seen or heard from him in six months—and that was just dandy with her. Had he ever mentioned to her any enemies he might have had, or people who might have been out to make trouble for him?

Alexandra giggled some more at that one. "Oh, no. You know how Alan is. Even if a million people hated his guts, he'd never tell a soul. He likes to pretend he's everybody's best friend."

Soon after that, Claire and Joe got up to leave. At the door, Alexandra stuck out her hand. "Claire, thank you once more. Let's just hope that dirtbag never wakes up."

Claire realized now was probably the only chance she'd get to disabuse the woman. "Sorry, Alexandra. But the truth is, I didn't do it."

Alexandra rolled her eyes. "Oh, well. I suppose your lawyer told you to say that."

"No, actually, it's the truth."

"Yes, of course. You take care now . . ."

After that they went by Ed Farnsworth's house one more time, but it was dark and no one answered when they tried the doorbell. Then they drove back to the hotel again, and Joe tried calling both Farnsworth and the Radners. He listened to more recorded messages, and left brief messages of his own.

He tried the number of the lady in Oakland, Beth Hyland. She answered.

Joe was prepared. He said he was Jerry Tennyson from Syndicated Data Corporation, and he was taking a survey of the working habits of Bay Area women. Did she work outside the home? How many hours a week? Was she . . . ?

But then Beth Hyland evidently changed her mind about answering any more questions, because Joe gently put the phone back in its cradle.

"What happened?" Claire wanted to know.

"The usual. She got suspicious—or maybe impatient or bored, who knows?—and hung up. Too bad, too, because I was trying to lead it around so we could be sure she'll be there tomorrow morning when we drop by." He looked at the bedside clock. "It's past ten now. If we try to catch her tonight, it'll be eleven at least. Not a good time of night for two strangers to be knocking on anyone's door to ask them questions." He snared Claire's hand and pulled her so she was standing between his thighs. He looked up at her. "A better move would be to get out of here at the crack of dawn, and see if we can catch her before she has a chance to leave the house for the day." He ran a hand under the collar of her shirt, a gesture that was both fond and questioning. "What do you say?"

"Sounds good." She tried to move away.

He held her still. "Hey."

"Um?"

"What is it?"

"Nothing." She was lying, and they both knew it. She was trying not to give in to the depression that seemed, once again, to be turning the edges of her reality a dull gray. She pasted on a smile. "Just tired, I guess. Let's get some sleep, okay?"

He looked at her for a moment more, then nodded. "Good idea."

They slept wrapped up together. But in spite of the comfort Joe's strong arms gave, Claire did not sleep well.

They rose at six and tried the Farnsworth and Radner numbers once more. No luck.

Joe turned to Claire once he'd hung up from the second call.

"You don't have to say it," she told him before he could speak. "I know. We have to give up on them."

"For now," he reminded her, trying, she knew, to interject a note of hope into a gloomy situation.

She made herself smile—she was forcing smiles a lot lately—and said she understood.

By six-thirty, they were checked out of the hotel and on their way to try to catch Beth Hyland at home.

They were in luck this time; she was home.

But she wouldn't come to the door. She spoke to them through a side window, as they stood on the big porch of her California bungalow-style house.

"I have already talked to the police about Alan Henson, and I don't intend to talk to anyone else. Please get off my property."

"But Ms. Hyland—" Claire began.

From inside the house, another voice—a man's voice—cut in. "She said she won't talk to you. Either get lost, or we'll call the police."

"But I—"

"Claire," Joe said softly. He was shaking his head.

She knew he was right, of course. If the woman wouldn't even come to the door, they were unlikely to convince her to reveal anything to them, assuming she *had* anything to reveal in the first place.

But, oh, Lord, this was it. Beth Hyland, hiding in her house, unwilling to so much as answer her door, was Claire's last hope. After this, she and Joe would get back in her car and keep driving until they reached Pine Bluff and the courthouse, where they had to report to Sheriff Dan at twelve noon—or else.

After this, there was nothing more she could do. She would go before the grand jury the day after tomorrow. In all likelihood, they'd hand down an indictment. She would go to trial for a crime she had not committed—and she might as well not kid herself. The chances were at least even that she would end up in prison.

For something she hadn't done.

"Please!" She fairly shouted the word. "Please, you have to talk to me!"

"Claire—"

"Get the hell off this property!" the man inside ordered again.

"But I—"

"Call the police, Beth," the man said. "I've had enough of this crap."

"Claire..." Joe reached for her.

She shook him off and fell against the heavy wooden door of Beth Hyland's house. "Please. Ms. Hyland! Please talk to me..." She pounded with her fists on the ungiving wood.

"Claire." Joe tried to take her arm. "Claire. It's no good. We have to go. Come on, Claire."

"We're calling the police, you crazy bitch!" the man inside announced.

Claire kept pounding, feeling the rough wood scrape her knuckles, not caring, begging the woman inside to please open up, while the man in there yelled obscenities and demanded she get the hell off his porch.

"Claire..." Joe tried again.

She blocked him out and went on beating at the door that was so securely locked against her.

And then Joe grabbed her right arm in mid-pound and spun her to face him.

"Let go of me!" she snarled.

He shook her. Hard.

When he stopped, she stared at him, stunned.

Then he said, "It's no use. We have to go. Do you understand?"

Numbly, she nodded. Then she instructed in an expressionless voice, "Let go of me, please."

He dropped his hands to his sides. As soon as he released her, she turned and went down the porch steps to the street where her car waited to take her back to Pine Bluff.

When she reached the car, she got in on the driver's side and stared out the window, waiting for Joe, who'd stayed behind long enough to exchange a few more words with Beth Hyland and the man in the house.

Within minutes, he was beside her, pulling open her door. "I think I should drive," he said.

She didn't argue. She got out, handed him the keys and went around to the passenger side. She stared out the window some more as he started the car, pulled away from the curb and drove away.

Chapter Thirteen

"Beth Hyland agreed not to call the police," Joe volunteered some time later, after all the tricky interchanges were behind them and they were safely on course, headed along Highway 80 toward Sacramento.

"She did?" Claire didn't glance at him. She kept her gaze out the window on the dry, rolling hills and the faded-denim sky.

"Yeah. I don't think she really wanted to make trouble."

"Right. She's a real sweetheart."

"I don't know if I'd call her a sweetheart," he said. "But I don't think she'll call the police."

"I guess I should be grateful." Claire knew she sounded petulant, but she went on, anyway. "Now Sheriff Dan won't have to arrest me—again."

Joe sighed. "Damn it, Claire. Let's get something straight here. If anyone calls in another complaint on you, the sheriff will probably be forced to revoke your bail."

Claire stared at him. She knew he was right, but she hadn't really let herself think about that up till now. She reminded him, "You didn't bother to point that out last night."

"I know." He stared grimly at the road.

"Why?"

"Because you looked so damned pitiful when you heard we had to give up and go home. I thought it would be worth it, just to see you perk up a little. But my idea was that we'd just walk away if things got the least bit tense. I was sure Dan would never know we went back out asking questions after I swore we would quit. I didn't count on you making a scene like that." He gave her a quick, understanding glance. "Look. I know you're as desperate as they come about now. And what you did back there, that crazy scene, I *do* understand the frustration that caused it. I also know I'm not blameless here. I *was* the one who pushed you to go on, even after I promised Dan we'd leave it alone. And I was also the one who led you to believe there wasn't much Dan would do if someone else complained about you. But the truth is, Dan Brawley has stuck his neck out about as far as he can for you. You've got to realize that he could be forced to lock you up for good, if Wayne Leven—who runs things strictly by the book—hears what we've been doing. Do you want to go back to jail?"

Claire stared down at her lap, feeling ashamed of herself. "No. And I'm sorry, Joe."

"Don't be sorry," he said. "Just think first next time."

"Okay."

For a moment, neither spoke. Then he said, "Listen. I'm sorry. About shaking you like that."

She shrugged. "It's okay. It got my attention. And right then, there wasn't much else that would have done that."

Claire truly wasn't upset about the shaking he'd given her. It had shocked her at the time—as he'd intended. But it had been a carefully calculated move, and it had worked with a minimum of fuss. He'd done what he had to do, and he'd done it for her own sake.

She couldn't fault him for it, and she didn't. Ever since that day last week—Lord, had it only been a *week* ago when he'd come to warn her about Alan Henson?—he'd done everything he could for her. He'd proved himself the best friend she'd ever be likely to know. And then, when she couldn't believe all he'd done for her, he'd done more.

He'd known that the trip to San Francisco would be futile, yet he'd undertaken it anyway, because she begged him to. She'd been so idiotically naive. She'd insisted on believing that some new piece of evidence might come to light if she were to wander around the Bay Area, asking the people Alan Henson had duped if they knew anything about his near-demise that they hadn't bothered to tell the police.

Lord, she'd been a fool. A fool about everything. Thinking for all those years that the world was fair.

And then, actually believing that she could do something to help herself out of the trap that was slowly swallowing her alive.

A fool, yes. A naive, innocent fool. Born innocent—and too dewy-eyed to get wise.

Even now, when she should have learned her lesson about this pointless excursion, she couldn't stop thinking about the people they'd never reached—the Radners and the man in Sausalito. And then there were all the ones like Beth Hyland, who had yelled at them, and refused to let them get near.

Oh, Lord, the truth was, *any* of those people might have done it—or hired someone else to do it.

Claire fisted her hands in her lap. She clenched them so tightly that her nails bit into her palms. She hated—*hated*—that they had learned nothing, that Joe had been right.

They hadn't the resources or the clout of the police. Only blind luck might have given them something to go on from one of the people on the list. And luck had not been with them.

She had wasted four days of her life and learned nothing. And they were days she could never get back, precious days, once-in-a-lifetime days that she could have spent at the ranch with Joe, forgetting her troubles instead of pursuing them.

And now the time had come to tell Joe about the baby. She was fresh out of excuses for keeping the truth from him. At first, she'd felt justified in not telling him because she herself hadn't decided what she wanted to do. Then she'd held off because she didn't want him to know until they'd finished their business in San Francisco.

Now the only reason she had for holding back was the selfish one: as soon as she told him, she would lose him. This new intimacy they shared would evaporate like a morning fog over San Francisco Bay.

Oh, he wouldn't desert her, she knew that. Joe was a real man—even more of a man than he gave himself credit for being. He would stick by her. He would probably even insist that she marry him. Even though he'd told her both times she'd begged him to love her that he was never going to marry—that he didn't believe in marriage, or in bringing children into a world like this one.

In this, her darkest time, he'd shown himself to be the best friend she'd ever known. And for that, he'd get a wife he didn't want and a baby he hadn't asked for. And if she went to prison, he'd have to make some hard choices about how to take care of that baby until her release. . . .

"Claire?"

She felt his quick glance. But when she looked, his eyes were focused on the road. "Umm?" She made herself face him, until he glanced her way again, and their eyes could meet.

Sweet heaven, had there ever been eyes like his? Or goodness, or strength like his?

Her love was a knife, turning in the deepest part of her. To love as she had always loved him, *would* always love him. And to know that as soon as she told him she was pregnant, he would ask her to be his wife—he would offer her the one, impossible, shining dream of her life. But not because he *wanted* to—because it would be his *duty* to.

He looked at the road again. "What's the matter?"

Tell him, her conscience instructed. *Tell him right now.*

"Claire?"

"I..."

"Yeah?"

"I just..."

"What?"

"I...really don't want to talk about it now." *Coward,* her conscience coldly accused.

His eyes found her, then shifted back to the highway again, but he didn't push her further. Instead he suggested, "Get the pillow from the back seat, why don't you? Rest a little. We've got a good three hours until we reach home."

Home, she thought grimly. *Where we get to report to Sheriff Dan that we'll be good from now on.*

She said, "Yes, I think I will close my eyes for a while." *The better to block out reality, my dear.* "I didn't get that much sleep last night."

"I noticed."

Claire got the pillow and put the seat all the way back. Soon enough, the whisper of the spinning tires lulled her into a fitful sleep.

* * *

When they pulled up behind the courthouse, Sheriff Dan was waiting right there in the parking lot, sitting behind the wheel of his big white 4X4.

Claire knew he was waiting for her, that he'd hung around the parking lot in an attempt to catch her before she went inside and gave Wayne Leven the opportunity to ask what was going on. Right then, she understood that what Joe had said about Dan must have been true. The sheriff had stuck his neck out for her.

Dan Brawley made a big show of casually getting out of his truck. He hitched up his belt and strolled over to the car. He leaned in Claire's open window.

"How're you doing, Short Stuff?"

"Okay, Sheriff Dan."

Dan tipped his Stetson at Joe. "Right on time, Joe."

"Just like I promised, Sheriff."

Dan looked at Claire again. "Well, it's good to see you back safe and sound." He coughed then, as if trying to find the right way to say what was coming next. Then he plunged in. "Now, Claire. You know I hate to see you in this trouble..."

He looked so uncomfortable that she helped him. "Go ahead, Sheriff Dan. What is it?"

"Well, it's just that running off like that was not wise. And from now on, as long as you're out of jail on bail, I want to be able to count on you to stay in the county, fair enough?" Claire nodded. Dan wanted a little more than a nod. "Can I have your word on that, Claire?"

Claire bit her lip, and then forced herself to promise. "Yes, Sheriff Dan. You have my word. I won't leave the county again as long as I'm out of jail on bail."

"And you'll stop trying to do my job for me." His smile urged her to give up playing amateur sleuth—and to admit the futility of such foolishness. Claire thought it a patronizing smile. She wanted to get angry, to shout at him that as long as she still had breath in her body, she wouldn't stop trying to find out what really happened to Alan Henson—especially since the sheriff's office of Excelsior County wasn't trying at all anymore.

But instead, she forced herself to remember that he had put himself on the line for her in not revoking her bail immediately as soon as he learned she'd gone outside the county limits. Sheriff Dan was a good man with a job to do. Shouting at him wouldn't accomplish any more than throwing herself against Beth Hyland's locked door had done.

"Well, Claire?" the sheriff prompted.

She nodded again. "Yes. All right. Next time I want to do police work, I'll apply at the sheriff's office for a job."

Sheriff Dan seemed relieved. "That's what I was hoping you'd say." He looked across the seat at Joe. "And as for you, Joe—"

Joe cut him off with a shrug. "Hey, Sheriff. Last I heard, it's a free country. Claire's got some problems right now, so maybe you have a right to rein her in. But me, I'm just a guy with a curious mind. Is there a law against me asking people questions?"

The sheriff snorted. "Hell. I suppose not."

"Good," Joe said.

"Just . . . be careful."

"I will. And thanks. For . . . everything."

"It's all right. Did you learn anything?"

"Not a thing you don't already know."

"Would you tell me if you had?"

"You bet." Joe shifted Claire's car into drive. "See you later, Sheriff."

"Good enough." Dan Brawley stepped back from the car. "Stay out of trouble."

"We will." Joe waved as they backed out of the parking space and slowly drove away.

Once they'd turned the corner of the courthouse, and the sheriff's imposing form had disappeared from view, Claire slumped back into her seat and closed her eyes. "There," she sighed. "That's over with." Then she thought of her mother and made herself sit up. "You'd better stop at the motel."

But Joe drove past the turn to her street. "You can call from the ranch."

"But, Joe—"

"Your mother said she could handle things for you. Let her do it."

"Joe," Claire argued as the car trundled over the bridge, "I told her I'd stop in as soon as we met with the sheriff."

"You can talk to her in twenty minutes. From the ranch."

"Why call when we can stop in person just as easily?"

They were across the bridge. "Because if you stop now, you'll just find some big problem that you'll decide you have to solve. You don't need any more problems right now." Joe pulled up at the stop sign on the way out of town.

"Don't tell me what I need, please." Claire tried to stay reasonable—she knew Joe was only thinking of her. But she felt as if the world was closing in on her. Now, even Joe seemed to think he had a right to tell her what to do. "Turn this car around, Joe."

He said nothing, only turned left and drove up the hill that led out of town. Indignation knotted Claire's stomach, but she saw the futility of arguing further right then. She sat back in her seat and kept her lips pressed tightly together as they drove the twisting dirt roads to the ranch.

When they arrived, she leapt out of the car and slammed the door behind her. Gonzo and Relay bounded up, and she was forced to settle them down and greet them before she was allowed to flounce into the house—an exercise in high drama that was somewhat spoiled because she had to wait at the door for Joe to unlock it.

Once inside, she went straight to the phone in the kitchen and dialed the motel. Her mother answered on the second ring.

"Snow's Inn. How may I help you?"

"Hello, Mother. It's me."

"Claire! How are you?"

"Fine. Just fine." She studiously refused to look at Joe, who had followed her to the kitchen and was standing, watching her, in the doorway to the hall.

"Are you at the ranch now?" her mother wanted to know.

"Yes, we just got in."

"Are you all right, Claire? You sound a little strained. Did you see Dan?"

"I'm okay, Mother. Really I am. And I spoke with the sheriff just a little while ago. The problem is . . . all worked out."

"I'm glad to hear that. But I thought you'd be stopping in here."

"I meant to, but Joe wanted to come right back here."

"Well, that's no problem. Everything is fine here, anyway."

"Good. Tell me everything."

"Are you sure you want—"

"Absolutely. I want to hear how things are going."

"Well, I'm doing quite well here, as a matter of fact." Ella launched into a detailed explanation of the challenges she'd surmounted in the past few days. She'd put Verna right to work on the back bungalow. It was spotless now, all ready for Claire to decide what she wanted to do next about it. Oh, and speaking of Verna—the poor woman had been under the weather, she'd even called in sick today. But Ella had called Amelia and she was cleaning the rooms right now. Business was brisk. All the rooms were full, and Ella had taken several reservations for the coming months. She *had* had a little trouble with that couple in number three, but she'd gone and knocked on the door and told them to keep it quiet, or she'd have to ask them to leave. That had settled them down. Oh, and she'd had to write a few checks—to Eaton Slade, the handyman, who'd come in to fix a leaky faucet in number six, among other things. And to both Verna and Amelia—hadn't payday been yesterday?

"Yes, Mother. I forgot all about it. Thanks for taking care of it for me."

"You are very welcome. Oh. I almost forgot. Someone called from your lawyer's office, to remind you that you're supposed to meet with him at eight Monday morning, before the hearing. I told them you wouldn't forget."

"Good."

"All right, then. That's all the news here. Now, tell me all about your trip," Ella cheerfully commanded.

Claire evaded. "We had a great time, but I'll explain all about it later, when we can sit down and talk."

Tactfully, her mother asked, "Then will you be staying at the ranch again tonight?"

Claire looked up, then, and right into Joe's waiting eyes. She raised her chin. "No, Mother. Now that I think about it, I've decided it's time I got my things together and came home."

"You have?" Ella sounded nonplussed. Clearly, Claire's answer was not what she'd expected.

"Yes. I think it's time, really, that I took up my responsibilities again. Life goes on, after all."

Ella asked if she was sure.

"I am. I'll be there soon." Claire said goodbye and hung up.

The room seemed unnaturally quiet. Joe and Claire looked at each other.

Joe broke the silence. "What the hell? What's going on?"

She was careful to stand very erect; he must know that she made her own decisions, that she was mistress of her own life. "I'm going home, Joe. I—I can't hide here forever. It's time I got back to my life."

"You're angry, right? Because I didn't take you to the motel before I brought you here?"

"Yes. You had no right to do that. But that's not why I'm going."

"Then why?"

"I just told you—because it's time I got back to my life."

Ha, a voice inside her head scoffed. *It's time to do more than get back to your life. It's time to tell him your secret...*

But she just couldn't do it. Not yet. She was a coward at heart.

"Look, Claire." He left the doorway and approached her, stopping at the edge of the table, across from her. "You don't have to go anywhere." He sounded so concerned, so caring. Would he sound that way when he learned what she was keeping from him? He continued, "Stay here. At least until Monday. Then, after the hearing, when you know..." He faltered. She understood. Just like everyone else, he wanted to make reality less ugly for her. "... where you stand, you can take it from there."

She breathed deep. "I know where I stand, Joe. In very hot water. And I'm through pretending things are going to work out. It's more than possible they won't work out. Staying here is only hiding my head in the sand."

Liar, her outraged conscience accused. *You just want out, quick, so you don't have to tell him. You'll do anything right now, even give up a few more precious days with him, not to have to tell him. But be honest, with yourself at least, even if you insist on continuing your lies to him. You're not leaving because he didn't stop at the motel when you asked him to. And you're not leaving because you have to get back to your life. You're leaving because you can't bear to look this man in the face and say what has to be said....*

She spoke frantically, to silence that condemning voice in her head. "Look, Joe. You've been wonderful. You've done more than any friend in the world could ever be expected to do. But I have to stop leaning on you. I have to stand on my own two feet and face what is happening to me."

Joe swore under his breath. "All right. Fine. You want to go back to the motel, I'll come with you."

"No."

"Why not?"

"I told you. I have to get on with my life. No one can help me with that. I have to...straighten out my affairs, and I have to do it on my own."

He stared at her. She felt that his eyes were trying to see into her head. "What the hell is going on here?"

"I just...I have to go." She marched straight toward him—it was the only way she could get to the hall that led to the bedroom. She prayed he wouldn't try to stop her.

Her prayers were futile. He grabbed her arm and pulled her up against his chest. "What is this? Something strange is going on. What's bothering you?"

I'm going to have your baby.... "Nothing. Everything. Please. Let me go."

"Why won't you talk to me?"

"Joe. I mean it. Let me go."

"Damn it, Claire!"

"Let me go!"

"Tell me."

"Nothing. There is nothing."

"I ought to—"

"Joe, you're hurting me!"

For a moment more, he held her, his grip like a vise. And then, his eyes suddenly cold, he let her go.

She turned and went to the bedroom, where she swiftly gathered up everything of hers that wasn't already in the suitcase in the car.

As she turned to leave, she met him coming in, carrying his own big duffel bag that he'd brought in from the car. He edged around her, as if she were someone he didn't want to touch even in passing, and set the bag down by the closet.

She turned to go, hoping, praying, that she could escape before he said another word.

"Claire," he said from behind her.

She forced herself to face him once more.

He stood by the closet, his strong arms crossed over his broad, hard chest. "Whatever it is, I'll find out."

Her mouth went dry. She swallowed. He was right, of course. He would find out. In the end, it wasn't the kind of thing she could hide anyway.

And she didn't *want* to hide it. She just wanted . . . not to lose him.

Which was absurd, since she had never had him in the first place.

And, of course, she *wouldn't* lose him. He would stand by her, insist on marrying her. That's how he was.

But, deep in his most secret heart, his trust in her would die. . . .

He must have seen the agony she was feeling. He softened his stance and coaxed, "Come on, Snow. Tell me. You can trust me, damn it."

Oh, Joe, don't you see? Of course, I can trust you. It's you who should never have trusted me. . . .

He took a step toward her. "Come on." He reached out a hand.

She longed to stay. But if she stayed, she'd end up telling him. And she couldn't do it. Not now. Later. Lord knew when. Just later. "No. I'm going. Thanks for . . . all you've done." She turned and bolted for the door.

Chapter Fourteen

Joe let her go.

What the hell more could he do, short of using force, to stop her?

The answer was nothing. Not a damn thing.

He dropped to the bed and sat unmoving, listening intently. Faintly, he heard her car door slam outside, the engine rev to life, and the sound of tires crunching gravel as she backed toward the house and then drove through the split in the fence.

Soon enough, except for the low, steady hum of the window air conditioners he'd put in during his recent home improvement phase, there was quiet.

She was gone. Everything was back to normal again; he was alone.

But what she'd said wouldn't stop echoing in his head.

You've done more than any friend could ever be expected to do....

Friend. The word galled him. It was the word he'd always used to keep her at a safe distance. And now, *she* had used it—to push *him* away. He supposed it was kind of funny. In a way. If having a woman tear your guts out with your own words could be considered funny.

You've done more...

Joe threw back his head and laughed. It was a raw howl of a laugh, one with no warmth or humor in it at all.

Hell. He hadn't done a damn thing, except take advantage of the tough time she was having enough to let her talk him into making love with her again. She'd told him it would comfort her, to be in his arms. So he'd given her comfort, and gotten plenty for himself, as well.

But as far as what might really have helped her, he'd done exactly zilch. He'd failed her in their pathetic attempts to find out who really shot Alan Henson. And, in the end, he wasn't going to be able to protect her from paying for a crime she didn't commit.

Joe knew, of course, that she was innocent of shooting Henson. There had never been the slightest doubt in his mind about that.

He knew she was innocent for two reasons: one, she had said so. And two, because, if she *had* shot him—something she would only have done in self-defense—she would have called an ambulance right away and *then* called the sheriff's office. It would never have occurred to her to do otherwise. She wouldn't have hesitated to face the consequences of her actions; and she would have been absolutely sure that justice would triumph in the end.

That was what was ripping her apart now. She was learning that she lived in a world where justice sometimes lost out to blind circumstance. It was breaking her heart.

He'd accused her a few minutes ago of keeping something from him. But now, thinking back, he knew that had to be just wishful thinking on his part.

He'd wanted there to be something, some secret, that he could drag out of her. Something he could really help her with, since he'd failed her so miserably with everything else.

But, of course, there was no secret. It was all right out there in the open for everyone to see. Her world was coming apart at the seams. She was going before the grand jury in less than forty-eight hours, and she wanted to get on with her life until then. Nothing mysterious about that.

Joe fell back on the bed, rubbed his eyes and closed them for a moment. When he opened them again, he was looking at his duffel bag by the closet across the room. On top of the bag was the steno pad he'd taken to San Francisco. The damn thing was almost completely full. Of useless notes. He'd scribbled his little heart out, getting down every bit of meaningless information that popped into his brain.

Joe sat up and swung his feet to the floor.

The damn notebook drew him.

There was that feeling he kept having about all this. That feeling he used to get sometimes when he was tracking some low-life fool and thought he'd exhausted all the possibilities of where the guy might be.

It was the what-is-wrong-with-this-picture? feeling. The feeling that he was looking right at what he needed to know, but just wasn't seeing it.

In such situations, the notebook helped the most. It had all the *pictures,* in the form of everything he could remember about everyone he'd talked to concerning the case.

Joe stood up and went to the duffel bag. He bent and got the notebook, and then sat in the rocking chair and began flipping through the pages.

"Claire, I really would like a private word with you."

Claire hung her dress in the closet and turned to look at Ella, who had appeared in the door to the hall. The last thing she wanted was a "private word" with her mother.

"Can't it wait a while, Mother? Right now, I'm just not up for it." She went to her open suitcase and began transferring its contents back to her dresser drawers.

Ella ventured into the room. "Dear, there are a few things I'd like to tell you, if you would just give me a moment or two."

"Mother, right now, I—" The front desk buzzer cut Claire off.

"Oh, no." Ella turned for the door. "I'll be right back. I'm sure it's only Amelia. She's having a rough time of it today."

Claire was curious. "Why?"

Ella paused in the doorway. "Because of Verna."

"What do you mean?"

"Well, it turns out Verna's left things a mess. And Amelia is having trouble getting the rooms cleaned because of it. It's not the end of the world. I'll attend to it. Don't you worry yourself."

Claire stood by the door to the hall for a moment, watching her mother's retreating back. There was really no reason not to just do as Ella had suggested and return to emptying her suitcase and putting her things in order.

But this problem with Verna seemed something she should get on top of. After all, she had come back to put her life in order. And if her head housekeeper wasn't doing her job, it would be better to deal with it now.

Claire followed her mother out to the lobby, and found Amelia cracking gum like crazy and looking thoroughly discouraged. Still, she straightened up a little when she saw Claire.

"Hey, Claire. How you doing?"

"Fine. What's going on?"

Ella turned. "Claire, I thought I told you not to worry about this right now."

Claire spoke firmly. "Thanks, Mother. You've been terrific. But it's time I started doing my job again."

"But, dear, I—"

Claire cut to the point. "Tell me what's happening, Amelia."

Amelia gave a good chomp on her gum. "Disaster, that's what. Capital D."

"Explain."

"Well, I don't like to rat on Verna. You know Verna and me always got along. But something serious is up with her. It's like she hasn't done half her work over the past week. Everything's behind. I'll be lucky to get the rooms cleaned by midnight tonight, with all the backup stuff I've got to do before I can actually clean the bathrooms and make the beds. I mean, the cart took me an hour to straighten up." She was referring to the housekeeping cart, on which she carried all the cleaning supplies and fresh linens as she went from room to room. "All the spray bottles were empty, and the mops actually *smelled*. And I've got both washers going, but all the sheets and towels are dirty. And now I'm out of detergent. Like *totally*." Amelia was so disheartened, she actually dropped into a chair right in front of her boss and blew a huge, pink bubble, waiting until it popped halfway across her face before reeling it back in. "I just don't get it. Verna always keeps on top of the supplies. She writes down what we need when it's low, and we never run out."

Ella did some clucking. "Well, she just hasn't been feeling well. I swear, she looked positively gray the other day when I asked her to scrub down the back bungalow...." Ella continued for a few moments in the same vein, chiding herself, feeling sorry for poor Verna.

Claire barely heard her. In her mind, she was seeing the dark stain on the rug in the back bungalow, and wondering if it was possible that Verna could have—

No, not Verna. Quiet, no-nonsense Verna. It couldn't be Verna....

Still, all the things she and Joe had discussed about Henson and his particular charm for women echoed in her head.

Would he have been able to charm Verna? She was so steady and practical, not the type to fall head over heels for anyone or anything.

And yet, she *was* a widow, who lived alone, who cleaned motel rooms for a living. She was one of those people other people take for granted, someone who keeps the world running, and gets little attention or recognition for a lifetime of dependable, day-in, day-out service. Deep in her heart, she *could* be lonely, and hungry for love.

And though Verna didn't seem the type of woman Henson would chose to charm, Claire and Joe had learned that the man never missed a trick. Certainly he wouldn't be beneath chatting up the housekeeper when she came in to clean his bungalow. And if she had any money at all...

"I gotta have detergent," Amelia whined.

"I understand," Claire said. "Are we out of anything else?"

"Window cleaner. And boy, do we need it. You should see the smears that those two little kids in number four left on all the windows and mirrors in there. Gross."

"Mother, can you watch things here for a little while longer?"

"Of course. I'm here as long as you need me. But I—"

"Good. There's a small box of detergent under the sink in my kitchen. You can use that for the next two loads. In the meantime, I'll go over to the grocery store and pick up enough of what we need to last until I can make my next trip to Grass Valley. And while I'm at it, I think I'll just drive to Verna's, to see if she's all right...."

* * *

At the ranch, Joe had moved from the bedroom rocker to the kitchen table. He'd found himself a big yellow legal pad—he liked bigger sheets of paper when he was formulating theories—and his hand was flying across the lined, yellow sheet. He was making notes about his notes.

He wrote:

An amateur—gets off one shot, probably in heat of passion, and then doesn't even stick around to see if the guy is dead. Probably assumes Henson is dead. And then finds out the next day that he's not.

Someone Henson ripped off. Someone with access to Claire's gun. The more I think about it, it's unlikely someone would have wandered in and just happened to discover a weapon behind the counter. Maybe, all along, we haven't given enough thought to the access problem, the factor of opportunity.

Sheriff and Leven blinded by all the circumstantial stuff, the stuff that points right at Claire. Claire and I blinded by the list, by wanting it to be someone on the list.

But Henson must have gotten to people who never made it to the list. And it's extremely likely that he got to someone local. Someone in Pine Bluff.

Most likely, a woman. A lonely, needy woman....

Claire drove straight to Verna's house, not stopping even to buy the window cleaner and detergent she'd promised Amelia. The cleaning supplies could wait.

But the tight knot of anticipation in her stomach, the way her heart pounded with hope and, yes, fear, too—those things couldn't wait. Those things had to be attended to right now.

As she turned left at the stop sign across the bridge and headed up the hill that led out of town, she recalled her promise to Sheriff Dan. She'd given her word she'd stop doing his job for him.

A small smile played on her lips. Well, fine. She *wasn't* breaking her word—or if she was, Sheriff Dan would never know it. After all, Verna *was* Claire's employee, and Claire was concerned about her. It was as simple as that. Claire's mother had said Verna was sick. Claire wanted to check on her. That was all.

But you could have called her.

No, I couldn't see how she really is over the phone. I wanted to check on her in person, and that's what I'm doing. There's no law against that. . . .

Claire thought of Joe. Perhaps it would be wisest to take the turnoff to the ranch, to find Joe and ask him to come back with her to Verna's, in case there really was anything to this crazy hunch of hers.

Claire shook her head. Ten to one, this would turn out to be a wild-goose chase. Claire had known Verna Higgins all her life. Verna was a peaceable soul, not the type to shoot a man in a fit of passion—or in cold blood, either, for that matter.

In spite of the way her stomach clenched and her heart beat in her throat, Claire was pretty sure of what she would actually find when she knocked on Verna's door: Verna in her housecoat, watching Saturday afternoon TV.

No, Claire wouldn't bother Joe. She'd already dragged him all over San Francisco for no reason. Enough was enough. She could handle this herself. Behind her, the dirt road that led to the ranch disappeared around a bend.

Soon enough, up ahead between a pair of tall pines, she could see the top of the dirt road that cut down to Verna's house. And then she was upon it. Crossing the opposing lane of traffic, she pulled off onto the shoulder and started down toward the little house that clung to the side of the mountain beneath the dappling shadows of the big trees.

Claire stopped the car several yards from the front porch. She sat for a moment, looking out the windshield at the house. It looked deserted. The blinds were drawn on the three front windows—the big ones to one side of the door, which probably served the living room, as well as the slightly smaller one on the other side, no doubt to a bedroom.

She could see no sign of Verna's gray compact car. But that could easily be in the garage, which adjoined the house and appeared locked up tight.

Claire got out, and stood by her driver's door for a moment, suddenly reluctant, after her headlong rush to get here, to go up to the porch and knock on the door.

Claire stared at the house, and actually considered getting back in her car and returning to town and calling Sheriff Dan. She could tell him her suspicions and let him handle it from there.

Claire shook her head.

No, she wasn't that woman anymore, that trusting woman who turned things over to the proper authorities because that was the right thing to do. She couldn't just let someone else handle it. She wanted to handle it herself.

Besides, she was probably making a big deal out of nothing at all. In any case, it was time to stop dawdling and get to it.

Claire squared her shoulders and marched to the porch, up the three steps and to the front door. She knocked briskly and then waited.

Nothing happened.

She called. "Verna! It's me, Claire. Are you in there?"

No one answered. She wondered if, like that night at Joe's, she'd have to break a window to get in.

She left the porch and walked around the side of the garage, where a small, cobwebby window allowed her to see that Verna's car, at least, was here. She continued on, around the garage, to the back of the house. The windows there were dark, as well.

She mounted the short stoop to the back door, pulled open the squeaky screen and knocked. When nothing happened, she tried the door handle. It turned.

"Verna? Are you there?" She pushed the door slowly open. "Verna?" She wrapped her fingers around the top of the door, and peeked around it.

She saw a small, dim kitchen and she saw open boxes on the floor, half-filled with kitchen utensils.

She also saw Verna, standing about four feet away from the door. Verna wasn't wearing the housecoat Claire had expected. Instead, she was fully dressed, and in her shaking hands she held a small revolver. The gun was pointed straight at Claire.

Chapter Fifteen

Verna said, "I guess you better come in."

Claire held her breath and wondered what her chances were of making a run for it.

"Don't even think it." Verna gestured with the gun. "Come in and close that door."

"All right. Take it easy." Slowly, Claire pushed the door open enough to slide through it. Then she closed it gently behind her.

"Keep your hands where I can see them."

Claire raised her hands in the air. "Okay. Now what?"

"Just...shut up. Just let me think." Verna's hands—and the gun she was pointing at Claire—kept shaking. Claire tried not to imagine what would happen if one of her fingers slipped.

Verna gestured with the gun some more. "Okay. In there." She circled around until she was between Claire and the door. Then she herded Claire through the doorway that led to the front room. Claire had to step over more half-filled open boxes to get through the kitchen.

"Sit down," Verna instructed when Claire had moved fully into the front room and stood near a faded, floral-patterned couch. Claire didn't argue. She nudged aside a box with tissue paper sticking out of it and sat at one end of the couch. Verna lowered herself into a heavily padded reclining chair across from her.

The women regarded each other.

The room was very warm. Claire could feel the sweat, partly from the heat and partly from her own fear, breaking out on her brow, her upper lip and beneath her arms.

Verna was sweating, too. And her hands, which still held the gun trained on Claire, were also still shaking. Claire had the terrifying urge to ask, What are you going to do with me? She held it back.

Verna looked more than merely desperate. Something inside her seemed to have snapped. There was a rim of white around her mouth. Her eyes had a wild, trapped gleam. Claire already knew what Verna was going to do with her, even if Verna didn't yet quite know herself.

Claire's elbow nudged the tissue paper that spilled out of the box beside her. It made a soft, crackling sound.

Verna spoke up. "Yeah, I'm packing," she said impatiently, as if in answer to a question that Claire had never uttered aloud. "I'm leaving. But I'm having a hard time deciding what to take. My car's not very big. I'll have to leave a few things."

Claire nodded. What should she do? Humor this wild-eyed stranger who seemed, somehow, to be no longer the Verna she knew? This woman who held Claire's life—and the secret life of a tiny baby—in her quivering, sweaty hands? She supposed it was worth a shot.

"Yes, I . . . imagine it's difficult. Making up your mind."

Verna's mad eyes narrowed. "I know you blame me. Don't pretend you don't." Her voice went plaintive. "But what was I supposed to do? They thought it was you, and I let them go ahead and think that. What else could I do? I didn't want to go to jail. But this...acting like nothing happened, it's making me, I don't know, crazy. I have to get out."

Claire, who was trying not to think of what she saw in store for herself when she looked into Verna's exhausted, mad eyes, asked carefully, "You're talking about what happened with Alan?"

Verna scrunched up her face. "What else is there? Of course. What happened with Alan. Don't play stupid. You know. I know you know."

Claire swallowed. "Yes. I do. I understand. About Alan."

Verna made a short, tight noise. The madness in her eyes receded a little; they were suddenly brimming with injured tears. "What was I supposed to do? What did he think I'd do?"

Claire ventured, "You loved him..."

Verna's eyes grew feverishly bright. "Yes, yes. You know. You understand. I loved him. I'm...not young. Not pretty. I was never pretty. I met Martin. We married. He was a good man. We had a good life, even though the...children never came. And then he died. And I thought, well, that's it. That was all of it. You've had what you will have. But then..."

"You met Alan."

"Yes. Alan." Verna smiled, a dreamy smile. She still held the gun on Claire, but she had relaxed a little. Her hands were steady now. "I met Alan. And life was...new again. I couldn't believe it was happening to me, of all people. That magic, that loveliness. But it was. I loved him from the first morning when I tapped on the door of the bungalow and he stuck his head out and smiled. He said, 'Hello there, come

right in.…' He was wearing a maroon silk robe, with his
initials on it. He was fresh from his shower, and the room
smelled of his after-shave. I was embarrassed at first. I asked
him if maybe I should come back later, when he was
dressed. But he said he was making coffee. Would I like a
cup…?''

Verna's dreamy voice faded. She rested her head against
the high back of her chair. Her eyes drooped, and the hand
with the weapon in it began to droop in the same way.

Claire watched the gun, as the hand that held it softly
drifted down to rest on the arm of the recliner. If she moved
swiftly, propelled herself straight across at the other woman,
and then knocked the gun…

Verna's eyes shot open and her head snapped erect.
''Don't move. Don't get ideas.'' Once again, Claire found
herself looking down the round, gray mouth of the quivering gun.

''I haven't,'' Claire assured her. ''I won't.''

''Good. Where was I?''

''He, um, offered you coffee.''

''Oh, God.'' Verna wiped sweat from her brow with her
free hand. ''Yes. He offered me coffee. And I shouldn't
have, but I said yes. Yes, yes, yes…'' Verna's eyes went
dreaming again, but this time she kept them wide open and
the gun remained pointed straight at Claire's heart. Verna
blinked. ''After things became…intimate—'' she blushed
''—he said we had to be *discreet* about us, that he had a few
things going on here in town that would be ruined if anyone knew about us.''

Verna sighed. ''Of course, I knew what he meant. He was
trying to get something going with you. But I also knew you
never looked at anyone but Joe Tally. So I knew that would
pass. And Alan and me would leave town together, eventually. So I met him in secret. It was easy, since I cleaned his
room five days a week. And you never checked on me. You

trusted me. I was a dependable employee. I don't think a soul in the whole town knew what was going on."

The dreamy look in Verna's eyes began to fade. "I gave him everything, the whole twenty-five thousand I had left from Martin's insurance. He was supposed to be investing it for me. He said he knew a way to double it in a year."

Claire shook her head, feeling compassion for Verna in spite of her own plight. She knew the rest without hearing it. "Oh Lord, Verna. I'm sorry...."

Another tight sound escaped the plain woman in the reclining chair—a sound between a mad bark of laughter and a sob. "Right. So am I. Oh, God, so am I. I was such a fool." Now Verna seemed unable to remain still. She stood up. "Don't you move."

"I won't."

Still keeping the gun trained on Claire, Verna skirted an open box in the middle of the floor and went to the window by the front door. She peered around the corner of the shade. Then she turned back to Claire. "God. I can't believe how stupid I was. When you told me that night that he was leaving, I still thought everything was fine. I thought that *we* were leaving. I left the office and went straight to him...and he told me the *truth*."

Verna's face twisted up again, and her voice grew thin. "He was packing already, planning to just skip out...by himself. He tried to sweet talk me a little, but only a little. He didn't even put much effort into covering up the truth. And the truth was that I was nothing...*nothing* to him. And, as for my money...he just gave me that grin of his. My money was safe with him, he said. He'd be in touch...."

Verna sucked in a long breath, steadying herself. The mad light in her eyes blazed up once again. "I left. I was going to come back here, get my own gun, and go tell him if he didn't want *me*, that was fine. But he'd better give me my money, or else. But I passed the office, and I thought about that gun you always kept behind the desk, and I had my key with me...."

Slowly, Verna approached the couch where Claire sat. Claire tried to keep eye contact with her, though all she thought of was the neat, round mouth of the gun.

"And the rest, well, I guess you can figure it out for yourself. I—I didn't plan to shoot him, though. I didn't. I *loved* him. But even when I pointed the gun at him and told him to give me my money back, he went on smiling. And it was too much, just too much. I pulled the trigger. He fell against the dresser. When he hit the floor, he didn't move... I thought he was dead, I swear it. So I got out of there.

"I waited, all night. I almost went crazy with waiting. And then in the morning, I had to go up to the schoolyard and get the damn *float* ready."

She loosed a mad snort of laughter and backed up a few feet, recoiling at the memory of what she'd been through. "Can you believe it? I'd shot the man I loved, and I had to be in charge of the Snow's Inn Independence Day float!" She turned, a fraction, toward the recliner. "And then, just after the damn parade, the news hit. It was all over town. You'd found him, and he *wasn't* dead. He was in a coma. My God, a *coma*..."

Now Verna began to cry, huge, soggy tears that streamed down her face and dribbled into her mouth, over her chin, everywhere. Her nose ran. She sobbed, deep, hiccuping sobs.

"Oh, Verna..." Claire seized the moment when Verna's guilt and regret totally controlled her. She stood up.

"Stop. Stop right there." Verna wiped at her nose with the back of her hand and waved the gun wildly at Claire. "I told you not to move!"

"But Verna—"

"Shut up. You just…shut up. You…you shouldn't have come here. You shouldn't have, Claire. You didn't leave me any choice, coming here."

Claire put up her hands. "Verna, it's over. Face facts. If you shoot me, there'll be no one to pin it on. They'll figure out this time that it's you."

"I'll be long gone."

"You can't hide forever. Think, Verna. You don't even have any money, you said so yourself…"

"I'll steal it. I'm a criminal now, I'll do what I have to do. That's how it is these days. Women like me don't have any choice." The gun wavered again, and Verna looked as if she might crumple. "Oh, how did all this happen? Oh, Lord. What should I do?"

"Give me the gun, Verna." Claire stepped closer, hoping against hope that, for once in this whole mess surrounding Alan Henson, luck would be with her. If only she could disarm the other woman before Verna actually fired.

Verna continued to back away. She had cleared the recliner. Behind her was the open packing box she'd skirted earlier to go to the window. "No, you step back now. Don't you come any closer. I mean it, Claire. I'm warning you…" Verna steadied the gun. Claire saw her own fate in Verna's bright, mad eyes just as Verna took one more step backward—and lost her balance when her heel hit the box.

The contents of the box clanged and rattled. Verna teetered. Claire bent at the knees and launched herself at Verna's legs.

Both women hit the floor. "Oof," Verna said.

And the gun went off—a deafening crack in the close, hot room.

The shot went wild, and Claire writhed up the length of Verna's body, grabbing for Verna's wrist. Her fingers closed around it. She squeezed, in an attempt to wrest the weapon from the other woman's moist hand.

"Don't you . . . I'll get you . . ." Verna muttered between soft, intent grunts and groans.

Claire didn't speak. She was fighting for her life and the life of her unborn child against a bigger, heavier opponent. As the two of them wrestled frantically for control of the gun, Claire tried to keep the top position.

But Verna was bigger, and she used her weight to advantage. With a heavy grunt, she got their struggling bodies turning.

And then Verna was the one on top. She scowled down at Claire. Then she lunged back and pointed the gun in Claire's face. Claire saw the small, round mouth of death.

Somehow, she managed to free an arm and knock Verna's arm up and out just as the gun fired again. The shot exploded. Beneath the ringing in her ears, Claire heard one of the windows by the front door shatter. Glass tinkled and chimed as it hit the screen, and then slid out beneath the shade to pepper the floor beside the door.

Verna, set off-balance by Claire's move, collapsed with another "Oof" on top of Claire, cutting off her air. Claire took the split second of advantage to roll their entwined bodies once more and gain the top herself.

She looked down into Verna's sweating, twisted face as Verna struggled to aim the gun at Claire once more. Claire thrashed and grabbed, catching Verna's outstretched arm just as she brought it back in again.

Now the gun was cradled between their two bodies, Claire's hands around Verna's hand, as Verna beat at Claire with her free arm.

The gun went off again. Claire heard the sound all through her body, right *after* she felt the hard shove against her shoulder. For a moment, dazed, she thought Verna had punched her there. But a quick glance showed her the blooming flower of red that was staining her shirt. And she felt the heat, the burning, the pain. She had been shot.

She looked in Verna's eyes. And she saw pure bloodlust.

"I'll get you..." Verna grunted. "You're done. You're finished...."

Claire knew the next shot was coming. With superhuman effort, she managed to shove Verna's hand upward. The gun discharged, a rolling thunderclap, seeming to catch up the echoes of the other blasts, and expand on them, until the whole world was one loud, unending boom. Claire felt a hot, slicing sensation along the side of her head.

She was hit for the second time. Verna crowed in mindless triumph. Claire looked down at the twisted face beneath her, dazed, as Verna smacked her a good one, on the side of the head, using the gun as a cudgel in the same spot the bullet had just creased.

Verna crowed again.

For Claire, the world went fuzzy. Her head grew heavy, numb. Dizziness sent the whole drab, hot room spinning.

Claire fought on, though the blow to the head had been a bad one. She forced her mind to keep functioning, her body not to give up. For the sake of the baby, the tiny innocent baby. And the chance for life it would never have if the madwoman beneath her had her way. Claire managed to grab Verna's wrist, and more or less pin the gun to the floor above the other woman's head.

Verna fought like a tiger; it took all Claire's weight to hold the gun hand down. How many shots were left? Claire tried to get her deadened mind to recall. Two, probably, if the gun was like most revolvers. If Claire could only last through two more shots...

Craa-ack! Another wild shot, echoing loud and then splintering the ceiling.

One more, Claire thought, only one more....

Verna fought to bring the gun between their bodies again. Claire took a final, dangerous chance, and released the other woman's hand.

"Ha!" Verna crowed, and brought the gun in, aimed it... With all the fading strength she possessed, Claire reared back on her knees. Though her injured shoulder seemed to scream aloud in protest, she drew back her arm and whacked Verna's wrist with her left hand.

The gun went flying, hit the side table by the recliner, and then spun on across the floor. Claire collapsed on top of Verna.

Verna shrieked in foiled rage. She bucked, her whole large body gathering and then shoving. Claire felt herself going up and over. She fell backward across the open packing box.

Verna rolled to her knees and began crawling, scrambling for the gun.

Through a veil of her own blood and ever-increasing lightheadedness, Claire made out the ceramic lamp on the table by the recliner. She dragged herself upright, felt the world go spinning crazily, and managed, somehow, to stagger around the back of the recliner where she could pick up the lamp.

She reached out both hands, lifted the lamp and tottered the few steps to where Verna was just wrapping clutching fingers around the trigger of the gun.

Claire dropped the lamp on the back of Verna's head in the split second before Verna managed to turn and fire.

With a soft "Oof," Verna passed out facedown on the floor, squeezing the trigger one more time as she faded from consciousness.

The last shot buried itself harmlessly in the plaster of the wall.

Claire blinked and swayed, thinking woozily that, at last, there would be quiet...that she could sit down until the world stopped whirling around.

But the quiet never came. Behind her, the front door was kicked from its hinges. It crashed against the jamb. And, though she could hardly see for the way everything was spinning and shifting, she knew who it was, anyway.

It was Joe, sliding around the side of the door, and aiming his own gun at her. Staggering, barely able to stay upright, she still couldn't repress a smile. He was something— only minutes behind her in figuring out who shot Alan Henson.

He took in the situation at a glance, and lowered his gun. "Claire. Damn it, Claire..."

Unconsciousness rose up and rolled toward her, a massive gray wave. "It's all right, Joe. I handled it. Verna's only knocked out. And I'm a little dizzy. But I'm pretty sure the baby's all right..."

Suddenly, her silly legs wouldn't hold her up. She was sinking. And Joe was there, catching her, cradling her across his lap.

"Getting...blood all over the place..." she sighed. "Love you. Always. Never stopped...."

His face was so close, his gold eyes afire with both anguish and tenderness.

The gray wave descended, and she knew no more.

Chapter Sixteen

The world was water, gray water. She swam in the gray
ness and felt soothed. At peace. Far above, she could see the
water's surface. Beyond that was the glaring light of con
sciousness.

"Claire? Claire, can you hear me?" Joe was calling her
from up there, where pain and reality waited.

She didn't want to go. It was so peaceful here, where she
floated without cares or...

"Claire! Wake up. Damn it, Snow..."

So much for peace. Joe wanted her.

She looked at the surface, and she swam toward it. Up, up
and up. And then she broke the surface. Her head pounded
when she did it, and her shoulder throbbed and burned, but
she opened her eyes, anyway.

"Okay, okay," she croaked. "I'm awake. Stop shout
ing."

"Thank God." He took in a long breath and released it. Then he carefully smoothed her tangled, blood-matted hair away from her forehead.

Now that the adrenaline rush had left her, every muscle in her body throbbed—not to mention the agony that pounded in her head and blazed in her shoulder.

Joe was talking. "I've got to find a phone. Call an ambulance and the sheriff's office. Do you hear me, Snow?"

"Yes. I hear. I do."

"But there's no phone in this room. I have to leave you, to do it."

She realized his chest was bare. "Joe...your shirt..." And then she understood. He was pressing his wadded-up shirt against her injured shoulder.

He took her right hand, put it on the makeshift bandage. "Here. Keep the pressure on this." He slid out from under her. She cried out at the pain.

"Claire?"

"I'm okay. Really. Okay."

Then she heard groaning. She was still disoriented enough that she thought for a moment she was the one doing it.

"Damn," Joe muttered as he picked up Verna's spent revolver. "Verna's coming to."

Though her head and shoulder protested shrilly, shredding her nerve endings with agonized alarms, Claire dragged herself to a sitting position, and leaned, panting, against the back of the reclining chair. She could see then that Verna was the one groaning. As Claire watched, Verna moaned and turned her head.

"Give me your gun..." Claire volunteered. "I'll cover her while you find the phone."

"In a minute," he said, setting both guns well away from Verna. He grabbed the cord of the broken lamp and yanked it until it came free from the shattered base, then he tied Verna's hands behind her back with the makeshift rope.

Verna moaned as he bound her, but didn't put up any kind of a fight.

Over by the open box in the middle of the floor, there was a roll of twine. Joe used it to tie Verna's ankles together.

Verna was crying by then, soft, defeated sobs.

"Joe," Claire said gingerly. "I don't think she'll do anything now. She's done fighting. I really—"

He shot her a furious look. "I'm not in the business of reading minds, Claire. The way I know she's through is I make it impossible for her to do any more."

"She's had a really rough time—"

"Lots of people have a rough time," he said flatly. "It's no excuse to go over the line." He jerked the last knot tight and stood up. He looked down at Verna. "Okay, Verna, where's the phone?"

"K-kitchen," Verna managed between sobs.

Joe turned and looked around. Then he knelt by the flowered couch and tore a long strip off the dust ruffle at its base. He went back to Claire and held his gun out, butt first. "Cover her. I'll tie that shirt to your shoulder."

Claire swallowed another cry of pain as he swiftly bound his shirt over the wound.

He stood up. "Keep that gun on her. I'll make the calls."

Claire nodded. He left the room. Verna lay limp on the floor, her body shaking with slow, deep sobs, but otherwise not moving. Still, Claire kept the gun trained on her until Joe returned.

Patty Severin, the physician's assistant who had been running the Pine Bluff Medical Clinic since Claire's father died, arrived in the ambulance ten minutes later. At Claire's insistence, she examined Verna first and pronounced a hospital visit unnecessary. Verna had sustained a concussion but should be all right. Patty's prescription was two pain relievers and rest—and Verna should seek help immediately if she experienced prolonged dizziness or extreme nausea.

Sheriff Brawley arrived just after Patty was through with Verna and had turned her attention to the bigger job of patching up Claire.

"Okay, what's going on here, folks?" He stood in the broken-in doorway.

Verna, whom Joe had reluctantly untied and allowed to sit on the couch when Patty Severin arrived, raised her chin high. "I ... shot Alan Henson," she said firmly. Claire looked at her and saw that she appeared relieved to be telling the truth at last. Her eyes were no longer wildly bright, but level and full of sad determination. "Claire found out it was me," Verna added. "I went crazy and was going to—"

Sheriff Dan put up a hand. "Save it. In a minute, I'll take you in. You can tell it all, over at the courthouse."

Verna hung her head. "Whatever you say."

Sheriff Dan approached Claire, who was sitting in a corner chair as Patty gently prodded the side of her head and checked her eyes with a penlight.

"You gonna be all right, Short Stuff?"

Claire, whose head felt as though there was someone in there swinging a sledgehammer and whose shoulder throbbed in counterpoint to the hammering in her head, pulled away from Patty's ministrations long enough to look the sheriff right in the eye. "Now that I know I won't go to prison for something I didn't do, I'm going to be fine."

The sheriff said nothing for a moment. Outside, a siren scream could be heard, approaching, coming on louder and then louder still. Over the expanding wail of the siren, the sheriff explained, "Sometimes we mess up. It begins to look like we messed up royally this time."

Claire gritted her teeth as Patty began bandaging her head. "Yes, it certainly does."

The siren outside grew louder still as the vehicle came down the dirt road and stopped in front of the house. Then, abruptly, the mechanical wail was cut off. Outside, a car door slammed.

The sheriff smiled. "We can put off taking your statement until later, if you'd prefer."

"Yes," Claire said. "I'd appreciate that."

Right then, Wayne Leven appeared in the doorway. "What the hell's going on?"

Sheriff Dan turned to his undersheriff. "Looks like we got a confession in the Henson shooting, Wayne."

Leven shot a triumphant glance at Claire. His lip curled in a knowing smile. "She's finally willing to admit she did it, huh?"

Sheriff Dan shook his head. "No, Wayne. Not Claire." He gestured at Verna. "It's Verna here."

Leven's mouth went slack. "The housekeeper did it?"

"You got it, Wayne. Let's take her in."

Verna was escorted from the house and into the back seat of Sheriff Brawley's 4X4, just as a deputy sheriff's truck pulled up. The deputy came inside and announced that he had been ordered to "Secure the area, until we've had a chance to perform a full investigation."

"He means we should get lost," Joe explained.

Patty said that was fine with her. She wanted to take Claire back to the clinic to look at her shoulder, anyway, to see if she felt safe treating it herself, or if a trip to the hospital in Grass Valley was called for. She and Claire rode in the ambulance, and Joe followed behind.

At the clinic, Joe went to get Ella while Patty led Claire to the examining room.

Patty found that the shoulder wound was a clean one. "Small caliber, thank heavens," Patty muttered, and noted that the bullet had gone right through and out the other side.

Patty gave Claire a shot to kill the pain before she cleaned and dressed the wound, which she explained she wouldn't suture. Gunshot wounds were better left to drain. "It makes more of a scar, though," she admitted, and left the room for a moment.

Claire sat alone and thought of the scar on Joe's shoulder, and smiled at the idea of having one to match. She was more able to smile by then; the powerful painkiller was beginning to kick in. As a matter of fact, she felt kind of peaceful, kind of ready for a long rest. . . .

Just then Patty returned and finished dressing Claire's shoulder. Then she began filling another syringe.

In Claire's foggy mind, a thought surfaced: the baby. What might all these things Patty was shooting into her veins do to the baby?

"Wait," Claire instructed as Patty swabbed Claire's good shoulder. "Just wait a minute. Please."

Patty paused. "What is it?"

"Oh, God."

Patty laid a kind hand on Claire's arm. "What? Tell me?"

"What shot did you give me?"

"Just the painkiller. Why?"

"What else will you give me?"

"An antibiotic. To stave off infection. What's the problem, Claire?"

She managed to force the words out. "What effect . . . will those drugs have on the baby, if I'm pregnant?"

"What are you telling me, Claire?"

Claire sighed. There was nothing to do but admit. "I'm pregnant. About seven weeks."

Patty looked solemn. "You should have told me."

"I . . . didn't think of it, until now."

"Okay. I can understand that." Patty gave a wry chuckle. "You *had* been shot twice and bopped on the head with a gun, after all."

"Yes, but I should have thought of it, I know. And there's something else...."

"Yes?"

"I don't want anyone else to know, until I've told ... the father."

Patty nodded. "Of course. I'll keep it strictly confidential."

Claire knew Patty Severin well enough to be sure she could trust her integrity. She was relieved about that, at least. She asked, "So what about the drugs you gave me, and plan to give me?"

Patty launched into a mini-dissertation on the pros and cons of pregnant women and prescription drugs. "Generally, nowadays, we advise pregnant women to avoid drugs altogether, if possible. But gunshot wounds are ... serious. There's the high possibility of infection, for one thing. Luckily, you're caught up on your tetanus. You had that shot four years ago, so we don't have to decide whether to chance giving you that or not. But you're going to have to suffer a little more discomfort than you would have if you weren't pregnant." Claire groaned. Her father had been a doctor, after all. She knew what medical people meant when they said "discomfort." Claire was going to live through hell on earth before the goose egg on her head went down and her shoulder began to heal. Patty went on, "Painkillers aren't good for the baby, so you'll take only what you feel you can't do without."

"I'll take none."

"Claire. Be realistic."

"I'll be okay. What about the antibiotics?"

"Your records show no allergies to ampicillin."

"Right."

"That should be safe enough to take. I'll give you a shot of it now, and send some home with you."

"Fair enough."

Patty gave her the last shot. "Your mother's waiting in the reception area," she said as soon as that was done. She handed Claire a bottle of ampicillin capsules—and another of the painkiller Claire had already decided she wouldn't use.

"I don't want these," Claire said.

"Claire. Take them with you. You don't have to use them, but keep them just in case..."

Claire decided not to argue. She'd flush them down the toilet as soon as she got home.

Patty went on, "Your mother will take you home and put you to bed. You're going to be feeling pretty ragged for a few days, so get plenty of rest. I'll come by your place tomorrow to change that dressing."

Patty went to the door. Claire jumped down from the examining table, and stumbled a little when she hit the floor.

"Careful," Patty cautioned.

"Yes. Absolutely," Claire agreed. She could feel the pain in her shoulder and in her head, but they were distant things. Mostly, physically, she felt a sort of numb well-being. That shot of painkiller had really done its work. If only it wouldn't hurt the baby....

Patty seemed to read her mind. "Claire. Don't worry about it. The chances that one shot of painkiller did any damage to the baby are slim to none. You just don't want to make a habit of them, that's all."

"You mean that? It's probably okay?"

"Cross my heart." Patty was gesturing her to walk ahead. Claire, reassured, floated out into the hallway.

Ella was there in the waiting room. Her face was very pale. "Oh, honey, Joe told me everything. Are you all right?"

"I'm fine, Mother. Really." Claire was looking around. "Where *is* Joe?"

"He'll be back later. He took Eaton Slade and went to Verna's again to get your car."

Claire bit her lip. The little balloon of painkiller-induced well-being that enclosed her sprung a small leak.

She was pretty sure she had said something about the baby just before she'd passed out in Verna's living room. Could this be the beginning of exactly what she'd feared? Was Joe avoiding her now, because he couldn't forgive her for the way she'd betrayed his trust in her?

But that was ridiculous. What she'd said had been hardly coherent. He might *suspect* the truth now, but he couldn't know for sure until he talked to her. And Joe wasn't the type to go jumping to conclusions without doing everything in his power to get the facts.

Unless he didn't *want* to know the facts—like Claire herself, all those weeks after she first missed her period, when she *knew,* but didn't want to face the truth.

Ella was watching her. "Claire? What's the matter?"

"Nothing. Just . . . wiped out, I guess." She couldn't resist pointing out, "And there was really no need to worry about the car now."

Ella shrugged. "Joe thought there was."

Claire had to suppress a surge of irritation at her mother. Ella said "Joe thought there was," as if that were reason enough to do just about anything.

"You've certainly changed your opinion of what Joe Tally thinks," she said, and even through the haze of the painkiller, it sounded testy, though she had meant to keep her tone sensible and calm.

Ella nodded. "You're right. I've been wanting to talk to you about that, but you put me off earlier. So I'll just wait until you're feeling better. And right now, since we've taken up so much of Patricia's Saturday, let's not waste any more of it."

"Fine. Let's go home." Claire sounded whiny and she knew it. She whined some more. "And not to your house. To the motel."

"Of course. Now do stop whining, dear."

"I've been shot twice and whacked on the head with a gun. I'll whine if I feel like it."

Ella, ever the genteel Pine Bluff aristocrat, nodded at Patty. "Thank you for all you've done, Patricia. Would it be acceptable if we took care of the insurance papers at a later time?"

Patty agreed that would be just fine.

Claire stuck to her resolve not to use the painkillers. As a result, the next few days were about the worst in her life. Her mother stayed right by her side. And Joe was in and out all the time. He was gentle and attentive—but, somehow, he seemed to have retreated from her.

The second day after her battle with Verna, when the acetaminophen Claire allowed herself seemed to do no good and pain was screaming through every nerve of her body, she shared sharp words with Ella, who just couldn't understand why Claire had developed a sudden aversion to pain medicine. Ella insisted that Patricia must have something she could give Claire. Claire shouted she would have nothing—and that was that.

Joe stood in the background, watching, saying nothing, careful not to get involved in this war of wills between mother and daughter. But Claire felt him watching her; she felt that he *knew*.

She longed to talk it over with him, to have it out in the open for good and all. But more than wanting to get it over with, she dreaded facing him at last and watching his trust in her fade forever at the same time as he agreed to give the baby his name.

At night, she longed for his arms around her. But he never stayed to share her bed. Since Ella slept on the couch in the living room, Claire tried to convince herself he was only thinking of her mother's sensibilities, as he had always done. But she didn't really believe that.

The truth was, he was withdrawing from her. And if she had any integrity at all, she was going to have to turn him down when he offered to marry her. She would love him forever—but never, ever, would she trap him into a marriage he didn't want.

Meanwhile, as Claire wrestled with the pain in her healing body and the deeper agony in her heart, Verna Higgins pled guilty to all the charges against her. Zack Ryder took over the job of defending her, because Claire called him herself and asked him to do it. Zack felt he could get Verna off on an insanity plea; he was also taking a ridiculously small fee, since Verna was penniless. Ella was already working to establish a fund for Verna with the help of the members of the community church.

In the hospital in Grass Valley, Alan Henson slept on. There was doubt now that he would ever wake up. And the rumor was that they would move him soon, to a more permanent nursing-care home in the Bay Area, nearer the home of his wife, Mariah.

Though time seemed to crawl, Claire's strong body actually healed quickly. She was also relieved to find she experienced no vaginal bleeding, nor any symptoms that the baby was in danger. A week after she was shot, she went to the clinic for a full examination. Patty's prognosis was that both she and her baby were coming along just fine.

It was a Tuesday, ten days after Claire knocked on Verna Higgins's back door and found herself looking into the mouth of a gun, that Claire finally decided it was time to send Ella back to her own house. She was ready to take complete control of her life once more.

She told her mother over breakfast. Ella was surprisingly agreeable—she was not averse, she said, to sleeping in her own bed again.

"How about if I stay this last night? And tomorrow morning, I'll move the things I've brought over here back to my house."

"That will be fine," Claire allowed.

"And, dear, now that you feel well enough, I'd like to talk to you about a few things...."

Claire sipped her coffee and sighed in resignation. She'd known this talk was coming. Her mother had been hinting at it for days. Might as well have it over with.

"Okay, Mother." Claire got up, refilled their coffee cups, and then sat back down across from Ella. "Tell me all about it."

Ella smiled—a half-relieved, half-anxious sort of smile—and lightened her coffee with canned milk as she always did. When she set the can down, she plunged right in. "Well, first, I *would* like to know if something's wrong between you and Joe."

Claire glanced away, at the locust tree beyond the window over the sink and the shafts of golden morning sun that fell in on the sill. "Mother, I..."

Ella waited a few seconds and then urged, "Speak up, dear. You can tell me. What are you thinking?"

Claire looked her mother in the eye. "What I'm thinking is I'd rather not talk about Joe and me."

"Now, dear—"

"I mean it. I don't want to discuss it."

Ella shook her head. "You're just like your father sometimes, did you know? Always keeping things in, bearing the weight of the world on your shoulders, when there are people who would love to take a little of the burden them-

selves, if only you'd let them. Your father had a hear
attack, remember? And I'll always believe it was fror
keeping everything in and bearing all the burdens by him
self."

Claire spoke gently. "Mother, Patty Severin says I'm i
great shape. And I *have* let you take some of the burden. *A*
lot of the burden, as a matter of fact. And you've beer
wonderful. I can't thank you enough. But what's betweer
me and Joe is something I have to work out alone. Please tr
to understand."

Ella studied her daughter for a moment. Then, "Oh, a
right. But I'm here. If you need a listening ear."

"Thanks. Is that all, then?" Claire started to get up t
clear the table of their breakfast things.

"No, it isn't."

Claire sat back down.

"I, actually, I have something I feel I really must get of
my chest."

Claire was curious, in spite of the fact that usually th
things her mother had to get off her chest were things Clair
didn't want to hear. "What is it?"

"It concerns . . . how wrong I've been. All these years."

"About what?"

Ella looked down at her lap and then raised her head high
"About Joe Tally."

Claire stared at her mother. It didn't take a genius to se
that Ella had changed toward Joe, but Claire had never ex
pected her proud, often self-righteous mother to come righ
out and admit how unfair she'd been for twenty years.

"Close your mouth, dear," Ella instructed tartly. "And
anyway, what is so surprising?"

"Well, I—"

"When I'm wrong, I admit it. That is, as soon as I rea
ize I'm wrong. And I have been very wrong about Joe.
have judged him not as himself, but by his background. I'v

et gossip and the opinions of others rule my thinking. I have been a terrible snob, and I am very, very sorry."

"But—"

"Just let me finish this."

"All right . . ."

"I began to see that my . . . judgment might be faulty on the day you found Henson on the floor of the back bungalow. Honestly, dear, I thought that man was the answer to all my prayers for you. He had such nice manners, he dressed so well and he drove a good car. And, of course, he catered to me shamelessly in order to get closer to you. And I lapped it up. I do like to imagine that your father, bless his heart, would never have fallen for that con artist. But *I* did. I'm ashamed to confess that, if poor Verna hadn't shot him, I just might have given him my money and ended up penniless in my old age. But that's neither here nor there at this point. What matters now, is that I understand how wrong I've been. And I see now why you love Joe Tally. Even a blind woman could see it, with all he's done for you since the trouble over Henson started. And I'm sorry. For all the years I've stood in the way of the two of you finding happiness together."

Claire didn't tell her mother that if Joe had only been willing to let himself love her, even the iron will of Ella Snow couldn't have kept the two of them apart. She only asked softly, "Is that all?"

Ella, whose eyes had become suspiciously moist, took a tissue from her pocket and blew her nose. "Well, yes it is. Were you expecting more?" She dabbed at her eyes.

"No, that's enough. That's . . . much more than enough." Claire got up and crossed the short distance to her mother's chair. "Oh, Mother, I . . ."

Ella reached up her long arms and pulled her daughter down. The women held each other. Ella spoke against Claire's hair, "I love you, dear. And I'm proud of you, too.

Never forget I'm here for you, that you can turn to me, as long as there is breath in my body."

"Oh, Mother. Thank you. I won't forget."

"Good, then. And I like to hope that, whatever's wrong between you and Joe, you'll work it out. You will, won' you?"

Claire straightened up. "I don't know. Let's just . . . wai and see, okay?"

"In other words, 'Mind your own business, Mother'?"

Claire gave a weary chuckle. "Something like that."

"Well, I've done my part." Ella blew her nose and wipe her eyes one more time. "The rest is up to the two of you, suppose."

Claire didn't answer. She set to work carrying the dishe to the sink.

That night, Claire and Ella sat companionably in the liv ing room watching a movie on the VCR. The bell rang ou front, and Claire told Ella she'd get it.

She went through the door to the lobby and found her self looking into Joe's strange golden eyes through the glas in the top of the door.

Her heart turned over in her chest. And she longed, for split second, to duck and hide from Joe as she had done tha night after they'd arrested her for shooting Henson. But thi time she didn't hide. She knew what he had come for.

And she knew that, at last, the time for absolute truth wa upon her.

Chapter Seventeen

He took her to the ranch.

Ella was absurdly delighted to see them go. She helped Claire pack an overnight bag and urged her daughter to "Just stay there as long as you like, dear. I'm all set up here, anyway, and there's no reason I have to leave. You just enjoy a little time away...."

When they pulled into the yard, the dogs were there, wriggling and whining. Claire made much of them, and then, carrying her overnight bag, she followed Joe into the house. Inside the door, she set the bag down. She was sure that if she did stay the night, she'd be sleeping in the guest room. But she didn't want to get into all that—the sleeping arrangements that seemed so banal and yet told so much—right then.

She thought she felt the quick brush of Joe's glance when she set the bag down, but he was behind her. It was probably only her imagination.

He said, "How about a beer?"

She started to shake her head, remembering the baby. But then she said yes, anyway, knowing she'd take no more than a sip or two. Somehow, to say no seemed an open admission that she was pregnant, and though she'd be telling him within moments, the urge to go on protecting her secret was still with her.

He went to the kitchen and came back with two long-necks. "It's a beautiful night. Let's go out on the porch."

She took the cold, sweating bottle. His fingers brushed hers lightly. The touch tingled all the way up her arm. "Sure. That would be nice."

They went out and sat side-by-side on the glider. The dogs came sniffing up, walked in circles, and lay down, with little *wuffs* of contentment, nearby.

The moon was a last-quarter crescent over the dark trees. Claire could hear crickets and the lazy croak of a single frog. Somewhere far away, a coyote howled. In the back pasture, Demon, nervous at the predator's cry, let out a long whinny.

Joe began it. He took a long pull off his beer. Then he said, "It's time to talk, I think. About the baby first of all."

Claire gave up any pretense that she would drink her beer. She bent and set it beside the glider on the porch. Then she sat up again and looked down at her hands, then back up at the moon.

"Lord," she said. Her voice was hardly more than a whisper. "This is even harder than I thought it would be."

His voice was gentle. "I figured, when you said 'the baby's all right,' that you meant you were pregnant."

Claire managed a weak sound of assent.

He went on, "And then, when you wouldn't take your pain pills, your mother became suspicious, too."

"Oh, God..." She glanced at him, then away. "Patty swore she wouldn't say a thing."

"She didn't. But last Friday you had a full physical, including a pelvic exam. Lorna let your mother see the bill." Lorna Dell was the clinic's office manager. "And don't blame Lorna," Joe insisted. "Your mother had been handling all the paperwork up until then, so Lorna just assumed—"

Claire waved a hand. "I get the picture. You don't need to say any more. What I can't believe is my mother hasn't said a word to me, except to tell me that she was wrong about you all these years and that she hopes we'll..." Her voice failed her. She finished lamely, "Work out our problems."

Joe actually chuckled. "She's sure we're going to find happiness together."

Claire sighed. "Tonight, if at all possible. Am I right?" Suddenly, her mother's eagerness to see Claire drive off in Joe's pickup with her overnight bag on her lap made a lot of sense.

Joe nodded. "Yeah, she wants us to work things out. For the baby's sake, if nothing else. At least that's what she told me."

Claire wished she could melt into a puddle and sink through the porch boards. "Oh, God. What exactly did she say to you?"

"She told me in no uncertain terms that you never had a thing to do with Alan Henson—so the best thing for everyone would be if I owned up to my responsibility and gave the baby my name. Someone like me, she pointed out, who was born *out of wedlock,* should surely understand that what a child needs most of all is two parents committed to giving him or her a decent start in life."

"Oh, Lord. That sounds just like her." Claire's face was flaming. She was grateful for the shadows of nighttime. She couldn't look at him. Staring off toward the tall trees beyond the road, she said, "She's afraid you'll think the baby might be—"

"I don't." He put his hand over hers. "I knew there was nothing between you and Henson from that day in your living room when you told me so."

Still not quite able to meet his eyes, she looked down at their entwined hands. "Thank you," she whispered, moved beyond measure to realize that he still trusted her. In spite of everything, even knowing about the baby, *he still trusted her*. She had said there was nothing between her and Henson, and he believed, *still* believed, without question, that that was so. Perhaps there was hope after all....

But then she quelled such crazy, impossible thoughts. Just because he believed the baby was his didn't mean he was longing to marry her.

She forced herself to speak. "Joe, I'm sorry about my mother. It's just...the way she is. If there's going to be a baby, she wants me to have a husband."

"Even if the husband in question is that dangerous, trouble-making loser, Joe Tally?"

Claire looked at him then. She *gaped* at him, actually. After all they'd been through, after all he had done for her, didn't he realize yet how absolutely first-rate, how incredibly, fantastically *wonderful* he was?

She jumped to her feet, almost upsetting her untouched beer and causing Gonzo to whimper and raise his head in doggy consternation. She marched to the porch rail and whirled to face him.

"That is it, I have had it. If you don't stop putting yourself down..." She had no words to describe the horribleness of what she would do. She sucked in an indignant breath. "I *hate* when you do that."

He set his empty beer on the porch and stood up. Slowly, he came toward her.

Down in her stomach, a hundred butterflies took flight. It was crazy, but the look in his eyes was the same look he'd given her the night they'd made the baby. It was a look of heat and wanting....

Oh, Lord, it wasn't possible. But it was happening. He was coming closer. He was *not* withdrawing. He was *not* shutting her out.

When he was less than a foot away, he reached out and touched the side of her face. She felt the warmth of that caress, the cherishing gentleness of it, through every inch of her body. He murmured her name. "Claire..."

She made a soft, questioning sound. "Joe...?"

His hand moved downward, over the fine column of her neck. It glided light as a breath over her still-bandaged shoulder, down the swell of her breast, until he could cup that breast.

He said hoarsely, "Your breasts. I think... they're fuller than that first night. You're so beautiful, Claire. With our baby inside you..." He thumbed her nipple. She felt it blooming. She released a long, slow sigh.

"I waited," he said, as he continued to touch her, his hand cupping and stroking her breast and then gliding up once more, to caress her neck, her face, to smooth back her hair. "I waited, until you were well enough. It was hell, I'll tell you, coming back here alone every night, when all I wanted was to hold you, to be with you.... But I knew your mother would care for you, and I thought it would be better, since your mother's so old-fashioned and I wanted to show respect for her. But now, it's enough. I don't want to wait anymore..."

She let her eyes droop half closed, thinking how she'd missed him, blocking out all thought of the future, as she'd always done with Joe. With Joe, there was no future. There was only tonight....

And then he said, "Marry me."

The world froze on its axis. A clean shaft of joy pierced her heart. But the joy didn't last.

After all, a marriage proposal was no more than she'd expected. She'd always known he'd offer to marry her. Just because he was doing it in such a beautiful, sensual way, didn't mean he really *wanted* the marriage.

She sidestepped, enough to send a clear signal that she didn't want to be touched right then. He dropped his caressing hand. She returned to the glider and took her seat again. He leaned on the railing, waiting, watching her.

"Well?" he asked warily. "Do I get an answer or not?"

"Oh, Joe." She bit her lip. "How can I do this to you? You've always sworn you never wanted marriage, and yet here you are, trying to do the right thing by a woman who chased you for twenty years, and then just *happened* to get pregnant the first time you made love with her."

"The condoms were too old," he said levelly. "I thought so even then. But I wanted you, so I took a chance."

"I had my doubts about them, too."

"So we were both a little bit to blame."

"Joe, I made a big deal about how it was my 'safe time'—"

"Was it?"

"Yes, but—"

"So you told the truth. And nature overrode you. Maybe we both should have been wiser, but we weren't. It was *both* of our faults. So we'll get married and share the responsibility for what we created."

"Oh, Joe. It wouldn't be fair to you. I've always known where you stand on the subject of marriage. I asked you to marry me twice, remember? Both times you said you would never get married—or bring innocent children into a rotten world like this is."

He shook his head. "You still don't get the whole picture, do you?" He hitched a leg on the railing, folded his hands on his knee and looked down at them. "But, hell, why should you? I've spent twenty damn years trying to keep you from seeing it."

"What?"

He looked up at her, and then he rose and came to sit beside her again. She felt the warmth of him, the strength, and she had to steel herself not to lean against him. She turned her head enough so that she could stare off over the trees again.

"Look at me, okay?"

"Okay." She met his eyes.

He admitted, "Yes, I've always said I wouldn't bring a kid into a world like this one. But now the kid is coming in spite of what I said. It's a done deal—and I'm finding it doesn't seem like such a bad idea after all. The last few days I've been thinking it over. And I've decided that after what I had as a kid, I want *my* kid to have a hell of a lot more. And I think, between the two of us, we can give him—or her—more. So you're right, at least partly. I do want to marry you so our baby will have two parents, just like your mother said. But, damn it, Claire. Even if there was no baby..." His voice, for the first time that evening, seemed to fail him.

Claire stared at him. She sensed what was coming. But how dare she actually believe it? "What? What? Oh, Joe, do you mean—?"

"Hell, I..."

"Yeah?"

"Well, all these years, while I've been constantly reminding you that we are *friends* and no more, I've been..."

Claire realized she was holding her breath. She let it out slowly. "You've been what?"

And he said it. "I've been in love with you."

Pure joy flooded her then, and this time it didn't fade.

Joe continued, "But I've always known you could do a hell of lot better than a guy like—"

"Don't say it." She pressed her fingers to his lips. "Don' ever say it again. There *is* no one better. You are good, and loyal and strong and kind. You're the man I love."

He shrugged. "Whatever."

She frowned. "'Whatever.' What is that supposed to mean?"

At last he reached for her, pulling her close, urgent, but also careful of her injured shoulder. He spoke against her hair. "It means I'm through fighting it. It means, after twenty years, I've finally given up trying to convince you to stop loving me. I surrender, Claire." He pulled back enough that she could see his face. "We are much more than friends. We're lovers, and soon we'll be husband and wife. And then, before you know it, God help us, there'll be this kid looking up at us, calling us Mom and Dad. That's how it is. Learn to live with it, okay?"

"Yes," she murmured. "Yes, yes, yes…" Her hands slid up to circle his neck.

He kissed her. For a brief eternity, there was nothing else in the world but the night and two lovers and the sweet promise of their desire.

At last, though, the kiss came to an end.

"I want us to be married right away," he told her. "And I've been checking into becoming the police academy's oldest living graduate. Brawley's going to help me. What do you think of that?"

"I think it's good. Wonderful. Terrific."

"I'm glad." He looked at her tenderly for a moment, then continued. "I've got some money put aside, not a lot, but some. It'll be a challenge, I know—newly married, with a baby coming, and there you'll be, with your husband off in school. But I think we can manage, somehow."

His expression turned rueful. "I can't offer you a perfect, mapped-out life, Claire. I wish to hell I could. But, damn it, I love you. And the time has passed when I can make myself leave you alone. So maybe we should just accept this... thing between us, and get on with our lives."

She grinned at him. "Joe, you can stop convincing me. I said yes five minutes ago."

With a muttered, "Thank God," he grabbed her close once more.

Claire melted against him, at last allowing herself to believe that it had all come out right after all. Their baby would have his time of innocence, protected by two people who loved him with all their hearts. And she would spend the rest of her life where she'd always longed to be: at Joe Tally's side.

The world was as she had always believed. A place of beauty and goodness—if a person was willing to seek the goodness. And to fight for it against all odds.

* * * * *

Silhouette

SPECIAL EDITION®

It takes a very
special man to win

That

SPECIAL

Woman!

She's friend, wife, mother—she's you! And beside each Special Woman stands a wonderfully special man. It's a celebration of our heroines—and the men who become part of their lives.

Look for these exciting titles from Silhouette Special Edition:

August MORE THAN HE BARGAINED FOR by Carole Halston
Heroine: Avery Payton—a woman struggling for independence falls for the man next door.

September A HUSBAND TO REMEMBER by Lisa Jackson
Heroine: Nikki Carrothers—a woman without memories meets the man she should never have forgotten...her husband.

October ON HER OWN by Pat Warren
Heroine: Sara Shepard—a woman returns to her hometown and confronts the hero of her childhood dreams.

November GRAND PRIZE WINNER! by Tracy Sinclair
Heroine: Kelley McCormick—a woman takes the trip of a lifetime and wins the greatest prize of all...love!

December POINT OF DEPARTURE by Lindsay McKenna
(Women of Glory)
Heroine: Lt. Callie Donovan—a woman takes on the system and must accept the help of a kind and sexy stranger.

Don't miss THAT SPECIAL WOMAN! each month—from some of your special authors! Only from Silhouette Special Edition!

Relive the romance...
Harlequin and Silhouette
are proud to present

A program of collections of three complete novels by the most requested authors with the most requested themes. Be sure to look for one volume each month with three complete novels by top name authors.

In June: **NINE MONTHS** Penny Jordan
Stella Cameron
Janice Kaiser

Three women pregnant and alone. But a lot can happen in nine months!

In July: **DADDY'S HOME** Kristin James
Naomi Horton
Mary Lynn Baxter

Daddy's Home ... and his presence is long overdue!

In August: **FORGOTTEN PAST** Barbara Kaye
Pamela Browning
Nancy Martin

Do you dare to create a future if you've forgotten the past?

Available at your favorite retail outlet.

◇ HARLEQUIN❜ ♥ Silhouette

Silhouette®

SPECIAL EDITION®

MORGAN'S MERCENARIES

by Lindsay McKenna

Morgan Trayhern has returned and he's set up a company full of best pals in adventure. Three men who've been to hell and back are about to fight the toughest battle of all...love!

You loved Wolf Harding in HEART OF THE WOLF (SE #817) and Sean Killian in THE ROGUE (SE #824). Don't miss Jake Randolph in COMMANDO (SE #830), the final story in this exciting trilogy, available in August.

These are men you'll love and stories you'll treasure...only from Silhouette Special Edition!

Silhouette®

SPECIAL EDITION®

WILD RIVER TRILOGY

by Laurie Paige

Come meet the wild McPherson men and see how these three sexy
bachelors are tamed!

In HOME FOR A WILD HEART (SE #828) you got to know
Kerrigan McPherson. Now meet the rest of the family:

A PLACE FOR EAGLES, September 1993—
Keegan McPherson gets the surprise of his life.

THE WAY OF A MAN, November 1993—
Paul McPherson finally meets his match.

Don't miss any of these exciting titles—only for our readers and only
from Silhouette Special Edition!

Silhouette

SPECIAL EDITION®

From this day forward

Coming in August,
the first book in an exciting new trilogy from
Debbie Macomber
GROOM WANTED

To save the family business, Julia Conrad becomes a "green card" bride to brilliant chemist Aleksandr Berinski. But what more would it take to keep her prized employee—and new husband—happy?

FROM THIS DAY FORWARD—Three couples marry first and find love later in this heartwarming trilogy.

Look for
Bride Wanted (SE #836) in September
Marriage Wanted (SE #842) in October

Only from Silhouette Special Edition

Silhouette Books has done it again!

Opening night in October has never been as exciting! Come watch as the curtain rises and romance flourishes when the stars of tomorrow make their debuts today!

Revel in Jodi O'Donnell's STILL SWEET ON HIM—
Silhouette Romance #969
...as Callie Farrell's renovation of the family homestead leads her straight into the arms of teenage crush Drew Barnett!

Tingle with Carol Devine's BEAUTY AND THE BEASTMASTER—
Silhouette Desire #816
...as legal eagle Amanda Tarkington is carried off by wrestler Bram Masterson!

Thrill to Elyn Day's A BED OF ROSES—
Silhouette Special Edition #846
...as Dana Whitaker's body and soul are healed by sexy physical therapist Michael Gordon!

Believe when Kylie Brant's McLAIN'S LAW —
Silhouette Intimate Moments #528
...takes you into detective Connor McLain's life as he falls for psychic—and suspect—Michele Easton!

Catch the classics of tomorrow—*premiering* today—
only from ▼ *Silhouette*

Silhouette Books
is proud to present
our best authors,
their best books...
and the best in
your reading pleasure!

Throughout 1993, look for exciting
books by these top names in
contemporary romance:

DIANA PALMER—
Fire and Ice in June

ELIZABETH LOWELL—
Fever in July

CATHERINE COULTER—
Afterglow in August

LINDA HOWARD—
Come Lie With Me in September

When it comes to passion,
we wrote the book.

BOBT2